To my husband who has been my number one fan and has supported me throughout this entire process. To my children, who provide me with the motivation to fulfill my dreams. I hope to teach them that they can do anything they put their minds to.

REIGNITE

A.M. Roberts

Content Warning

Reignite is a romance that may contain triggering situations such as rape, stalking, kidnapping, physical and sexual assault, graphic sexual scenes, and graphic language.

As an author, my goal is to foster a deep connection between my readers and the characters within my story. This includes conveying the resilience required to endure and transcend trauma while still being able to discover humor, joy, and love in life.

To those who identify as survivors, please know that you are not alone. If you or someone you know has experienced sexual assault, I encourage you to reach out for support by contacting the National Sexual Assault Hotline at 1-800-656-4673.

PROLOGUE

The moment she walked through the school doors, I was captivated. There was something about her—an undeniable pull. I knew, deep in my bones, that she was meant to be mine. But I'd seen the power of a strong woman firsthand. My mother embodied that strength, using it to gather the courage to abandon both my father and me, chasing a dream that didn't include the burden of a toddler. She had taught me that strength in a woman was a dangerous thing. Unpredictable. Destructive.

Watching her navigate the ruthless world of entitled rich kids, I couldn't help but admire the way she moved through it all, unscathed. She was fierce - stronger than most of them realized. I knew I had to build her up, make her believe in me - in us.

But what I never saw coming was the aftermath of my final step: breaking her. After graduation, she became silent as if she never knew me. No communication, no lingering glances. She simply disappeared - gone without a single look back. I thought I had her; I thought she was mine. But in that moment, I realized how wrong I had been all these days.

Now, I see it clearly. I didn't break her - not entirely. But I did leave my mark. Cracks. Flaws in her perfect mask.

I will finish what I started... yes. I will break her.

She's mine. I always get what's mine. That's who I am.

1.

Dani

The overpowering scents of alcohol and old cigarettes overwhelm me, making it difficult to catch my breath. Gradually, a sense of discomfort creeps in. It's confusing. Then, my gaze falls upon my torn panties discarded on the floor. My dress is in tatters as well. Glancing down at the bed beneath me, I see sheets stained with blood. Panic sets in. I struggle to breathe, unable to...

"Dani!" I jerk awake, disoriented and gasping for air. My heart is pounding in my chest as I sit up too quickly, causing a wave of dizziness to crash over me. My roommate, best friend for the past seven years, is sitting beside me, her familiar presence a comfort in the chaos of my thoughts. For a moment, I'm lost in the darkness, the haze. And then I feel a hand on mine, warm and grounding.

"You had another bad dream, didn't you?" Izzy's voice is soft but firm. I blink rapidly, trying to clear the remnants of the nightmare from my mind.

I nod, unable to speak at first. The nightmare still lingers, heavy in my chest. It's the same one - always the same. "Yes," I whisper softly - my voice barely audible.

"Was it the same one?" Izzy inquires, placing

a reassuring hand on mine. I nod in response. This nightmare has haunted me for years; despite my efforts to lock away the memories of my prom night. They always resurface in my dreams.

Prom was supposed to be a memorable evening, but for me, it turned out to be a nightmare. It ended with my innocence being taken from me without consent by someone I thought I loved deeply. Tommy Hansen, a popular, charming boy in our school, surprised me by asking me out at the start of our senior year. Unlike the other wealthy students, most of whom lived lavish lifestyles, I was more reserved. My father was in jail, and my mother, though well-intentioned at times, often left me alone to pursue her own interests. She claimed it was for our betterment, but in reality, she was seeking personal gain through relationships that never lasted.

Despite my parents' shortcomings, I excelled academically and earned a scholarship to a prestigious school in Ohio. Although I try to believe my academic achievements were solely based on merit, I can't ignore the possibility that my mother's involvement with the school's headmaster played a role. Learning the truth was devastating, but all my mother could offer was a nonchalant, "You can't ever say I didn't do anything for you," as she took a drag from her cigarette.

When Tommy unexpectedly asked me out, I was caught off guard, unsure how to respond. A part of me was eager to embrace his offer, while another cautioned me that it might be a ploy. Despite my doubts, all I could manage was a hesitant nod. Thus began my journey as his girlfriend, transforming me from a girl with no friends to the most popular girl in school. Finally, I felt a sense of belonging and, more importantly, found the love I had always yearned for in the perfect guy.

Fast forward to prom night, and my memories are hazy, except for the car ride to the prom with Tommy. He couldn't contain his excitement, talking about the amazing night ahead and expressing his eagerness to be with me. Although I never explicitly agreed to his intentions of intimacy, perhaps out of a desire not to follow in my mother's footsteps, I reasoned that love should entail such intimacy, right? Sensing my apprehension, Tommy offered me a water bottle, urging me to drink up for relaxation.

Taking a gulp, I was taken aback as the warm liquid burned down my throat. It was definitely not water. Despite only drinking a few more sips from the bottle, my recollections of the night are fragmented. They involve snippets of dancing and the surreal moment of being crowned prom queen, all while feeling like I was on cloud nine.

Sometime in the early hours of the morning, I awoke in a rundown motel room feeling disoriented, as if I had been asleep for an eternity. The overpowering smell of alcohol and old cigarette smoke made me queasy. To my horror, I discovered my dress torn and my undergarments discarded on the floor. *Where was Tommy?* My mind raced to make sense of the chaotic scene before me. Pain in my lower region drew my attention to the bed, where I saw bloodstains, disheveled sheets, and pillows on the floor. Overwhelmed, I rushed to the bathroom and vomited, unable to comprehend what was happening. Suddenly, I heard footsteps approaching me from behind.

"You're finally awake," Tommy said, lighting a

cigarette.

"What have you done to me?" I asked, tears streaming down my cheeks.

"Nothing you didn't ask for. You were all over me last night," he smirked.

Confused and in disbelief, I struggled to remember the events of the previous night. "I don't remember. I barely took a few sips," I whimpered, pressing my icy hands against my face, struggling to recollect anything. Tommy stooped down, bringing his face close to mine. I used to adore that face. He was strikingly handsome with his blond hair, blue eyes, and chiseled jawline. His physique was tall and muscular, as you'd expect any quarterback. But at that moment, Tommy appeared deranged, even repulsive. This wasn't the young man who snuggled with me during scary movies, strolled with me along the trail, and vowed to love me for all eternity. He certainly wasn't the young man who had constantly reassured me that my virginity didn't matter to him because he loved me and was willing to wait until I was ready. I no longer recognized my boyfriend; he instilled fear in me. His gaze bore into me as he took another drag of his cigarette, blowing the smoke directly into my face, and causing me to cough.

Tommy leaned closer, his once-handsome face now a grotesque mask of smugness. "Exactly," he said, his voice low and mocking. Your memory seems to be failing you. Trust me when I say that this was what you wanted. It might be a good idea to freshen up," he remarked before getting up and making his way out of the bathroom.

I recoiled, the words cutting through me like a

knife. "No," I whispered, my heart shattering. "I never wanted this. I know I didn't. You told me that you would wait. You promised..."

He laughed, a cold, cruel sound that made my skin crawl. "I lied," Tommy interjected, turning back toward me with a smirk in his eyes. Tommy's once familiar face now seemed menacing, a stark contrast to the person I once trusted. "Did you honestly believe I would wait forever for you to realize you didn't want to be a prude? Did you think I would wait to get inside that tight little pussy of yours? I showed patience for far longer than I had anticipated." He scoffed, raising his unapologetic gaze to meet mine, chuckling softly. "Yet, it was well worth the wait. Feeling your tightness gripping my cock as I thrust into you? Undoubtedly worth it." He paused briefly, as if contemplating saying more but thinking better of it. Abruptly, he quipped, "Thanks for the lay," as he strolled toward the exit.

With those words, my world crumbled. The boy I once loved – the boy I had trusted – was a stranger now. He wasn't the sweet, charming Tommy I had known. No, this was a man I barely recognized.

I was left there, alone in the aftermath, my heart breaking into pieces.

****

After spending some time sitting with me, she quietly lets me know that she had made breakfast and to join her when I am ready. I take a few minutes to get myself together and open my door to the delightful aroma of eggs and bacon sizzling on the stove. I exit my room with only a few quick strides leading me into the kitchen. In our cozy apartment, every room seems to be within an arm's reach.

"This smells amazing," I exclaim, my mouth watering.

"Of course it does. I figured you could use a delicious hot breakfast before your interview. I also have some coffee brewing for you after the rough night you had."

"You're the greatest," I reply, pulling out a chair and settling into it.

"I know," Izzy says with a sweet smile, prompting me to roll my eyes, knowing well that sweetness isn't quite her style. Isabella Fiore is a lively Italian with boundless energy, unafraid to speak her mind. Our dynamic works because she never lets me dwell on negativity for long, while I help ground her when needed. We first crossed paths at the start of our senior year in high school and instantly connected. Our bond has remained steadfast—even though we couldn't be more different.

Izzy also has a unique ability to find the positive in every situation, brightening any room she enters. Both men and women are drawn to her confident, positive aura. It doesn't hurt that she's stunningly beautiful, with thick, glossy black hair cascading down her back, flawless olive skin, captivating green eyes, elegant cheekbones, and a radiant smile. Though petite, she is blessed with a perfect figure that commands attention. Comparatively, I might not be unattractive, but I feel rather ordinary next to Izzy.

"So, how are you feeling about your interview?" Izzy inquires as she serves eggs onto my plate.

"Alright," I respond, looking up to see her raised eyebrows. "Okay, I'm nervous. I understand the importance of securing a job. However, I'm not particularly excited about working for a group of self-assured, wealthy men who each have a different woman every night." I had come across the job listing for a personal assistant role at Stonebrook, a highly reputable, successful marketing firm. After conducting my research and reading various professional and gossip-related articles about the company and its co-CEOs, I was well aware of the type of men they were. Despite their good looks, I knew what to expect. I only applied because I couldn't continue letting Izzy cover my share of the rent. While she insisted that she didn't mind, I felt uneasy about accepting handouts. I believe in earning my own keep. I learned early on that I had to strive hard for everything I wanted in life; otherwise, it could slip away easily. That was a lesson my mother never grasped.

2.

Dean

I never felt the need for an assistant. I was accustomed to handling everything solo, yet Jay somehow arranged interviews behind my back.

"Why the hell would I need an assistant, Jay?" I question.

"Why the fuck not?" Jay casually replies, lounging in my chair with his feet on my desk. Despite our similar appearances, our personalities couldn't be more contrasting. I focus on the business we co-founded, seeking structure and consistency, while Jay is carefree and, disorganized, with the maturity of a prepubescent boy.

"So, you want me to pay someone to do nothing?" I inquire.

"Not nothing. They can assist you with various tasks. Fetch your coffee, make copies, or even provide other services," Jay suggests with a smirk, implying something inappropriate.

"If I wanted that kind of service, I'd hire a hooker," I retort, dismissing Jay's absurd proposal.

"But would they get you coffee?"

"Get the fuck out and maybe actually do some work?"

"What fun is that?" Jay finally shifts his feet off of my desk and starts to rise. Stepping into the hallway, he glances back. "By the way, you have a few interviews set up and the first one is in fifteen minutes. Enjoy!"

"Fucking bastard" I mutter quietly.

I've managed quite well without an assistant. Carla, our diligent secretary, lends her support whenever I require it. However, I've noticed her fatigue lately, and she has expressed a desire to spend more time with her children and grandchildren. Perhaps it wouldn't be such a burden to delegate the trivial daily tasks to someone else, allowing me to concentrate on the larger responsibilities at hand.

I can only hope that genuine potential walks through those doors. I'll be furious with my brother if I waste half a day's effort. I know him and this interview process is bound to be a disaster. If I want tits and ass, I'd simply go to a bar. I need to focus on work, not be sidetracked.

"Mr. Anderson," Carla's voice crackles over the intercom. "Your first interview is here." I can hear the amusement lacing her tone.

Here we fucking go.

3.

Dani

I find myself in a position I never imagined I would be in. The thought of being someone's assistant, or worse, a subordinate to a wealthy man, was not appealing to me at all. However, financial constraints pushed me to seek employment. Izzy is more than willing to cover my share of the rent with her family's wealth, but I can't take advantage of her generosity. She is the only true friend I have ever had, and I refuse to complicate our relationship by involving money, regardless of her giving nature. Izzy has always been humble about her family's wealth but wanted to find her own way in this world. Despite having the means to live in a more luxurious place, we both chose to maintain our independence and settle for the modest apartment that we now call home.

As I approach the entrance of Stonebrook, I brace myself before stepping inside. The reception area exudes an air of sophistication with plush leather couches and verdant plants adorning the space. A young woman sits behind a sizable desk, engrossed in her work. Summoning all the courage I can muster, I approach her. "Hello. I'm here for an interview." She continues typing, seemingly oblivious to my presence. Just as I am about to repeat myself, she glances up briefly.

"Name?" the young woman huffs.

"Danielle Cliff."

"Ah, yes. You can use these elevators behind me," the receptionist gestures. "Go up to the top floor. You will be meeting with Mr. Dean Anderson. His secretary will inform him of your arrival."

I express gratitude before I head up. Moving around the desk, I reach a point where I can see two elevators on the back wall. Stepping into one, I take a moment to calm myself with deep breaths. Despite having attended interviews in the past, I can't shake off the nerves. The elevator doors open before I can second-guess myself. The floor layout is straightforward. There's a desk close to the elevators and a smaller waiting area compared to the grand lobby downstairs, where two other young women are seated. I noticed a few closed offices and what seems to be a couple of conference rooms.

Approaching the desk, I observe an older lady, possibly in her sixties, sitting there. I have to hold back a giggle. She's dressed in a very professional skirt suit, but her red poofy permed hair and excessive makeup catch my attention, giving her a rather unconventional appearance.

"Can I help you?" she asks, looking up at me over her modern, black-rimmed glasses perched at the end of her nose.

"Yes. I have an appointment with Mr. Anderson."

"Name?"

"Danielle Cliff."

"Please have a seat."

"Thank you," I respond, heading towards the chairs. I pick one against the wall, facing the office doors to observe people entering and exiting.

As I glance at the two women who I assume are also here for the same position, my confidence dwindles. They both look striking. One is tall, with long straight black hair, green eyes, and legs for days. The other is blonde with a dark tan, bright blue eyes, and a fit physique that exudes femininity. Now I feel plain and doubt my chances of securing the job. I lack experience as a personal assistant, but I wonder how challenging it could really be. Realizing I'm nervously biting my nails, I swiftly tuck my hands into my lap.

I hear the sound of a door opening and glance up. Another individual with blonde hair strides confidently out of the office, smiling. She passes by the desk heading towards the elevators and quickly disappears. The ringing of the secretary's phone catches me off guard. After a brief conversation, she summons Tara into the office without lifting her gaze. Tara, the dark-haired beauty, rises and vanishes behind the door.

I have been sitting in this chair for approximately half an hour and finally, my name is called. Rising slowly, I approach the door, suppressing a wave of nervousness-induced nausea. As I cross the threshold, I stumble, ending up on my knees with my purse and its contents spilling onto the floor. To make matters worse, when I look up, I find an incredibly handsome man gazing at me with intense dark eyes – the same face I had seen while researching the company. *Breathe,* I remind myself as I attempt to salvage my dignity by swiftly collecting the scattered items and composing myself.

"Are you okay?" The man asks with a subtle smile playing at the corner of his mouth, clearly entertained by my mishap.

My cheeks flush crimson.

"I'm fine," I reply, feeling his presence even more striking in person. His short, thick dark hair sets off his captivating blue eyes that almost appears gray, framed with long eyelashes bright against smooth tan skin. His white shirt hugs his well-built physique, indicating he is a regular at the gym.

"Please, have a seat," he gestures toward the chair in front of his desk. Moving more cautiously this time, I reach the chair and sit down as gracefully as possible. "So, you're Danielle. Your resume indicates no prior experience as a personal assistant," he remarks without meeting my gaze.

"That's correct."

"Why did you apply?"

"I need employment. While lacking direct experience as a personal assistant, I conducted thorough research on the company and believe I can excel in any assigned task."

"Numerous experienced people have applied for this role. Why should I select you?" he leans closer, questioning me.

"I am a results-oriented individual. My sole purpose here is to fulfill assigned duties efficiently. I am diligent and confident that you would not regret hiring me," I respond, growing more assured with each query.

"If hired, can you maintain a professional

relationship with staff and leadership?" His question took me aback. In this moment, I sense a deeper meaning lurking beneath the surface, and the whispers it conveys leave an unsettling taste in my mouth

"If you are implying that I would engage in inappropriate behavior, you are mistaken. While you may possess charm and wealth, I am not interested in conceited individuals with a revolving door of women. I am appalled that a professional like you, would assume that I would try to misuse my position for personal gain. Not every woman will fall at your feet," I declare firmly, standing up and turning towards the door.

"Need I remind you that, you indeed, did fall at my feet," he smirks.

I knew this was a mistake.

"Watch your step as you leave."

With those words, I shoot him another glare and practically storm out of his office, heading swiftly to the elevators. *What an arrogant prick,* I think. I know I shouldn't have reacted in that way, and I'm certain I did not secure the position, but I have no desire to work for someone who assumes I would act unprofessionally or attempt to sleep with them. I resolve to search for job opportunities elsewhere. Perhaps my favorite café has openings. I begin to think of delightful pastries and beverages that would help ease my anger towards Mr. Anderson as I make my way to the café to inquire about any openings.

4.

Dean

I may not have handled that situation as professionally as I should have. I had a list of questions prepared for her, but after she entered the room, I was no longer interested in hearing generic responses to typical questions. I was eager to learn more about her unique qualities and what she could bring to the table that other candidates could not. Even before she spoke, I sensed she was different. The previous candidates who had come into my office seemed to rely on flirting to make an impression, but I knew none of them were the right fit. Despite my certainty, I felt they all deserved a fair assessment and a review of their resumes before finalizing my decision.

As I sit at my desk, gazing at the paperwork before me, I find myself unable to shake the memory of that woman. Being so fixated was unusual for me, but her spirited demeanor had left a lasting impact. Her entrance replays in my mind repeatedly—the graceful curve of her back as she stumbled, the brief glimpse of her cleavage as she hurriedly gathered her belongings, the blush on her cheeks from embarrassment. I wished to evoke a similar reaction on another pair of cheeks. Shit. Where did that thought come from? Despite encountering many attractive candidates vying for the assistant position, Danielle was the first to truly capture my attention. She possessed beauty with her long, flowing brown hair, mocha-colored eyes, and a figure adorned with curves in all the right places.

I did not intend to offend her with my question, nor did I assume she had ulterior motives, yet I found myself engrossed in her impassioned response. I have had women falling at my feet throughout my adult life, though not literally. This situation was novel. I typically avoided mixing business with pleasure due to past experiences that left me wary of forming personal connections, despite what others might believe about me lacking emotion. Some may even say I have no heart. Professionalism was paramount when considering having a female colleague in close proximity. Never before had a woman challenged me or reprimanded me during an interview, and I was taken aback by how unexpectedly aroused I became. The sensation of my cock bulging against my slacks intensifies, prompting me to relieve the tension discreetly. Locking my door, I succumb to the urge, picturing Danielle's alluring movements, the swaying of her breasts as she retrieved her items, and the captivating sight of her ass in those form-fitting pants as she turned away. With each stroke, the pressure mounting since I first laid eyes on her dissipates as I reach a release.

I must be a masochist as I find myself in a challenging situation, determined to convince her to return and work for me. In the past, I made it a rule to avoid getting romantically involved with my employees due to the complications and drama it usually entails.

Therefore, wanting her to work for me feels like a self-imposed punishment. However, given today's events, I am unsure if she would willingly agree to meet with me. I take a deep breath, composing myself in order to focus on preparing a contract that would capture her interest enough to accept my offer.

****

I wanted to avoid seeming too eager, so I decided to wait until the following day before reaching out to her. "Carla, can you please call Ms. Cliff and inform her that I would like to schedule a second meeting?"

"Isn't she the one who had a little tumble?" Carla inquires, a hint of amusement in her voice.

"Yes, that's her," I respond with a chuckle.

"You're considering offering her the job?" Carla's surprise slightly irks me, but I know better than to snap at her. Despite being my subordinate, she has always had a nurturing approach towards me, unafraid to call me out when needed. And, like my brother, she is not afraid of me as most people in the office are. She always seemed to have my best interests at heart. Losing her would be a tough blow for the company and it would be incredibly challenging to replace her if she were to leave abruptly because I acted childish.

"Yes, I am," I confirm, seeking her approval, though not entirely necessary. I value her perspective, maybe even more than my own brother's.

"So, you've actually made a hiring decision?" I

internally groan. Speaking of the idiot.

"If she accepts the offer, then yes, I will have made a hiring decision," I said, trying to keep my voice neutral.

"Is she hot?" Jay piped up, eager for details.

I frowned. "Absolutely no sleeping with her," I warn him.

"Ah, so that's a yes then? And just for the record, asking a simple question doesn't imply any ulterior motives. I don't form attachments; I just provide a good fuck and send them on their way," Jay responded, giving me a knowing look.

"Your interactions with my personal assistant will be strictly professional," I said firmly. "You know my stance on mixing business with..."

"Pleasure," Jay interjects, raising his hands in mock surrender. "Yeah, got it. You're quite the stickler. Not everyone is like Gabby," he adds, noticing my stern expression and quickly backing off. I shake my head, instruct Carla to make the call, and head back to my office to focus on completing the remaining tasks at hand.

5.

Dani

A phone number that I don't recognize appears on my phone. Typically, I avoid answering unknown numbers, but not today. "Hello?"

"Is this Ms. Cliff?"

"Yes?" I respond with uncertainty.

"This is Carla from Stonebrook Marketing. I'm calling to let you know that you have been invited to a second meeting with Mr. Anderson." A second meeting? Holy shit. This is completely unexpected. However, didn't he grasp that I had essentially told him to fuck off in a professional manner? Would this follow-up meeting focus on the job itself, or would it turn into an attempt to humiliate me because he's not accustomed to being rejected by women? I am tempted to decline. I want to convey to Carla that she can relay a message from me to Mr. Anderson to fuck off. Nevertheless, the café isn't hiring and working for a prominent company like this could open doors to more significant opportunities. Would I regret turning down this second meeting? "Ms. Cliff? Are you still on the line?"

"Yes. I apologize. Yes. I'm still here."

"Will you agree to a second meeting?" Just as I am

about to decline, my mouth betrays me.

"Yes. When?" Fuck. Why do I have to be so curious?

"This afternoon at 3."

"I will be there." I hear a click. I glance at the time. Shit. I only have 2 hours until I need to be there. I quickly jump in the shower to freshen up. I make it to the doors with just ten minutes to spare. I walk briskly past the receptionist this time, hoping I don't waste any more time by having to give her my name, but she doesn't even look my way.

My mind races as I ride the elevator up to the 22nd floor. Why does this building have precisely twenty-two floors? Why not just make it an even twenty? Am I a glutton for punishment? Accepting a job where I have to take orders from someone else? Working for a boss accustomed to getting whatever he wants whenever he wants? In a building where someone finds twenty-two floors perfectly acceptable and not at all peculiar? Maybe I was the only one who found it odd. The doors open, interrupting my thoughts.

I approach Carla, noticing her more natural makeup look compared to last time, but her signature poofy hair remains the same. She gestures for me to sit down without delay, reaching for the phone, presumably to inform Mr. Anderson of my arrival. Uncertainty clouds my mind about the purpose of this second meeting. Could it be that I am being considered for the job? I made a complete fool of myself with that outburst for assuming that he was being inappropriate; not to mention my ungraceful entrance. Would anyone hire a person who raises their voice during a first interview?

"Ms. Cliff?" I hear my name and look up. "You may enter now." I acknowledge the instruction and proceed cautiously, determined not to repeat past mistakes.

As I enter the room, my eyes are drawn to the figure seated behind the desk. He remains tall, dark, and handsome. His flawless complexion, sharp cheekbones, and a tense jaw line, even in relaxation, captivate my attention. Although not particularly religious, I find myself pondering if this impeccably crafted individual evokes pride from a higher power.

"Are you planning to remain standing, or shall we begin once you take a seat?" His words bring a flush to my cheeks. I hope my embarrassment goes unnoticed as I settle into the chair.

"If you're trying to ask me out, you're wasting your time." I declare, folding my arms and legs defensively. He looks at me, eyebrows raised.

"That's not why you're here, but it's duly noted." I gulp loudly, shifting in my seat, scolding myself for being presumptuous. I'm torn inside, and he seems to be relishing it. Asshole. "You're here because I want to offer you the job," he announces, setting his pen down, and finally focusing completely on me.

I chuckle. "I'm sorry, did you just say I got the job?"

"Yes, I did."

"Why?"

"Why?" He echoes, looking puzzled.

"I just thought that after I raised my voice at you, you wouldn't even consider me for the position."

"Ms. Cliff, I am the CEO of a highly successful

company. It's not the first time someone has raised their voice at me, and it won't be the last. I am seeking someone who can help me with daily tasks, someone I can trust to maintain professionalism and confidentiality, and I believe you are that person," he responds, clasping his hands on the desk. "I have prepared a contract for you to review, and I will need your signature if you agree, which I hope you will." He adds, handing me a document. I begin to read it and cough slightly upon seeing the salary.

"You can call me Dani. Is this serious?" I inquire, half-expecting him to burst into laughter and admit that this is all just a prank in retaliation for what happened the other day.

"Yes. I recommend going over the entire contract, but essentially, it outlines that I will provide you with a $75,000 annual salary for supporting me throughout the week, even on evenings and weekends if necessary."

"Do most assistants make that much? I thought being an assistant meant typical nine-to-five hours, Monday to Friday?"

"I'm paying you more than the average assistant because while you are expected to be here Monday through Friday, there may be occasions where I require your presence at a business dinner or work function without question."

"Why do I have to attend those events?"

"Primarily to take notes on my behalf."

"Notes?" Mr. Anderson leans in, his shirt snug around his sturdy frame.

"Ms. Cliff, a significant portion of my work happens

outside the office. This is the arrangement I propose. You applied to be my personal assistant, which entails accompanying me to some evening meetings. If this doesn't align with your expectations, feel free to decline my offer, walk out that door, and continue your job search." With that statement, he rises, strides to the door, and opens it. I contemplate leaving but the salary offered is beyond my wildest dreams, making it too lucrative an opportunity to pass up.

"Alright. I agree," I respond softly.

"Good." He heads back to his desk and retrieves a pen. "There are a few spots where you'll need to sign," he explains as I begin to sign the documents. "You can start on Monday. Arrive at 7:45 to ensure a prompt 8 o'clock start. Grab a large black coffee from the nearby coffee shop before coming in, and please, knock before entering my office when you arrive. I will brief you on your tasks then." I nod, passing him the stack of papers.

"Thank you. I'll see you on Monday."

6.

Dean

I observe Dani walking towards the elevators, still clutching the contract in my hands.

"Bye, Carla. See you on Monday," she utters, waving goodbye while waiting for the doors to slide open. I chuckle softly, shaking my head— witnessing Carla's surprised expression. Closing the door behind me, I make my way back to my desk piled high with paperwork to review. Letting out a sigh, the last thing I want to do is scrutinize contracts. I realize I need a break as I catch myself rereading the same line repeatedly. My thoughts drifted back to our second meeting, which had been far more successful than the initial one. It was a challenge to stifle my laughter when she mistakenly thought I had invited her here for a date.

I avoid dating. My schedule is too hectic for a relationship, and no one has piqued my interest since Gabby. Although I never considered myself the type to commit, I took a chance with Gabby. She was beautiful, intelligent, and outgoing. We shared wonderful moments together, becoming serious enough for her to move in with me. We professed our love for each other, but only one of us meant it. On our second anniversary, I had planned to propose. Returning home early that day to prepare, I discovered her in bed with someone else. Later, I learned she had been disowned by her wealthy family and needed me to maintain her lavish lifestyle. Some might say I now use women after being used, but I have always been upfront with the women I bring home, though I haven't brought a woman home in quite some time. I can't endure that kind of turmoil again and refuse to expose my emotions. Hence, hiring Dani was a poor decision. She evokes feelings in me that have long been dormant. I invited her to accompany me to dinner meetings and social gatherings. It was unconventional to bring one's personal assistant, prompting her to question my motives. While note-taking was the initial excuse, I truly wanted to spend more time with her and learn about her and her background. She was unlike any woman I had encountered before. Her challenging nature intrigued me.

A sudden knock on the door snaps me out of my thoughts.

"Come in," I call out.

The door creaks open, revealing my brother casually leaning against the frame, munching on a burrito.

"Do you really have to eat like a pig?" I tease.

"Do you really have to have a stick up your ass all the time?" he retorts.

"What's up?" I ask.

"Apart from bugging you about that girl you hired, I wanted to inform you that the Hansen meeting got rescheduled to tomorrow. I can't make it, so you'll have to go," he explains.

"But you're the main contact for that client," I point out.

"I have an important appointment I can't miss. Can you please handle it?" he asks, settling into a chair opposite me.

"I'm already swamped with clients, Jay. Are you even working around here?" I question.

"I'm always working," he insists.

"Charming people is not work," I quip. Jay's playful expression shifts to seriousness, a rare sight.

"Please, Dean?" he implores, causing me to lean back, puzzled.

"What's going on, Jay?" I push.

"I have a friend who needs help. I might be in and out for a bit, but I'll still manage my current clients. I just need you to handle this new one," he explains.

"Jesus... Jay, please tell me it's nothing illegal," I press. Jay feigns offense dramatically.

"I'm shocked you'd even think I'd do something illegal," he protests.

"Says the guy who got busted for indecent exposure," I counter.

"Hey," Jay retorts, raising a finger. "I was drunk, and the girl was a crazy bitch. I had to bolt out of there butt-ass-naked because she was threatening me. It was a matter of survival."

I chuckle, shaking my head. "Or a matter of being a complete idiot," I remark, eyeing him seriously. "As long as you promise me it's all above board and won't harm you or the company, I'll handle your new client."

"Thank you so much," Jay breathes a sigh of relief, getting up. "I owe you one. I'll leave the file on your desk later."

As he swiftly exits before I can even respond, I shake my head in contemplation. Jay and I, separated by a four-year age gap, have always shared a close bond. However, as time passed, our relationship started to show signs of strain. Jay's laid-back and carefree nature contrasts starkly with my more serious demeanor. He navigates life with ease, never appearing fazed or burdened by stress. Despite our differences, Jay has an innate understanding of our business, effortlessly matching my expertise. The challenge lies in keeping him focused.

I can't help but feel a twinge of envy towards Jay. While I pride myself on my intelligence and hard work, it seems that he effortlessly sails through life, obtaining what he wants. As his older brother, I have shouldered the responsibility of caring for him throughout our entire lives. I continue to clean up the messes he leaves in his wake, a duty I have carried for years.

Jay often jests about my uptight nature, failing to see the necessity of my focus and discipline. Yet, I am acutely aware that our success hinges on this balance. Attempting to regain my composure, I divert my attention to the documents before me, making a mental note to purchase whiskey on my way home.

****

I introduce myself with a warm smile, reaching out my hand towards Mr. Hansen.

"It's a pleasure to meet you," I say, eager to start our collaboration.

Mr. Hansen, a hint of surprise in his voice, responds as he shakes my hand, "Likewise, but I was expecting to work with Jay?"

Explaining the situation, I assured him, "Yes, originally you were, but due to unforeseen circumstances, I will assist you to ensure you receive the attention you deserve."

"Understood. Let's begin then," he agrees, ready to dive into our work.

We make our way to the conference room, a simple space designed for productivity, free from distractions. Taking our seats at the sleek conference table surrounded by high-end chairs, I lay out the necessary documents before us.

"Shall we start, Mr. Hansen?" I initiate the conversation.

"Please, call me Tom," he interjects with a friendly tone.

"Of course, Tom," I acknowledge, continuing our discussion. "Before we proceed, I must admit, I had expected to be working with your father?"

Tom opened up, sharing, "My grandfather actually. My grandfather's health is not at its peak, and the burden on him is immense. I stepped forward to assist in reviving his business. It was my initiative to bring you on board.

Although I'm not a native of New York, I have chosen to remain here until the company starts to witness some growth. I purchased a bigger building, hoping to open up a second location or move his original store there if his health continues to decline."

Expressing sympathy, I respond, "I am sorry to hear about your grandfather's situation. How about we alleviate some of the stress for him? It appears that your current sales have declined by approximately eight percent over the past year, with a continual decrease over recent years."

"Yes," Tom sighs deeply. "My grandfather has been successful in business for a considerable time, but times have changed, and he hesitates to embrace modernization. He is old school, set in his ways and reluctant to adapt. I am hopeful that with the support of your company, we can find a middle ground where he can still maintain some of his traditional approach to business while boosting our sales." I nod, absorbing his words.

Continuing the conversation, I assure Tom, "After researching your grandfather's company, I am confident that we can elevate your sales sustainably. I propose arranging a meeting for one of my marketing colleagues to visit you, inspect the business operations, analyze the financial data, and grasp the operational dynamics. This will enable us to tailor effective marketing strategies to enhance success and resonate with your target audience. Following this, I aim to meet with you, and ideally, your grandfather, to explore our options."

"Sounds promising. I will discuss this with him and get back to you soon." Tom rises from his seat, this time extending his hand in gratitude. "Thank you for your valuable assistance and time."

Exiting the conference room, I escort Tom to the elevators, bidding farewell once more before returning to my desk to document our discussions.

****

"How did the meeting go?" Jay asks. His call interrupts me just as I'm preparing to depart from the office.

I respond, "It went smoothly. However, it appears we will be collaborating closely with Mr. Hansen's grandson, Tom, rather than Mr. Hansen himself."

"Really? Mr. Hansen never mentioned that," Jay expresses surprise.

"Perhaps he was unaware when he spoke with you," I mention, slipping on my coat and grabbing my keys.

"Maybe," Jay hesitates.

Noticing his uncertainty, I remark, "You don't sound convinced."

"It was merely a passing comment about his grandson during a conversation," Jay explains.

Curious, I ask, "What did he say?"

Downplaying it, Jay responds, "It's probably nothing."

Concerned about working closely with Tom, I assert, "Jay, since I will be working with him, I prefer to be informed about all aspects of our clients." Jay falls silent momentarily.

"Jay?" I prompt.

After a pause, Jay finally responds, "Yeah, I'm here. It's just that I have been speaking on and off with him for months, trying to encourage him to take the step but not wanting to push him too far. Mr. Hansen mentioned how he wanted his grandson to take over the business, but Tom seemed disinterested. It seemed like he lacked ambition and was reluctant to relocate to New York to assume control."

Considering the situation, I mention, "Well, perhaps circumstances have changed. Tom mentioned he would stay until the business's sales improved and expressed concerns about his grandfather's declining health due to stress."

"I suppose. Just be cautious. Ensure you communicate with Robert as well. I wouldn't place complete trust in Tom just yet," Jay advises.

"I had already intended to do so. I'm heading home now, but I will catch up with you later," I inform Jay.

"Alright, see ya."

7.

Dani

Izzy leans in, swiping chips from my bowl. "Let's go out tonight," she suggests.

"Didn't you go out last night?" I counter, pulling my bowl protectively closer.

"Yeah, but without you," she replies.

"I can't. Work starts tomorrow, and I can't risk being late," I explain.

"You do suck at being on time," she teases, a hint of truth in her words. Despite my efforts, I always seem to run behind schedule. "I liked you more when you were carefree," she adds.

"You do realize I rarely went out even before this job, right?" I raise an eyebrow at her.

She smirks. "Yeah, you're a bit of a bore. Why are we friends again?"

"Because I make amazing hot chocolate, listen to all your drama, keep your secrets, and you're too lazy to find a new best friend," I remind her.

"True. You do make really good hot chocolate," she admits, standing up. "Well, at least watch a movie and have some wine with me. The hotel just got some

Buccella Cabernet in and I've been dying to try it."

"I'm in for the movie but the wine I think I'm going to skip."

"Nope. I forbid you. It's a sweet, red wine. You will love it. You're having some," she states as she starts pouring a generous amount of wine into two glasses.

As we sipped, she asked if I was nervous about starting work.

"Just a little. But how hard can it be, right?" I ponder, enjoying the wine. "Wow, this is delicious."

"Told you. But don't try to distract me. You realize that we are talking about you? Dani. The girl that trips over air?" My thoughts go back to my interview and my less than graceful entrance.

"Aren't you supposed to be supportive?" I ask, pretending to be mad.

"Just make sure you look cute. Maybe your boss will be less mad when you screw up if your face is too pretty to yell at."

"Ugh" I give her a disgusted look, rolling my eyes. "I would rather him just yell at me. I don't have any interest in him being attracted to me in any way." Izzy starts shaking her head.

"I don't understand you. He's so hot. And have you seen his brother? Why wouldn't you want their attention?" She begins to move towards our DVD rack.

"You know why. He's just another arrogant, rich boy blessed with good looks who believes he deserves everything because of it. I dated someone similar in the past. Where did that lead me?" Izzy halts her browsing, turning to me with a grave expression.

"Dani, I know what you went through was tough. But you can't judge every good-looking guy with money based on Tommy. Tommy is a fucking prick. A truly awful person. Not every guy fits that mold." She pivots back to the titles, continuing to browse.

"I didn't say every guy was like that, just every affluent guy." She glances back briefly, shooting me a disapproving look.

"Do you truly wish to remain single indefinitely? Perhaps we should indulge in a romantic comedy to guide you," she suggests, presenting a selection of films in the genre. I respond playfully by sticking out my tongue.

"I won't be alone forever; I simply haven't met anyone worth pursuing," I counter.

"And do you plan to find them by staying cooped up at home every evening? You need to get laid. Perhaps someone can fuck the boring out of you," she provocatively suggests.

"Sorry, but no amount of fucking will transform me into a different person. I will still prefer cozy nights at home, clad in sweats, engrossed in a book while savoring a mug of hot cocoa."

"Except that your vagina would be happy. At this rate, you may have to brush off the dust from your cobweb-covered labia," she teases.

"I'll watch any movie you want if you just stop talking about my vagina," I reply, hoping to change the topic.

"Fine. I choose this," Izzy states as she grabs a DVD

and tosses it over to me. I react quickly, barely catching it. Pretty Woman. I should have known since it's her all-time favorite movie. I groan, but anything was better than discussing my sex life, or lack thereof. Despite the teasing, it was comforting to have her by my side, making the night more enjoyable than a night out could ever be.

****

I slowly open my eyes to the gentle embrace of daylight filtering through my window. Startled, I leap out of bed and glance at the clock. Panic surges through me - only 45 minutes left before I need to be at work. How did I oversleep like this?

Without wasting a moment, I dash into the shower. Shortly after, I am hastily dressed in a sophisticated dark gray knee-length pencil skirt paired with a crisp white button-down blouse neatly tucked in. Snatching my matching gray jacket and purse, I hurry out the door frantically to hail a cab.

As I step outside, the bright sunlight pierces through my sunglasses, shielding my eyes from the morning glare. The lingering effects of last night's wine lingers, adding an extra challenge to my already chaotic morning.

I hear the familiar ping of my cell phone, indicating a new text message. Retrieving it from my pocket, I read Izzy's words with a sigh.

Izzy: You really suck at being on time.

I can't help but roll my eyes at her playful jab.

Swiftly, I type out my response, teasing her in return.

Me: You really suck as my best friend.

I hit send and wait for her reply.

As I glance down at my phone, a cheeky emoji stares back at me, its tongue playfully sticking out. I chuckle and slip the device back into my pocket, hailing a cab without missing a beat. Grateful for not having to wait, I instruct the driver to take me to Stonebrook.

Checking my watch anxiously, I hope to arrive on time. Suddenly, my eyes catch sight of a quaint coffee shop just a block away from my destination. Could this be the place my new boss mentioned?

"Stop!" I urgently command the driver, handing him some cash before dashing out of the vehicle. Rushing inside the coffee shop, I order a large black coffee for my boss, inwardly cringing at the thought. Who actually drinks black coffee? Oh, right, billionaire CEOs do.

When I step outside, I realize I only have five minutes left before I am officially late. I must appear quite comical, half-walking, half-running into the building. I greet the receptionist briefly as she observes me rushing toward the elevators. I really should learn her name. Entering the packed elevator, I breathe a sigh of relief, but as more people join on the next floor, I accidentally get jostled by the person in front of me. The coffee I'm holding gets knocked over, causing it to spill all over my new white blouse. And let me tell you, it's fucking hot! "Oh, fuck!" I exclaim. All eyes in the elevator turn towards me. I try to conceal the mess and quietly apologize as the doors open once more.

"No need to fret over spilled coffee."

"There is a need when it feels like it's scorching my fucking skin off," I retort without even glancing at the man beside me. I hear him chuckle.

"Well, I suppose we ought to start some paperwork for worker's compensation then. And maybe fetch a towel," he snickers. Finally, I raise my head to look at him and realize who he is. Oh shit! Jay Anderson. My boss's brother and business partner. He is undeniably good-looking, towering over me with his height, even as I wear heels. He has a pleasing build, similar to his brother with broad shoulders but leaner. His brown shaggy hair falls effortlessly against his face, complemented by hazel eyes and a smile that could soften even the coldest heart.

"Um, uh, no need for paperwork," I stutter.

"I don't recall seeing you around here. Are you new?" Jay asks. I nod.

"It's my first day."

"Wait. You're not my brother's new personal assistant, are you?"

"Yes, I am." As the elevator arrives at our floor and the doors slide open, he extends his hand, gesturing for me to exit first.

"So, that coffee belongs to him, then?"

"It did."

"That's going to ruin his entire day."

"You seem quite pleased about that."

"His suffering is quite amusing." I shake my head. He must sense my unease because his expression turns serious. "Listen. If he gives you a hard time, just let me know. I'll handle it."

"Thank you, but I can manage my own battles."

"That may be true, but I'll be here nonetheless." I offer him a grateful smile.

"Thank you." He nods in return, then strides down the hall, disappearing into what I assume is his office. I approach Mr. Anderson's door and lightly knock, noticing Carla engrossed in a fashion magazine.

"Come in."

I timidly enter the room as instructed. The man is hunched over some documents, so I patiently wait for his attention.

"Please place the coffee on the desk. Your workspace is outside to the left, with tasks for today," he directs without looking up. I carefully set down the coffee and prepared to exit.

"So, you arrive late and bring me half a cold coffee?" Damn. I mentally curse my luck. Before I can apologize, he interrupts, "No need for excuses. Professionalism is key here."

Under my breath, I mutter, "Cold my ass."

"Something to say, Ms. Cliff?"

"I was late by two minutes and someone bumped into me, causing your coffee to spill all over me. It was scalding hot, in case you're wondering," I explain, gesturing to my stained blouse.

"Consider keeping spare attire if mishaps occur often," he suggests sharply. I shoot him a glare before leaving.

As I head out, he calls, "Miss Cliff?"

I pause, meeting his gaze. "Avoid white," he advises. Irritated, I exit, letting the door close with a bit more force than necessary. Carla notices my distress.

"Rough start?" she asks.

"Just a bit," I reply.

"If you need it, the restroom is nearby," she offers.

"Thanks," I reply, rushing to secure privacy. Examining my reflection in the mirror, I see that the situation is worse than expected. Soaked through, my white bra, now the color of coffee, is completely noticeable. No amount of scrubbing will get this out. Desperate, I message my savior for urgent help, hoping for a swift response.

8.

Dean

I hear a gentle knocking on the door, pulling my attention away from the documents spread out in front of me. As I glance at my watch, the time displays 8:02. She's late.

"Come in," I call out, keeping my head down to avoid distractions. I needed to focus on the work at hand; there was much to be done before my upcoming meetings with my teams.

I sense her presence in the room, waiting for my instructions.

"Please place the coffee on the desk. Your workspace is outside to the left, with tasks for today," I direct without looking up. As she places the coffee on the table, a blend of coffee and coconut wafts through the air, the latter likely emanating from her. Taking a sip, I realize the cup is only half full.

"So, you arrive late and give me half a cold coffee?" I remark, unimpressed by the situation. She attempts to apologize, but I am not one for half-hearted excuses.

"No need for excuses. Professionalism is key here," I state firmly.

"Cold my ass," I hear her mutter under her breath.

"Something to say, Ms. Cliff?"

"I was late by two minutes, and someone bumped into me, causing your coffee to spill all over me. It was scalding hot, in case you're wondering," she explains. For the first time since she walked into my office, I raised my gaze to meet hers. Fuck. This was not the scenario I had hoped for, as I felt my pants tighten around my growing length. She's covered in coffee - her wet, white blouse clings to her skin. I can't seem to take my eyes off her soft, flat stomach or ignore the fact that her bra is completely visible, showing off large and perfectly round breasts. I can't let her know how much I am attracted to her.

"Consider keeping spare attire if mishaps occur often," I suggest sharply. She shoots me a glare before leaving.

"Miss Cliff?"

She pauses, meeting my gaze. "Avoid white," I advise.

After she leaves in a huff, I contemplate my words. Perhaps my response was unnecessary and lacked professionalism. I could have chosen to overlook the revealing nature of her attire, but I didn't. Normally adept at charm, I realize it wouldn't be effective in this situation. I need her to take her responsibilities seriously.

I left her a list of tasks to complete, wondering if she would be able to manage them independently or if she requires constant guidance. With limited time on hand, I hoped she possessed the intelligence to proceed without interruptions.

Exiting my office hours later for a scheduled meeting with one of my teams, I glance toward her empty desk. Presuming she had gone to attend to the errands I assigned, I instruct Carla to guide my team to the conference room upon arrival, although I doubt they need assistance as we have weekly meetings.

Settling into the head chair, and reviewing the information in front of me, I focus on the upcoming meeting to momentarily distract myself.

****

After my meeting concludes, I leave my employees and make my way back to the familiar confines of my office. As I enter, my gaze falls upon Dani, deeply engrossed in her computer screen, her brow furrowed in concentration. Notably, she had swapped her attire, now clad in a sleek black button-up blouse that accentuates the warm hue of her complexion. Swiftly, I retreat into my office, a wave of relief washing over me as I observe my dry cleaning neatly hung and lunch awaiting me on my desk. Clearly, she was more than capable of handling her responsibilities. For now, I wasn't prepared to part ways with her just yet.

I settle at my desk - a routine I follow unless interrupted by a lunch meeting. Devouring my teriyaki grilled chicken with mixed vegetables, I attempt to tackle the mounting workload ahead. The sheer volume of paperwork before me signaled a long night ahead. This accumulation was uncharacteristic of me, with only one factor to blame - my preoccupation with the enigmatic figure stationed just beyond my door. Her distracted demeanor lingers in my thoughts, compelling me to unravel the mysteries of her mind. This desire, coupled with an unprecedented urge to dismantle her emotional barriers, unsettles me.

An hour passes, and an inexplicable force draws me toward her workstation. Uncertain of my intentions, I approach her desk, trying to engage in conversation.

"Ms. Cliff? Ms. Cliff?" I call out repeatedly, attempting to capture her attention as she appears lost in thought.

Startled, she meets my gaze, revealing an unfamiliar sorrow in her eyes. Suppressing my intrusive thoughts, I wrestle with the impulse to offer solace, a gesture I know to be inappropriate.

"Is everything alright?" I ask, eager to delve into her thoughts and satiate my curiosity.

"Everything is fine," she replies, her voice tinged with uncertainty. Her subtle biting of her lip only distracts me, drawing my focus to her enticing mouth. I quickly redirect my thoughts, reminding myself of the need for professionalism.

"I was checking on the progress of the invitations. It's imperative we expedite their distribution," I explain, striving to maintain a businesslike demeanor.

"Oh," she responds, a hint of alarm flickering across her features as she navigates through the task at hand. "I'm working on them."

"Please ensure they are ready by tomorrow," I instruct, my tone firm yet composed.

"Right. Mr. Anderson?"

"Yes?"

"Is there a specific theme I should be aware of?"

"No. We aim for simplicity. Classy. Formal. Black Tie."

"Understood."

I linger, studying her. Something is off with her.

"You sure you're okay?" I ask, my voice filled with concern.

"Yes. I'm good." With a nod, I retrace my steps into the seclusion of my office, bracing myself for a prolonged evening ahead.

9.

Dani

I receive a text from Izzy, informing me that she's coming over with a new bra and blouse. Relief washes over me as I still have errands to run for Mr. Anderson and I prefer not to look like a hot mess while doing so. I provide her with directions on how to get to me and express my gratitude profusely.

After fifteen minutes, I spot the elevator doors sliding open, and Izzy enters, looking flawless in snug skinny jeans and a revealing tee. I hear Carla starting to offer her assistance, but I quickly stride over and intervene.

"Carla, it's okay. She's with me." Carla nods and returns to her book.

"Hey. Thank you so much for bringing this to me." Izzy scans me and bursts out laughing. "Not funny."

"It's hilarious. Just what I'd expect from you."

I fold my arms and give her a stern look. She grins and hands me a bag. "Okay, gotta run now, but catch you later. Try not to make any more messes today."

Taking the bag, I wave to her and make my way to the restroom. Changing into the black blouse she had given me; I grab my purse and head for the elevators.

"Carla, I'm stepping out to run some errands for Mr. Anderson. I'll be back soon." For a moment, I'm not sure she heard me, but then she gives a slight nod.

Outside the building, a black car is waiting; the driver is beside the back door. "Ms. Cliff?"

"Yes?"

"I'll be your driver."

"My driver?" He opens the back door, nodding.

I hesitate.

"I'm Mr. Anderson's driver, Henry. He informed me that you would need my services for some errands." It made sense. Of course, he would have a driver.

"Okay," I say, getting into the backseat. Before I can tell him my destination, he pulls out and turns, already aware of where to go.

We hurry to the dry cleaners, where I collect a couple of his suits before heading to an Asian-inspired restaurant nearby. Placing his order for takeout, I settle the bill and step back, glancing at my phone even though I'm not anticipating any messages. The only person I confide in is Izzy. I also do have occasional chats with my friend Chad. Chad, undeniably charming, outgoing, and boisterous, was my polar opposite. Despite our contrasting personalities, we instantly connected when we crossed paths at a former workplace. Being inherently socially awkward, my past experiences with men only heightened my unease. I was always on guard, which was utterly draining. However, upon meeting Chad, I had this gut feeling that he was trustworthy, and my intuition proved correct. Moreover, he was gay, alleviating any concerns I had about unwanted advances.

It's not that I shy away from relationships or intimacy; it's just that I haven't met someone I can truly open up to. The fear of losing control grips me. Whenever I do engage in physical intimacy, I need to maintain complete dominance. It's usually with someone who's just average-looking and lacks a big ego. They visit my place, and once it's over, I promptly show them the door. No emotional attachments, no strings, no heartaches.

As I glance up from my phone, scanning the room, my eyes lock with his. Panic sets in instantly. I struggle to breathe, my head spins, and a wave of nausea hits me. I shut my eyes, then quickly reopen them to find his spot vacant. Frantically, I search the restaurant, but he's nowhere to be seen. Was it just my imagination? Despite my efforts over the years to let go of the haunting nightmare, the mere idea of his presence, his touch, terrifies me. Grabbing Mr. Anderson's lunch in haste, I return to the office.

Aware of his ongoing meeting in the conference room, I step into his office, hang up his dry cleaning, and leave his lunch on the desk. Uneasiness still lingers as I retreat to my workspace, preparing to tackle the next task: crafting invitations for Stonebrook's Annual Gala. The guest list sits in my email inbox, awaiting my attention.

Starting the task felt overwhelming, but researching Stonebrook's past galas seemed a good place to begin. As I revisit those memories, my mind keeps drifting back to Tommy and my seventeen-year-old self.

After Tommy assaulted me, I spiraled into a deep depression. All I wanted was to fade away, to pretend the world didn't exist. He turned my life into a nightmare, spreading vile rumors about me. The girls labeled me, while the boys saw me as an object. The worst part was the talk that I was just a conquest, nothing more than a bet, though that was never confirmed. It was hard to believe that someone would wait so long just to win a game, but after what Tommy did, nothing seemed impossible.

Even though we dated for nine months, "had sex" on prom night, and then he left me, I was the one ostracized. I tried to become invisible, avoiding social gatherings and keeping to myself in school. The confident girl I had once been vanished. I begged my mom to let me finish school from home, but she refused, reminding me of the effort it took to enroll me there. When she questioned my desire to stay home, I confided in her about the incident. Her response shattered me, blaming me for not giving in sooner, claiming men don't like to wait. Despite my love for her, that moment stripped away any respect I had left. If my own mother couldn't love me enough to defend me, how could anyone else?

Alone and abandoned, I sank deeper into despair. At seventeen, I lost my will to live, convinced the world would move on without me. With my mom out on another escapade, I found solace in her pain medication. In the quiet of my room, I swallowed those pills, questioning if she would even shed a tear for me.

I was descending into darkness, convinced of my insignificance in a world that seemed indifferent to my pain.

****

"Ms. Cliff? Ms. Cliff?" I heard my name being called, pulling me out of the depths of my darkest memories.

"Sorry, did you need something?" I ask, meeting Mr. Anderson's concerned gaze.

"Everything okay?" His unexpected worry catches me off guard.

"Of course. Everything is fine."

"I'm checking on the invites. They need to be sent out soon."

"Oh." Panic sets in as I realize my computer has gone to sleep. Hastily, I wake it up, trying to refocus on my task. "I'm working on them."

"Please have them ready by tomorrow."

"Right. Mr. Anderson?" I call out as he turns to leave.

"Yes?"

"Is there a specific theme I should be aware of?"

"No. We aim for simplicity. Classy. Formal. Black Tie."

"Understood."

As he lingers, studying me, I feign composure.

"You sure you're okay?" His concern pierces through my facade, but I can't let him in. I can never let him find out.

"Yes. I'm good." With a nod, he retreats to his office. Glancing at the clock, I realize there are only two hours left. I force my attention back to the screen, burying myself in research.

****

I arrive home at around 5:30 to a beautifully set table with dinner waiting and a bottle of wine. The sight fills me with gratitude toward Izzy. Emerging from around the corner, she greets me warmly.

"You're amazing. Thank you for dinner," I express my appreciation with a hug.

"Of course. It was your first day, and after what you've been through, I knew you needed this," Izzy replies thoughtfully.

"I do, and you don't even know the half of it," I confess, meeting her gaze.

"Please don't tell me you fell again. Unless you fell and your vagina landed on his dick. I would definitely be interested in hearing that story," Izzy teases, trying to lighten the mood. I shoot her a playful glare as we settle at the table, savoring a few bites before recounting the events at the restaurant.

"Do you really think it was him? What would he be doing in New York?" Izzy ponders.

"I'm not sure. Maybe it was just my imagination," I muse, taking another bite of pasta.

"Be careful, Dani. It's unlikely, but not impossible. If it happens again, promise me you'll tell me. We'll face it together," Izzy urges, giving me a stern look.

"Of course," I assure her.

"I mean it. You tend to keep things to yourself. I need your word on this," she insists.

"I promise," I reply sincerely.

After clearing the table, we settle in to watch a movie before I hop into bed early, hoping for a more positive start to the next day.

10.

Dean

This week flew by in a whirlwind of events. A crucial meeting was scheduled for Tuesday with Mr. Hansen, but it almost didn't happen due to his sudden company emergency. Together, Tom and I realized the immense amount of work lying ahead; however, the potential success of this endeavor could bring us substantial financial gains. Throughout the week, my days were filled with endless phone calls, back-to-back meetings, and poring over numerous documents. Jay and I barely crossed paths, both consumed by our hectic schedules. As Friday approached, exhaustion set in, and I longed for some relaxation. While weekends often demand as much work as weekdays, sometimes it's essential to recognize when to take a break. Although thirty-two might not sound old, the toll stress takes on my body now is vastly different from ten years ago.

"Hey, man."

I glance up to see Jay standing before me.

"Hey. What's going on?"

"Let's go out tonight."

"I'm not sure, Jay. I'm completely drained."

"You need a breather. A few drinks won't hurt.

Maybe get some pussy." I meet my brother's gaze. He's right. Perhaps not about the pussy part, but it has been a while since I truly enjoyed a night out.

"Alright. Shoot me the details, and I'll be there." Jay winks mischievously before taking off.

After wrapping up some pending contracts and tidying my desk, I finally leave the office. While on route, a text comes through.

Jay: McNally's at 8.

Glancing at the clock, it's already seven. Just enough time for a quick shower before heading out.

Twenty minutes later, I stand in front of my closet, pondering what to wear. It's been ages since I hit the town. I opt for my dark jeans paired with a simple black T-shirt, aiming for a relaxed look.

I enter McNally's and immediately spot Jay with a couple of our friends, Ben and Mark. Ben and Mark were my classmates back in school, and we became inseparable after being paired up for a project. Mark is tall and slender - sporting shoulder-length, blond hair and a youthful face. He is always laid-back and easygoing, exuding a surfer vibe despite never having surfed. On the other hand, Ben was the complete opposite. Shorter in stature with red hair and freckles, he proudly embraces his love for food and aversion to the gym, evident in his recent weight gain. Despite this, Ben's humor never fails to lighten the mood and bring laughter to those around him.

"Hey guys," I greet, shaking hands with my friends.

"It's been a while," Mark replies.

"I know. I've been swamped with work," I explain, Jay nodding in agreement.

After ordering a whiskey straight, I turn to Mark. "How's Andrea?"

"She's doing great," Mark beams with excitement evident on his face. "I'm actually planning to propose to her soon."

"Congratulations!" I exclaim.

"Don't congratulate me just yet. Let's see if she says yes first," Mark chuckles nervously.

"She will," I reassure him.

"Unless she decides to run off to California and find a real surfer with a bigger... surfboard," Ben jokes, prompting laughter from all of us.

"This surfboard suits her just fine," Mark replies confidently.

"Hey, isn't that Dani?" Jay interrupts, looking past us.

I glance over to see Dani with another girl – she is warmly welcoming a guy. She stands up from the booth and embraces him tightly, making my muscles tense up. Downing the rest of my drink, I order another one, feeling out of character. Jealousy isn't something I usually experience.

Dani looks stunning. She's dressed in a sleek black sleeveless dress that accentuates her figure, hinting at just enough allure with a touch of cleavage. The hem of her dress falls to mid-thigh, lifting slightly with each movement, a subtle tease.

"Dean?" I snap back to reality and face the group of guys.

"Yeah, that's her," I reply, watching the handsome guy slide into the seat beside her, wrapping his arm around her and eliciting her laughter. That should be me, but it can't be.

"Whoa, man. Everything okay? Who's she?" Ben inquires, raising an eyebrow.

"She's his assistant. Isn't she hot?" I roll my eyes at Jay's response, taking another sip.

"Your assistant? Wow. I need to get myself a personal assistant," Ben remarks.

"Seems like she's strictly off-limits, Dean," Mark jokes.

I shoot him a glare.

"She works for me. That's it. You all know my rule," I start, only to be cut off by their chorus of reminders about not mixing business with pleasure.

"You might want to reconsider that rule. If you don't, I might. However, her friend is really hot, too. Think they'd go for a threesome?" Jay interjects.

"Cut it out, Jay."

"Touchy, huh? Since when did you grow a vagina?" I shake my head, trying to brush off his comments as I finish my second drink. I know he's just busting my balls, but it still irks me.

"You might need to rethink that rule," Mark suggests, leaning in and whispering, "I recognize that look. That's how it all begins. Next thing you know, you're shopping for rings."

"There's no such look," I deny, though he sees through the facade, choosing not to argue back.

I lean back, observing her for a few minutes. She appears content. Serene. It's a side of her I haven't witnessed before. In the office, she's focused. Often, she seems on edge, especially in my presence. The idea that I might make her uneasy unsettles me, yet perhaps it serves a purpose. After all, I am her superior. We are not friends. We cannot be friends. Our relationship cannot transcend its current boundaries.

The man she is with rises and takes her hand, assisting her as she glides out of the booth. Her dress hikes up slightly as her thighs brush against the leather seats. I feel my cock stir. He guides her to the dance floor. I shift my focus to ordering another drink. I engage in light conversation with the others to avoid drawing any more unwanted attention. I take small sips of my drink, trying to maintain composure, then glance back to witness her body moving against his. My grip on the glass tightens as my free hand clenches into a fist. I have the urge to confront him. The notion of composure quickly fades. I swiftly finish my drink, attempting to drown out the inner voice urging me to intervene.

I excuse myself to the restroom. I relieve myself, unconcerned about the inevitable return trips. I wash my hands, splash water on my face, and lock eyes with my reflection. "Pull yourself together," I mutter. *She is your employee. You barely know her. She is no different from any other woman.* My reflection seems to smirk in response to my last thought, fully aware that she is different. I've been with numerous women, yet none evoke this sensation within me.

A sense of losing control.

And I am always in control.

11.

Dani

"Come on, get up," Izzy's voice breaks the silence as she snatches the blanket away from me.

"What?" I protest, reaching for the blanket in vain.

"It's Friday night. You made it through your first full week of work. We're going out to celebrate. I've even invited Chad, and he'll meet us at McNally's."

I sit up, surprised. "You invited Chad?"

"Yep. You deserve a night out. I need one too. Let's go, have a few drinks, and enjoy ourselves."

I almost protest, but deep down, I know she's right. After a long week, a fun night out with my closest friends sounds perfect.

"I have no idea what to wear," I admit, looking at Izzy.

"I've got the perfect thing. Follow me." Without questioning, I follow Izzy's lead. I slip into the dress she hands me. It's snug, revealing, and short - nothing like my usual style. But maybe, just for tonight, that's exactly what I need.

We venture out and stumble upon an empty booth, slipping right into it. Izzy makes her way to the bar to order our drinks. Upon her return, I notice two margaritas in her hands. It's not necessarily my go to drink, but I'm allowing myself to have some fun and trust in Izzy to help me with that.

As we settle in and chat, Chad approaches and joins us. It has been ages since I last saw him, and his presence fills me with excitement. Bursting out of the booth, I embrace him tightly.

"Dani! You look gorgeous as always," he exclaims.

"Thank you. You're looking great too. Have you been hitting the gym more?" I ask.

"I might have," he chuckles.

"Find a new hottie?" Izzy prods.

"So hot," he replies with a grin. I can't help but laugh.

"Let's all sit down," I suggest. Izzy holds up her finger to me before walking back over to the bar.

Chad then mentions my eventful week working for the CEO of Stonebrook. I acknowledged the intensity but highlighted the rewarding pay.

"And you get to be around one of New York's most eligible bachelors all the time," he teases.

"I don't stare at him all day. He's usually occupied in his office or meetings," I clarify.

"But you're still in his vicinity," Chad points out, causing me to chuckle. I finish the last sip of my drink.

"You need to catch up," Izzy announces cheerfully before returning with what seems like six double Vegas bombs.

"Alright," Chad exclaims, grabbing a few and passing a couple over to me.

We raise our glasses in unison.

"To good friends, good health, and good times," Chad proclaims, lifting his drink. Our glasses clink, and we down the shots. And then another. The effects start to kick in, but I push any worries aside. Tonight is about unwinding and enjoying ourselves.

"Dance with me," Chad suggests, extending his hand as he steps away from the booth. I take it, and we glide onto the dance floor. A lively, unfamiliar tune fills the air. Despite not recognizing it, our bodies effortlessly sync to the beat, moving in harmony.

Lost in the music for a few songs, we eventually make our way to the bar for another round.

"How's everything going?" Chad asks, taking a sip of his beer.

Fantastic," I respond, perhaps drinking a bit too quickly. He raises an eyebrow.

"Come on, Dani. Really, how are you? Any romantic interests catching your eye?"

I shake my head. "No one has piqued my interest."

"In a city like New York, really? Not even your boss?" Chad teases.

I chuckle. "Well, my boss is easy on the eyes, but he's my boss. Besides, there's no mutual interest there. When he's not barking orders, we're arguing. Only on a few occasions do we exchange in some polite conversation. But for now, I'm content with how things are."

"Dani, you are twenty-five years old. I understand if you have other goals besides finding a man and settling down, but you're choosing not to because you're scared. You can't let your past keep you from the potential in your future." Chad knows a little about my past. I didn't go into as much detail as I had with Izzy though. He knows what happened with Tommy but I never let him in on my depression or my attempted suicide.

"I get it, but don't let fear hold you back," Chad says.

I nod. "I'm not. Just waiting for someone who truly interests me."

"It's not just about that," Chad insists. "Life's full of opportunities. Don't miss out."

I reassure him with a smile, and we finish our drinks. Chad takes my hand and leads me back to our table but our group seemed to expand in our absence. Izzy was there with Jay, Dean, and two unfamiliar faces.

"Hey! Look who it is," Jay says, unwrapping his arm around Izzy. My eyes dart right to Dean, er, Mr. Anderson. The atmosphere was tense. Mr. Anderson's discomfort was palpable. I observed him take notice of Chad's and my hand clasped together and I quickly let go.

"Hello, Mr. Anderson," I greet, glancing at Jay before turning to Dean. "Mr. Anderson."

"Dani, please. We're at a bar. Just call me Jay. Always Jay, no matter where we are. I can't stand that Mr. Anderson formality," Jay insists. I nod, stealing a quick glance at Dean, his expression clouded with the usual gloom.

"Meet Ben and Mark, our buddies," Jay introduces

the two men. They greet me with warm smiles and waves, and I return the compliments.

"Oh, Chad, this is my boss, Mr. Anderson, and Jay, his brother and partner," I say to Chad, motioning towards the group. "This is Chad, and it appears you've already met my best friend, Izzy," I add, gesturing to Izzy, who is leaning in towards Jay.

I slide gracefully into the booth, with Chad following suit. A server casually walks by, and Jay promptly orders a few rounds of shots. We raise our glasses in unison, savoring the fiery liquid as it goes down. One shot follows another.

Dean remains silent amidst our chatter. He always seems on edge, even when he's out. Can the man ever truly unwind? My surroundings start to blur slightly, and my speech slurs. I crave some fresh air. Politely excusing myself, I step outside, greeted by the brisk night air that jolts me awake.

As I stand there, a figure approaches. Expecting Chad, I glance up, only to realize it's a young man. Shaggy blonde hair, leather jacket, tight jeans.

"Hey there, sweetheart. Waiting for someone?" His words hang in the air, unanswered by me.

Perhaps if I stay quiet, he'll disappear.

"Come on, don't ignore me. How about we leave this place?" I continue to shake my head, avoiding his gaze. My heart quickens its pace. *Please just leave me alone. Please just leave me alone. Please just leave me alone.*

He draws closer, reaching out to turn my face towards him. I instinctively pull away.

"No!" I assert firmly.

He smirks, undeterred. "Oh, come on. I promise you, we'll have a great time." With each step he takes, I take a step back, and the crowded street around us fades, leaving us in a solitary menacing alleyway.

"She said no, so why don't you back the fuck off?" A familiar voice breaks through the tension. Mr. Anderson. I never imagined I'd feel such relief at the sight of him.

The creep slowly raises his hands in surrender, muttering, "We were just talking."

"Fuck off," Dean strides forward. The man quickly retreats, not looking back. Dean grabs my arm, leading me further into the narrow alley beside the building.

"Are you okay?" he asks, catching me off guard with his concern.

Surprised, I reply, "Why do you care? You can't stand me. So why bother?"

"What makes you think I can't stand you?" Dean questions.

"Seriously?" I scoff.

"Maybe this is how I treat everyone I like," he suggests.

"That might explain why you're single," I retort, surprised by his rare laugh.

"That smart mouth," he remarks, stepping closer. My heart races, hoping he doesn't notice, but his smirk reveals otherwise.

"I didn't know you had a boyfriend," he observes, causing my eyes to widen for the second time.

"I don't," I clarify.

"You seemed cozy with him in there," he notes.

"Chad?" I chuckle. "He's good looking, kind, and charming. Everything I would want in a boyfriend. But I'm afraid he's off the market for females."

Dean raises an eyebrow, not catching my hint. "Chad is gay. Besides Izzy, he's my closest friend."

As Dean processes this information, I wonder why he's even interested. Surely, he's not into me, right?

"Would it bother you if I had a boyfriend?" I tease, emboldened by some liquid courage.

He steps closer until I'm pressed against the building, his proximity sending a mix of excitement and nerves. Normally in a position like this, I would be fearful but I'm not. I'm almost comforted by the woodsy scent of his body as it washes over me, along with a hint of whiskey.

"What if I were?" he challenges, his eyes fixed on mine.

"You're just teasing. You're not the jealous type," I counter.

"Not usually," he admits.

"So, why were you sulking earlier?" I ask, his gaze lingering on my lips.

There's no way he'd be interested in me, right? But here we are, inches apart, his lips inching closer to mine.

"I wasn't thrilled about another man touching you," he confesses, his hot breath sending shivers down my spine.

As our noses nearly touch, I struggle to believe what's happening. He's my boss, my incredibly hot boss.

"You could have anyone in there," I whisper. His expression turns serious.

"I don't want anyone else," he murmurs, his voice lower and more alluring than usual - sexy as hell.

"And what do you want?" I manage to ask.

Just then, Izzy interrupts, pulling us back to reality. "There you are!" Dean quickly withdraws, returning to his usual demeanor.

"What happened to you two? I didn't interrupt anything, did I?" Izzy inquires.

"Not at all," Dean replies, returning to his grumpy self. Turning back to me, he quickly mutters, "I'm glad you're okay. I'll see you Monday." As he walks past Izzy, he nods, acknowledging her. My gaze doesn't leave his back until he turns the corner and is no longer in my view.

"Okay. What the hell was that?"

"I'm not sure," I reply, walking with Izzy towards Chad. After saying our goodbyes, we catch a cab home. My mind races with confusion. Was my boss truly interested in me? And more puzzling, I found him so enticing. I wanted him to kiss me. The desire for his touch lingers, though I push those thoughts aside. It's unrealistic. We were both intoxicated.

He's successful, wealthy, and attractive, but with a revolving door of women except for one. I read about their breakup online while researching the company. I saw pictures, and she was beautiful. At the same time, I'm just his plain, broken assistant who picks up his dry cleaning. He'd never actually want me. He doesn't seem like a guy who does complicated things; but I'm complicated. I bury my dirty thoughts deep within, knowing they can never be.

12.

Dean

I turn onto my back; the weight of the thoughts that have kept me awake for hours pressing down on me. Her presence lingers in my mind - the scent of coconut still hanging in the air, the way she nervously bit her lip, the intensity of her gaze that seemed to pierce through me.

I can't shake the image of her, the way she stood there, helpless, as that guy tried to make a move. I couldn't stand it – not for a second. Watching him close the distance between them, watching him invade her space, it was unbearable. And hell, there was no way I was going to stand by and let him lay a hand on her.

Her expression changed when I stepped in, and there was a glimmer of relief and gratitude in her eyes. Perhaps she was just glad to be rescued from the unwanted attention. Yet, she allowed me to guide her away and be close to her. It felt like she was open to more, like she wanted me to kiss her. I wanted it too.

Tonight had been charged with tension, every word hanging between us, every glance a possible signal. We were standing at the edge of something, a line neither of us dared to cross, but neither of us could ignore.

I take a deep breath, my thoughts heavy. The whiskey had clouded my judgment, blurring all the lines between us. I knew exactly who I was - a man with a reputation for keeping things light and casual. And I knew exactly who she was - someone who seemed to crave more than just a fleeting connection.

In that moment, though, all I could think about was the rush - the thrill of the forbidden. I was her boss, and that alone should've been enough to stop me. But in my mind, I was already imagining the feel of her pressed against me, the taste of her lips, the danger of it all.

I close my eyes, letting out a long, frustrated sigh. Now, in the silence of the night, the clarity comes. Giving in to that impulse would've been a disaster. She deserved more than a fleeting moment of heat; she deserved someone who could offer her something real, something lasting. I wasn't that man.

And even if I was - if I could be - I wasn't sure I could let her in. I couldn't risk losing control, losing myself in the chaos of a connection I wasn't equipped to handle. I'm not the commitment type, and I can see it now - she's someone who craves deeper, meaningful bonds. Entangling myself with her would only lead to heartache.

I need to get a grip. I need something - anything - to distract me, to pull me back from this dangerous line of thinking. I'd promised myself that I'd find a way to keep my distance, to avoid whatever mess might be waiting if I gave in to this. But right now, all I feel is the pull of her, and I can't seem to escape it.

13.

Dani

It's Monday morning, and as I step into the café, the familiar scent of coffee envelopes me as I order Mr. Anderson's black coffee and a French vanilla iced coffee for myself. I wouldn't be truthful if I said I wasn't still replaying Friday night in my mind. The events of that evening had haunted me through a restless night, filled with anxiety about what awaited me this morning. Should I confront him and clarify what had happened, or should I act as if it were all a figment of my imagination? Would it be awkward? Did he even recall the moment?

"Danielle," the barista calls, snapping me from my thoughts.

"Yes, sorry!" I reply, hastily grabbing the coffee. With my heart racing, I exit the café and return to the office, attempting to steady my nerves.

Upon entering, I spot Carla deep in conversation on the phone. I offer her a smile, which she acknowledges with a nod. I make my way to my desk, setting down my coffee before powering up my computer. As I wait for it to boot, I muster the courage to knock on Mr. Anderson's office door.

"Come in."

I open the door slowly, placing his coffee on the desk before him.

"Thank you," he says, barely glancing up. I nod, retreating back to my own desk. Perhaps he didn't remember. Perhaps he was just as embarrassed as I was. The thought that he might be horrified at nearly kissing his personal assistant sent a wave of heat to my cheeks. I shouldn't have felt upset, yet the sudden surge of embarrassment was undeniable. Deep down, I knew it could never blossom into something real between us, and I certainly didn't want it to be just another fleeting encounter. Maybe it was a blessing we had been interrupted, but was it too much to expect a simple acknowledgment and a hello?

I try to shake off my frustrations as I glance at the list in my email, determined to get to work. Around ten o'clock, I grab my phone, toss it into my purse, and start toward the elevators. It is time to pick up the dry cleaning. Suddenly, before I could process what was happening, Mr. Anderson's office door swung open, and I found myself on the floor.

"Oh shit, I'm so sorry, Dani," he exclaims, reaching down to grab my hand and help me up. I instinctively touch my nose, only to feel the warm trickle of blood.

"Here." Dean quickly snatches a tissue from Carla's desk and hands it to me. I press it against my nose, hoping to stop the bleeding.

"Wasn't it enough to embarrass me Friday night? You have to do it again?" I mutter under my breath, clearly not quiet enough, as he catches my words.

"What does that mean?" he demands, his tone

sharp.

I shake my head. "Nothing. I'm late to pick up your dry cleaning." I storm off toward the elevators, still gripping the tissue to my nose. Tears sting my eyes —whether from the pain or the hurt, I can't tell. The elevator doors open, and I step inside, desperate to leave it all behind, even if just for an hour.

A hand shoots out as the doors begin to close, forcing them open again.

"Dude, where are you going? We have a meeting!" Jay calls out.

"I'll be up in a minute," Mr. Anderson shouts back. The doors close, and he turns to me. "Want to tell me why I embarrassed you on Friday?"

"It doesn't matter."

"It does to me."

I can't help but laugh.

"Why is that funny?" he asks, a frown creasing his forehead.

"You had me pinned against a wall in an alleyway, only an inch from my face, and then you have the nerve to ignore me when I bring you coffee like I'm some—" I falter, searching for the right words.

"Personal assistant?" he finishes for me. Not exactly what I had intended to say, but perhaps his phrasing was gentler. I shoot him a glare.

"So it's okay to toy with someone like that? Is this how you treat people? Women? If that's the case, it's no wonder you're never in a relationship. It's not fear holding you back; it's that no one can stand you for more than one night." For a fleeting moment, I see pain flicker in his eyes.

"I'm not in a relationship because I'm too busy being a successful businessman and I choose not to be in one. I'm not sure what you expected, but I am your boss, and you are my employee. I told you when you were hired that this would be strictly professional. We both had a few drinks, and maybe things got a little out of hand, but nothing happened, and that's how it's going to stay."

I struggle to mask the hurt in my eyes, unsure how well I succeed.

"Good. I'm glad we can agree. You wouldn't be able to handle me anyway." I turn away, but not before catching a hint of a smirk on his face. The elevator doors open, and I step out, turning back to face him.

"You'd better get back to your meeting. I won't be in for the rest of the day since I need to make a doctor's appointment." I begin walking toward the restroom. "And pick up your own damn dry cleaning," I shout just as the doors begin to close.

14.

Dean

I stare at the closed elevator doors, my mind racing. What the hell just happened? A part of me wants to chase after her, but I am already late for a meeting, and deep down, I fear it would only be a waste of time. I'd sort it out later.

I press the button for the top floor and make my way back. I don't understand why I thought I could simply return to work; she dominates my thoughts, especially the hurt flickering in her eyes. This was precisely why I avoided mixing business with pleasure—things always got complicated. If it felt this tangled after nearly kissing her, what would ensue if we crossed that line? Sure, dodging the conversation we needed to have was an asshole move, but we'd both had too much to drink, and I wasn't even sure how much she'd remember. Clearly, she remembered enough.

I kept glancing at my watch, half-listening to my marketing manager's updates. I should be taking notes, and paying attention, but I am completely checked out. Thank goodness Jay is focusing. As soon as the meeting ends, I shake hands and hurry out.

"Dean." I turn back to see Jay, concern etched on his face. "What's going on with you?"

"Nothing. I'm fine." I attempt to slip back to my office, but just as I'm about to shut the door, Jay wedges his hand in to stop me.

"You are not fine. You bolted out of the meeting and barely participated. You looked like you'd rather be doing anything else—like getting off to Mrs. Goldstein. That's not you. Hell, I'm usually the one who looks like that."

"I'm going to ignore that comment because my stomach is churning just thinking about it." Mrs. Goldstein had been one of my high school math teachers —sixties, heavier set, and notoriously wore clothes that were far too tight. I still remember the day she bent over in class, exposing her thong to everyone right after I'd eaten lunch. It was a memorable moment, but not in the best way. Jay chuckles. "I'm fine."

The skepticism on his face told me he didn't buy it. He won't let me off the hook until I provide something he could work with. I roll my eyes. "I might have accidentally hit Dani with my door, giving her a bloody nose."

"Oh shit," Jay laughs. "Is she okay?"

"Well, she's on her way to the doctor's office, so I hope so."

"Is she pissed?"

Mildly." I note his raised eyebrows. "Okay, she completely blew up at me about almost kissing her Friday night and then me dodging the conversation this morning. The bloody nose was just the cherry on top."

"Whoa. Wait, back up. What do you mean 'almost kissed'?"

"We were drunk. But thankfully, her friend

interrupted us, which was probably for the best. Now, if you'll excuse me, I need to get back to work."

"You are fucked, brother. So much for your bullshit motto." Jay winks and salutes as he backs out of the doorway. He just doesn't get it. We were drunk. There was no way anything like that would ever happen again— no matter how much I envision my face buried between those luscious thighs, tasting every ounce of her.

15.

Dani

I can hardly believe I'm sitting in a doctor's office right now. Thankfully, the bleeding has stopped. I don't think anything is broken, but better safe than sorry. As I wait for the doctor, my mind races through the events that just unfolded. I can't believe I lost my composure like that. I need to figure out how to apologize when I return, that is, if I still have a job, . I wouldn't blame him for firing me, even though he did slam my face with a door. Perhaps we're even now?

"Good morning, Miss Cliff. I'm Dr. Henley," he says as he checks my chart.

"Good morning, Dr. Henley."

"So, why don't you tell me what happened?" He examines my nose with a practiced eye.

"I was walking, and my boss opened his door. We collided."

"Understood. Well, I have good news for you: your nose isn't broken. It seems you won't have too much bruising, but don't be surprised if some appears. Ice it frequently, just a few minutes at a time. It might feel sensitive for a little while, but you should be back to normal in a few days."

"Thank you, Dr. Henley."

I check out of the office and quickly hail a cab. The last thing I want is for people to gawk at my swollen face. After what feels like an eternity, the cab arrives in front of my building. I step out, scan the area, and all the air rushes out of my lungs. Panic surges as I turn and sprint toward my apartment. My mind must be playing tricks on me—this can't be real. He can't be here.

"What's going on? You look like you've seen a ghost," Izzy says as she rounds the corner, concern etched on her face. "Dani?"

I glance up, caught off guard. "I, uh, thought I saw..."

"Don't tell me it was Tommy again."

"I don't know what's happening to me, Izzy. He can't be here. He just can't!" As if to confirm, Izzy rushes to the window and peeks outside.

"I don't see him anywhere, Dani. Are you sure you saw him?"

"I don't know. Maybe I'm just losing it." She offers a small smile and wraps me in a comforting hug.

"You've been under a lot of stress with the new job and that hot boss of yours. It's not impossible that your mind is playing tricks on you. And seriously, what happened to your face? You look like you've been in a fight."

"My boss opened his door just as I walked by, and BOOM! There goes my face," I say, mimicking an explosion with my hands.

"Oh shit! Are you alright? You should see a doctor!"

"I did. That's why I'm home. I refuse to go back to the office looking like this."

"Alright then. I'm heading out to grab takeout and a couple of bottles of wine. I'll be back in an hour."

"Thank you. You're the best."

"I know!" she calls out as the door clicks shut behind her. I take a deep breath and head to my room, feeling utterly drained. It doesn't take long before sleep overtakes me.

I find myself in Dean's office. He's so close that I can feel his breath against my skin. He leans in, kissing my neck and tracing along my jawline. I pull him closer, kissing him fiercely, as he grinds his length against mine. I want nothing more than for him to be inside me. As I start to unbuckle his belt, he suddenly grips my wrists, holding them down while continuing to kiss my neck. I struggle against him, but it's no use. When he pulls back, it's not Dean's face I see anymore. It's Tommy's.

I jolt upright, drenched in sweat. What the hell was that? My attraction and hatred for my boss, combined with my fear of possibly seeing Tommy again, has me completely tangled up. Taking several deep breaths to steady myself, I open the door to the delicious smell of tacos wafting through the air. Izzy knows me all too well; tacos are my comfort food when I'm stressed. I feel incredibly lucky to have her as my best friend.

****

After dinner and a few glasses of wine, I pick up

my phone from the bed and settle onto the couch with Izzy for a movie. Thankfully, it wasn't *Pretty Woman* this evening.

"Let's watch *The Proposal*," she suggests.

Seriously? She chooses a movie where the overworked employee and her grumpy boss end up falling in love? She flashes me a grin. Yep. Definitely intentional. I shake my head and glance at my phone. Three new text messages await me.

Dean: How is your nose?

Well, this is surprising. It almost sounds like he cares about my injury. But knowing him, he was probably just feeling guilty.

Dean: Will you be at work tomorrow?

There he is, slipping back into his usual self, polite only until he can ask what he really wants.

Dean: I'm sorry.

An apology? That was unexpected. Am I dreaming? I should probably text him back.

Me: Assuming I still have a job, I'll be in tomorrow, but you'll need to pick up your own damn coffee. There's no way I'm letting the cute cashier at the café see my face like this.

I didn't expect a reply, but soon enough, my phone vibrates.

Dean: I'll pick up my own coffee from now on.

Is that a joke? Or is he acting a bit jealous? I am probably overthinking it, but he is seriously confusing. One moment he acts like he despises me, and the next, he seems jealous. I'm getting whiplash from his mood swings.

Me: Should I also mention that the manager at the dry cleaners you go to is always flirting with me?

Dean: Nice try. Bert is old as dirt. Didn't think wrinkly cocks were your thing. Still on your to-do list.

Damn. I can't help but smile at that.

"What are you smiling at?" Izzy narrows her eyes, studying me.

"Nothing. I'm not smiling."

"You're smiling. When your lips turn up, that means you're smiling."

"I'm not smiling. I'm just stretching them out."

"Fine, don't tell me. Next time, you can buy your own damn tacos."

I gasp dramatically, clutching my chest.

"Yes. I said it!"

"Fine. Mr. Anderson texted me, and he said something I found funny. Why do you always threaten tacos to get information out of me? It's cruel."

"It works," she replies, taking a sip of her wine. "So, texting your boss?"

"He just asked if I was okay and if I was coming into work tomorrow."

"Mmhmm. Are you sure he just doesn't want to know if you're coming?"

I threw a pillow at her. "Quiet. No one talks while Betty White is on the screen."

16.

Dean

Dani: Damn. I was counting on the fact that you've never once picked up your own dry cleaning.

I sigh. This was not the first time she had hinted that I was just a spoiled rich boy, relying on others for everything. But I wouldn't have reached my level of success without hard work. While I am indeed wealthy, I handle a lot of my own responsibilities. Typically, people are drawn to me for my money, but she seemed put off by it. Yet, I had been fooled before. I need to steer this conversation to a close. I genuinely wanted to know how she was doing. When I sent those initial messages, I didn't expect a response at all. Of course, she had to mention another guy. I was certain she did it intentionally to provoke me. Even though I tried to keep my distance and not show particular interest, I couldn't hide my irritation at the thought of other men around her.

Me: Sorry to disappoint.

Minutes have passed since I sent the text. What is wrong with me? Here I am, hovering over my phone, waiting anxiously for her response. I hadn't even done that when I was with Gabby. I set my phone down, attempting to distract myself with some television. I don't watch much TV, but occasionally, it helps me drift off to sleep. Just as I was about to close my eyes, my phone dings.

Dani: Not as disappointed as Sandra Bullock is right now.

What is she talking about? As if reading my mind, another text arrives.

Dani: The Proposal. Sandra Bullock is packing up her stuff, ready for deportation.

Interesting. A movie about a boss-employee relationship. Was she hinting at something?

Me: Interesting movie choice.

Dani: Izzy chose it. She's into the rom-coms. I'm more of a thriller/horror kind of girl.

No hints, just coincidence. I hate to admit I feel a bit let down by that. I have to end this conversation before I say something foolish. I decide to say goodnight.

Me: I didn't picture you as a horror kind of girl.

Damn it, Dean. Get it together. Just say good fucking night.

Dani: I like the feeling you get when you know something big is about to happen. When your whole body stiffens, your heart races, and you become almost breathless just waiting for that moment.

Jesus Christ. Is she messing with me? I have really lost it. Now, my dick is reacting to her words, and all I can think about is her being breathless beneath me.

Me: I prefer that feeling during a different activity.

Shit. There goes my other head speaking for me.

What am I doing? I put my phone down and, before I can see her response, head for a cold shower. It doesn't do much to calm my arousal, so I resort to my hand, pretending it's Dani, recalling that night in the alley. Her in that black dress, her nipples hardening in response to me, and her creamy thighs sliding open for me. I finish quickly, clean up, and return to bed. I glance at my phone one last time.

Dani: Goodnight, Mr. Anderson.

I had fucked up. Three words that remind me of the nature of our relationship and what it could only be: professional. Why do I have to be such an idiot? It felt like I had intentionally turned women off for so long that I didn't know how to reverse it. I reply with a goodnight, set my phone down, and hope she won't be invading my dreams.

****

I wake up feeling unrested. I slept like shit and found myself up earlier than usual. Determined to shake off the fatigue, I push myself harder during my workout, extending it beyond my typical routine. By the time I arrive at work, it is already 7 a.m. Coffee in hand, I step into my office, ready to tackle the mountain of tasks ahead, particularly the Hansen file. The gala was just around the corner, this weekend in fact. I had extended invitations to both Tom and his grandfather, hoping to discuss a few more details and strategize. Our schedules have been packed with meetings recently, and Mr. Hansen has been elusive, making it challenging to carve out time for a conversation. If they continue to dodge me at the office, I would need to think outside the box; I prefer not to lose this account.

While many attend the gala for the free food, drinks, and a chance to unwind, I have a different agenda. It is a large event and every year I manage to connect with new clients amidst the celebration. Jay often told me to relax and enjoy myself, but I found true enjoyment in knowing that the business was thriving.

I lose track of time as I immerse myself in work until my stomach growls, reminding me of my neglect. I glance at my watch—10:30 a.m. I realized I hadn't had breakfast, and after my intense workout, my body was craving protein. I make my way to the elevators, my eyes instinctively drifting to her desk. Empty. Had she even come in today? I greet Carla with a mumbled hello before stepping inside the elevator. As I approach the lounge, I hear giggling—no, not just giggling; it was genuine, joyous laughter.

Curiosity piqued, I slow my pace and peek into the lounge. There is Dani, doubled over in laughter, tears streaming down her cheeks. I feel a wave of irritation wash over me; she has never laughed like that with me. My entrance was deliberate, meant to announce my presence. I spot Aaron, one of my marketing associates, looking overly pleased with himself, his gaze lingering over her body. I shove my hands into my pockets, fighting the urge to confront him.

"I don't pay either of you to sit around and chit-chat, so I suggest you both get back to work," I say, my tone sharp.

Dani shoots Aaron a brief smile as she slides off the counter. "Yes, Mr. Anderson," he replies. Aaron winks at her as he leaves the room, and if it weren't for his undeniable talent in his role, I might have fired him on the spot. Trying to shake off my frustration, I grab some protein bars and head back to the elevator, only to find Dani still waiting there.

"Your face looks good," I say, a clumsy compliment escaping my lips. She turns to me, her expression curious. "I mean, your nose. I'm glad it didn't bruise."

"Right," she replies, turning back toward the elevator as I follow her inside. *Great job making this fucking awkward*, I think to myself. I resolve to keep quiet and avoid her for the rest of the day, a plan that succeeds until she knocks on my office door. With a resigned sigh, I brace myself for the scent of coconut that will linger long after she leaves.

17.

Dani

I try to maintain my composure when he compliments my appearance. It is a rarity for him to say anything nice, so it catches me off guard—especially since it was the second surprise of the day. When Mr. Anderson entered the lounge, his fierce glare directed at Aaron made me wonder if his life was in danger. I couldn't help but speculate whether Mr. Anderson was more upset about us taking a break or if he was just annoyed by Aaron's flirty demeanor.

Aaron is undeniably attractive and has a knack for making people laugh, but I feel no spark between us. In fact, I was almost relieved when our conversation was interrupted; I wouldn't have wanted to reject him had he asked me out. The tension in the room was palpable, and I figured it was best to keep my distance until I needed to address an issue regarding the gala.

Mr. Anderson provided me with detailed instructions that made organizing the event much easier. However, I had just received a distressing call: our caterers were unable to fulfill their commitment due to a small kitchen fire. Taking a deep breath, I go to his office, remembering to knock first.

"Come in," he calls.

As I enter, I find him deeply engrossed in paperwork.

"Sorry to interrupt, but we have a problem." His eyes lift from the pages at my words.

"What problem?"

"With the gala. The caterers just called. They had a kitchen fire and won't be able to cater the event." I notice his jaw tighten.

"Damn it. It's less than a week away! Anyone worth hiring will be booked solid," he says, rising from his desk and pacing by the large windows that spanned the back wall.

"I might have a suggestion." He pauses and turns to face me. "You remember my friend Izzy? Her family owns a major hotel chain—the Italiana Hotel?" He nods, his eyes narrowing, so I press on. "They have an incredible restaurant. The food is authentic Italian, and I'm sure they would help us out."

"Okay."

"Okay?"

"Yes. Okay." He returns his focus to the scattered papers on his desk, signaling it was my cue.

"Great! I'll make some calls." He responds with a small grunt, and I turn to head back to my desk, ready to ask Izzy for another favor.

****

"You're such a lifesaver!" I exclaim, wrapping my

arms around Izzy in a tight hug.

"I know. But let's be honest, this is a huge opportunity for the hotel too. The Stonebrook Gala is massive, and it could open a lot of doors for us."

"Sounds like a win-win, then." I nestle deeper into the couch, cocooned in a blanket, cradling my famous hot chocolate. It's September in New York, and while it's not winter temperatures yet, there's nothing quite like the comfort of a warm drink and snuggles with my favorite blanket after a long, stressful day. Izzy wanders over and starts rummaging through our movie collection.

"What are we watching tonight?" I ask.

"Beauty and the Briefcase." I roll my eyes.

She laughs. "Just let me fantasize about you hooking up with your boss without giving me a hard time!"

"Shouldn't your fantasies include yourself?" I shoot back.

"You kinky bitch. I didn't think you were into threesomes!"

"I'm done with this conversation. That's not what I meant at all."

"Maybe you'll hook up at the gala. Oh my God! Imagine if he pulls you into a closet because you both can't wait to get to his place to tear each other's clothes off!"

"First of all, that's never happening. Second, I'm not even going to the gala." Izzy practically snaps her neck turning to face me, her eyes wide in disbelief.

"What do you mean you aren't going to the gala? It's a work party! You work there. We're catering. You love our food. You have to show up!"

"Are you seriously whining right now?"

"Yes," Izzy pouts.

"I can't stand when you whine."

"But it usually works, so I'll keep whining until I get the response I want."

"He didn't even invite me," I say, my voice faltering.

"Maybe he just assumes you know you are supposed to go."

"You really think I'm expected to be there?"

"Uh, yeah. I do. But if you're unsure, just ask him. Oh, the movie is starting." She shifts until she is comfortable, diving into the bowl of popcorn resting in her lap. I struggle to focus on the screen, but my thoughts keep drifting back to the gala. Am I really expected to go? I don't even have anything to wear! I slam my head back against the couch, trying to concentrate on the film while sipping my hot chocolate. Mmm, a nice hot beverage truly does help calm the nerves.

"Do we watch too many movies?" I inquire, curiosity lacing my tone.

"Never! I'm appalled that you would even question our movie-watching prowess," comes the confident reply.

"Yeah, you're right. This is perfect," I say, snatching a handful of popcorn.

18.

Dean

"Dani. My office." I command, leaving the door ajar for her entrance. As I settle into my chair, I try to brush aside how good she looks in the black dress that clings to her curves. My eyes betray me, darting up and down her figure, praying she remains unaware of my scrutiny.

"Mr. Anderson?" she says, her voice tentative.

"Is everything prepared for the gala on Saturday?"

"Yes, and I'll be picking up your tux tomorrow morning."

"Very good. You have everything you need for it as well?" I ask, noticing the wide-eyed look of surprise on her face. "What's wrong?"

"Oh, um, well…" she stammers, and I arch an eyebrow. Surely, she knows she's expected to attend this event?

"I wasn't going to go." Her response should suffice. It's not mandatory for her to be there, and while most employees will attend, not all do. Yet, a different thought begins to stir within me.

"You will be there," I assert firmly. Her jaw drops in astonishment, and my gaze instinctively follows the movement and I feel my dick twitch. I'd love to show her what she can do with that pretty mouth. I feel my pants tighten and shift in my seat, hoping she doesn't notice the effect she has on me. I reach for one of my company cards and hand it to her.

"What's this?" she asks, looking puzzled.

"One of my company credit cards."

"Do you need me to purchase something for the gala?"

"Yes. A dress for yourself and anything else you might need to accompany it." I watch as she bites her lip. Damn this woman.

"I can't accept this."

"You will. It's an important event. You need to dress accordingly."

"Why do you assume I don't already own a presentable dress?" she challenges, a smirk playing on my lips.

"Do you?" I lean back, watching her shift her weight and roll her eyes. If she were mine, I'd have her in my lap, punishing that defiance with a firm hand.

"No."

"Then it's settled." I turn my attention to the computer, hoping she'll take the hint to leave. But when she doesn't move, I finally speak without looking up. "You can go now." There's no way I'll survive watching her walk out of my office, but somehow, I know it's only the beginning.

****

"Mr. Hansen, it's a pleasure to finally connect with you."

"I must apologize for not keeping in touch; this is our busiest time of year. To be honest, I've been so grateful that Tom has taken an interest. It was quite surprising since he never seemed interested before."

"I understand completely. Will you be attending the gala this weekend?" I ask, swiveling my chair to gaze out the window.

"Unfortunately, I won't be able to make it, but Tom will be there."

"That's unfortunate. I was hoping to discuss your account with you in person. However, I'll have my assistant reach out to schedule a meeting here at the office."

"That sounds good, Mr. Anderson. If you need anything or have any questions, don't hesitate to talk to Tom. I must say, I'm impressed by how dedicated he's been to helping the company lately. I've never seen him so motivated."

"That's great to hear. I'll touch base with you later."

"Of course. Goodbye, Mr. Anderson." I rub my eyes as I hang up the phone, feeling the urgency of needing Dani to arrange a meeting with him soon. The sooner we can get this account moving, the better. It's a challenging account, but I have faith that my team will handle it effectively.

I glance out of my office and spot someone standing at Dani's desk. Is that Aaron? I throw open the door. "Dani! My office. Now!" I watch as she excuses herself and I step back.

"Yes, Mr. Anderson?"

"Do I need to find a new assistant?"

"What?"

"I'm pretty sure I didn't stutter." Maybe I'm being unreasonable. Okay, I know that I'm being a complete asshole and there's no justification for threatening her job, but I'm furious. She cannot flirt with some pretty boy right in front of me.

"Why would you need to find another assistant? Did I do something wrong?" She glares at me, crossing her arms, inadvertently pushing her chest up. Damn it.

"I thought I warned you about slacking off on the job."

"Aaron was just asking a few questions about the gala."

"Did he invite you to go with him?"

"I don't see why that's any of your business."

"You will not be going with him. You're going with me. You are my assistant, and I need your help to enhance my business that night." She looks furious, but there's no way I'm letting that fucking tool take her as his date.

"Fine," she replies after glaring daggers at me for several long seconds.

"And please email Mr. Hansen to set up that meeting. I'll send you the details."

Her expression pales, eyes widening momentarily before she quickly regains her composure and storms out of the office, slamming the door behind her. I shake my head, questioning my choices. Why am I forcing a woman I clearly find attractive to spend the evening with me when I can't even touch her? I must be a glutton for punishment.

19.

Dani

Did he just say Mr. Hansen? I quickly sit at my desk, trying to take deep breaths. I was so furious that I barely listened while walking out the door, but I was pretty sure I heard the name Hansen. It's not an unusual last name—there are probably tons of people with that surname. So why am I panicking?

After a few more deep breaths, I log into my email to find the information he promised. I click on it:

Mr. Ed Hansen

Hansen's Hardware

edhansen@urmail.com

Holy shit. I fire off a quick email to him as Mr. Anderson instructed, but I need to get out of this office. I can't sit here and focus; it's too much. Normally, I would ask Mr. Anderson if I could leave early, but I'm still annoyed with him; right now, everything feels overwhelming. I grab my things and tell Carla I'm not feeling well and am leaving early. She opens her mouth to say something, but I am already on the elevator.

With shaky fingers, I take out my phone and dial.

"Hello?"

"Izzy! Please tell me you're free right now."

"Whoa. Okay. Calm down. I'm at home. What's going on?" I step off the elevator, nearly colliding with two women. I mumble an apology before rushing out the doors to hail a cab.

"I'm on my way. I'll explain when I get there." I hang up as I step into the cab and give the driver my address. Surprisingly, it only takes about 20 minutes to get back home, which I am not complaining about. That means I had at least five less minutes of freaking out. I pay the driver, thank him, and run up to my door, barging in like a whirlwind.

"What the hell is going on? You look psychotic right now, by the way," Izzy remarks, taking a sip from a bottle of wine. Yes, a bottle. As if she could read my mind, she points to the counter. My own bottle. God, I love this woman.

"I just had an argument with Mr. Anderson, and he asked me to email one of his clients."

"That's terrible." Damn this sarcastic bitch.

"The client is Ed Hansen. Hansen Hardware." I give her a moment to process. She stares blankly at me. "Tom's grandfather?" Her eyes widen, and her mouth drops open slowly.

"What in the actual fuck? Seriously?"

"Yes," I sigh heavily, reaching for the bottle of wine as I sink into the couch. I take a few generous gulps, the rich liquid warming me from the inside out. After a moment, I jump up and head to the bedroom to change. I slip into some comfortable shorts and a tank top before returning to the couch, where my precious bottle awaits.

Izzy wanders over, keen to listen as I vent my frustrations. She has a knack for lightening the mood, sharing the most ridiculous facts she has learned, knowing that it helps calm my nerves. "Did you know," she began, "that space smells like seared steak? And bees can actually sting other bees." I chuckle at her enthusiasm, but her last fact catches my attention: "Sea lions can dance to a beat."

Before I knew it, the entire bottle was empty, and I was feeling the effects, especially since all I had eaten that day was some fruit for breakfast. All I want is to escape, and both Izzy and this large bottle of wine have proven incredibly effective in helping me forget.

Izzy turns on the music, and we begin to dance. Normally, I'm not a great dancer when sober, but somehow, when I'm drunk, the dance Gods seem to bless me, transforming me into a dance Goddess. Or maybe I just look ridiculous and don't care. Either way, I lose myself in the music, feeling better until a knock at the door interrupts my groove.

"Who can that be?" Izzy wonders aloud. I shrug and keep moving, tuning out the mumbled voices as I attempt to twerk.

"Nice dance moves."

I spin around too quickly and stumble, bracing for a face-first fall. Fortunately, a pair of hands catch me just in time. I look up to see Mr. Anderson.

"Mr. Anderson?" I realize I'm still in his grasp and

awkwardly step back, not exactly graceful. "What are you doing here?" I slur.

"I came to check on you since you left work so abruptly."

"Oh."

"But it seems like you're more than okay." His tone suggests he's more than a little pissed. He turns to leave, and panic bubbles inside me.

"I, work, stressed, needed some time." He raises an eyebrow, and for the first time, I notice how sexy his eyebrows are. I never thought of eyebrows as being sexy before but his are. Everything about this man is sexy. What am I thinking? He's my boss—rich and infuriatingly confident. He's also a dick. I wonder how big his dick is. Suddenly, I'm distracted by thoughts I shouldn't be having. Oh Christ, now I'm thinking about his dick.

"Are you okay?" I open my mouth, but no words come out. Just then, Izzy appears, saving me from further humiliation.

"Dani was on the verge of a panic attack and needed to leave. It happens sometimes." I stare at Mr. Anderson as he runs a hand through his hair, releasing a frustrated sigh. How can someone be that good-looking? Focus, Dani —don't get fired. I'm about to explain when my stomach starts to churn. Uh-oh. Not good.

"You don't look so good."

"I'm gonna—" I bolt to the bathroom and barely make it to the toilet before everything comes rushing back up. A hand grips my hair, lifting it away from my face, while another rubs my back. "Izzy, you don't have to do that."

"Does she do this often?" It's not Izzy's voice. Oh no. Can someone die of embarrassment? Because I'm pretty sure I might.

"Mr. Anderson. Please leave."

"I'm fine right here. And it's Dean. We aren't in the office right now." We sit in silence for a few minutes until my stomach settles. I feel horrible, managing just enough energy to flush, wash my hands, and brush my teeth. "Do you want to tell me what happened?"

"No."

"If there's a problem at work, you need to come to me about it."

"I was mad at you."

"Is that why you left?"

"No. That's why I didn't tell you I left." Suddenly, exhaustion washes over me. He must notice because he lifts me up and carries me to my bedroom, laying me down gently. I don't even question how he knows which room is mine or worry about the underwear scattered across the floor. I close my eyes, and before long, sleep claims me, though I swear I feel his fingers brushing my hair back from my face before darkness takes over.

****

As the morning light filters through the curtains, I awake feeling ravenously hungry. A slight headache throbs at my temples, yet I feel surprisingly better than I expected. I shuffle into the kitchen, only to find Izzy still fast asleep. Quietly, I grab a bowl and fill it to the brim with cereal. I open the fridge to pour in some milk when a voice pierces the silence.

"You're being stupid if you don't go fuck that guy."

I jump, bumping my head on the fridge door. Perfect! Just what I need to enhance my headache. Rubbing the spot I hit, I turn around slowly.

"What?"

"Don't play dumb. That guy came all the way here to 'check on you,' held your hair while you were throwing up, and then carried you to bed."

"So? It was embarrassing. He probably did it out of pity."

"Sure. A rich, successful, smoking hot guy just came over to help because he feels sorry for you," she scoffs, rolling her eyes.

"Oh, come on, Izzy. He's surrounded by gorgeous women all the time. There's no way he finds me attractive or interesting. I'm just plain and boring, with a ton of baggage."

"Baggage makes you interesting. Sure, you're not tall and model-thin, and your wardrobe outside of work is pretty lame. And you spend your evenings like my grandmother Ethel used to before she died, God rest her soul."

"Is this really meant to make me feel better? If you plan on becoming a motivational speaker, you should reconsider because you're terrible at it," I scoff.

"That's quite offensive. I'd make an excellent motivational speaker if you'd just let me finish," she retorts, crossing her arms defiantly. I let out a sigh.

"Go on."

"Thank you. Now, as I was saying before I was so rudely interrupted," I can't help but roll my eyes. "You don't need to look like a model; you are beautiful just as you are. Guys appreciate curvy women. You have a fantastic figure—he'd be foolish not to notice that. Sure, your fashion sense might need some work, your dancing skills could use improvement, and you do have a few old lady tendencies, but you are also kind, caring, and one of the strongest people I know. Honestly, he'd be an idiot not to see that. But I get it; you've built walls around yourself, and I doubt he knows you well enough to truly appreciate what makes you special."

I take a large bite of my cereal, crunching obnoxiously to drown out the conversation.

"And shoving food into your mouth tells me I'm right. Do you like him?"

"No! Maybe. I don't know. He's definitely hot, but he often acts like an asshole."

"Maybe you both just need to lower your walls a bit and let each other in."

"Are you going to give him the same motivational speech?"

"That's not a bad idea."

I shoot her a glare. "Don't even think about it."

"Or what? Best case scenario, you end up with a hot boyfriend or at least a wild night. Worst case, he gets weirded out and fires you." I slam my head on the table, forgetting about my headache for a moment.

"Fine. I won't give him a motivational speech. But I know what I saw last night and at the bar. Something is there. You have a date with him tomorrow, right?"

"What?"

"The gala?"

"That's not a date. It's for business."

"Sure it is."

"I have to get ready for work."

"Just talk to him today."

"About what?" I stand up to rinse my bowl and put it in the sink.

"Maybe explain why you freaked out yesterday?"

"No way."

"Fine. Then just thank him for taking care of you."

"I didn't ask him to."

"No, but he did it anyway. Thank him. Whether it's through words, on your knees, or bending over his desk, you make sure he knows you appreciate him." My eyes were rolling so much that I feared they might get stuck.

"On that note," I walk away, heading for the shower. I don't have time to linger, so I quickly wash and put on a cream, sleeveless dress with a slight V-neck, throwing on a black sweater before grabbing my purse and heading out the door.

I decide to stop by the café for a mocha iced coffee. With a little time to spare and still feeling peckish, I grab a muffin and settle at a table. Just as I take a bite, my phone buzzes from my purse.

Chad: Vomiting in front of the sexy boss man? Not my idea of hot foreplay, but to each his own, you kinky bitch.

I sigh, frustrated. Not him too. Damn Izzy for not keeping her mouth shut.

Me: It was either that or shitting on his chest. Somehow, I figured he wasn't into the latter.

Chad: You win. That's too much even for me.

Me: Did Izzy try to get you to team up against me too?

Chad: She just wants you to be happy. So do I. Don't hold back out of fear.

Me: Last time I trusted someone and didn't hold back, it nearly killed me.

If only he knew how true that really was.

Chad: But it didn't. So stop overthinking and have fun. Don't make me tell you stories about fetishes. Actually, I can find someone who gets turned on by vomit.

Me: Wait. You still belong to that fetish site?

After one of Chad's exes dumped him, he went on a dating site spree, signing up for as many as he could. I had no idea how he managed to keep track of them all, but he did for a while.

Chad: It makes for good stories. And blackmail.

I chuckle quietly. He once told me about a guy who was into trees—getting turned on by looking at, smelling, and even rubbing his hands over them. There were more stories that were just too bizarre to comprehend.

Me: I think I'll pass on the vomit fetish guy, and please spare me any more fetish stories. I just ate.

Chad: Are you sure you don't want to meet the vomit guy?

I can't deal with him right now. I checked the time and realized it's time to go. Tossing my phone back into my purse, I grab my coffee and head toward Stonebrook. Today was going to be great. It wouldn't be weird at all. I'd just thank him and carry on with my day. Taking a deep breath, I reassure myself: Not weird at all.

20.

Dean

I strive to concentrate on my work, yet my mind keeps drifting back to the image of Dani sleeping. I can't quite explain why I lingered to watch her, but I did. Her roommate had mentioned a panic attack, and though I wanted to believe her, past experiences have made me wary. Trust doesn't come easily to me anymore. I question why I ended up there at all. When I stepped out of my office and heard Carla say she went home because she wasn't feeling well, a familiar worry crept in. The last time I felt this way was with Gabby. To truly worry about someone, you have to care for them, and I can't afford to care about Dani. This is unraveling everything I've worked hard to maintain, breaking the vow I made to myself. Yet here I am, violating my own rules and starting to genuinely care for my clumsy, beautiful assistant.

My thoughts drift to her, particularly how she looked in those tiny shorts while trying to... what is it called? Twerk? I remember how her skin felt under my hand when I rubbed her back, and how her tank top clung tightly to her curves, her hard nipples visible beneath the fabric. I feel a surge of desire coursing through me.

A sharp knock at the door jolts me from my reverie.

"Come in."

Dani enters slowly. Her beauty strikes me. The tight dress she is wearing highlights her curves and reveals just enough cleavage to make my situation even more complicated. I shift in my chair, but it only serves to press my arousal tighter against my pants.

She bites her bottom lip and offers a small smile, and I feel embarrassed by how close I am to losing control.

"I just wanted to thank you for helping me last night. I know I was a mess, and you didn't have to do that for me."

"I wasn't going to leave you when you were unwell." I notice a flush creeping down her cheeks.

"You didn't even have to check on me, but I appreciate it." I nod, acknowledging her gratitude.

"Did you really have a panic attack?" I ask, sensing her tension.

"It wasn't a full-blown panic attack, just the beginning. I had to rush home because Izzy helps me manage it before it escalates," she explains, taking a deep breath.

"Did something happen here that triggered it?" I catch a flicker of vulnerability in her expression, but it vanishes just as quickly.

"No." I can tell she is holding back the truth, but I decide not to press her.

"Alright. If you need anything, just let me know. I emailed your tasks for the day. Once you finish, feel free to leave early to prepare for the gala tomorrow. I'll pick you up at 7 sharp."

"Okay." She remains in her spot, as if she were weighing something in her mind.

"Is there anything else?" I prompt, but she shakes her head.

"No." With that, she turns and leaves, closing the door quietly behind her.

There's something she's not sharing. I chuckle to myself, realizing that just as I start to care for her, I discover she's hiding secrets. I get that everyone has their mysteries, but I despise games and detest being deceived. I try to push the thoughts aside, but her words and actions replay in my mind. What the fuck is she not telling me?

****

"You want to explain why you're still here?"

I glance up to see Jay leaning against my doorway. "Work. Obviously."

"Take a night off, will you?"

"Why are you here?" I question, feeling suspicious since my brother never stays past 5.

"Just checking in on you."

"You could've called."

"I tried." I check my phone, and he's right.

"Sorry. I'm just behind and trying to catch up."

"It's nearly 9."

"Good thing I don't have a curfew."

"Something's bothering you," Jay observes as he settles into the chair across from me.

"I have no idea what you mean. Do you really have to do that?" I snap, motioning to his feet propped on my desk.

"Relax, bro." I shoot him a glare. "Seriously, what's going on?"

"Nothing."

"It's a girl, isn't it?" I sigh. "Oh wow! It is a girl! Who's the lucky lady?"

"No one."

"Not wanting me to know means I definitely know her." He watches me as I try to ignore him. "I'll figure it out. You know I love a good challenge."

"No. You love meddling in everyone's business." Jay shrugs.

"Got a date for the gala tomorrow?" I sigh again; he's relentless.

"Do you?" I ask, looking up at him. He leans back further, hands behind his head, grinning.

"Nah. Thought I'd keep my options open. And stop deflecting."

"No. Bringing a date to spend the evening with my assistant and I wouldn't go over well."

"Wait. Why's your assistant going with you?"

"I handle business at the gala. I wanted her there to take notes."

"You've never brought an assistant before," he says,

narrowing his eyes. I shrug.

"Never had one to bring." Suddenly, Jay jumps out of the chair, sending a stack of papers tumbling to the floor.

"No. You've never taken anyone from work to the gala. It's supposed to be a nice evening for employees and clients. You wouldn't make someone work unless... Jesus, Dean. You like her, don't you? Please tell me you're not forcing her to go with you tomorrow."

"I asked."

"Asked or told?"

"Does it matter?"

"Of course it matters. If you asked and she said yes, she might be into you too. If you told her, she's stuck spending her evening with you." I roll my eyes.

"Did she at least seem excited about going?" I choose to ignore his question.

"She was pissed, wasn't she?" He laughs. "Why not just tell her how you feel? I mean, I haven't seen you genuinely interested in a girl since Gabby."

"Don't bring her up." Jay raises his hands in surrender.

"I'm just saying this is a good thing. You should put yourself out there again. How long has it been since you last stuck your dick in something other than your own hand?"

"I'm not inclined to answer that."

"Exactly my point."

"It's not like I haven't been with anyone since

Gabby. I've been with plenty of women."

"Not for a while you haven't. And they came to you. You never chased any of them. Maybe it's just an itch you need to scratch. It's not like you have to have a relationship with this girl. Just give her a good fuck and get it out of your system."

"She works for me, Jay."

"Never stopped you before."

"And it should have!" I yell. Jay sighs.

"Not every girl is like Gabby. I can tell Dani is different."

"Maybe not. She's hiding something."

"Oh?"

"I don't know what, but she's been acting strangely. Whenever I ask about anything personal, she spits out some excuse that I can tell is a lie because she's a terrible liar."

"Maybe she doesn't want to discuss personal stuff with her boss." I rub my hands over my face and through my hair.

"Listen, since you asked for my wisdom—"

"I definitely didn't ask for anything."

"I'm going to pretend you didn't just interrupt me. As I was saying, maybe tomorrow you should take the chance to talk to her like a man rather than a boss. Let down some walls. You really like this girl? Then act like it. I know you, Dean. I see all your layers. You keep people at arm's length to avoid getting hurt, but you won't admit it. You act like an ass because it's easier for people to fear you than to like you. But that's life. You need to take risks. Everything worth having in life requires taking a chance."

"Says the guy who won't sleep with a girl more than once."

"That's a choice. I just haven't found anyone interesting enough to pursue beyond one night."

"Right."

"Just think about it. I may wish for a papercut upon your scrotum most days, but you're my brother, and I want to see you happy."

"A papercut on my scrotum?"

"It's incredibly uncomfortable."

"And you would know?"

"This is about you, not me. So stop overthinking and just enjoy the evening with Dani before someone else sweeps her up. I mean, she's got a great rack..."

"Get out." I push him toward the door. He smiles and winks at me before I slam the door shut.

He has a point, though. She really does have a great rack.

****

The evening of the Stonebrook Gala has arrived, and I'm on my way to pick up Dani. Usually, I feel relaxed on nights like this; I've been through them countless times. Yet tonight, I take deeper breaths and fidget more than usual. I haven't seen Dani since yesterday morning, and our brief conversation just now—when I let her know I was en route—only heightened my nerves. I'm feeling slightly fatigued, having struggled to sleep last night, my brother's words echoing in my mind.

Maybe I shouldn't have made her feel like her job was at stake just to convince her to come with me. Would she have said yes if I had simply asked? Was I leveraging my position to keep her close? The answer is a resounding yes. And I can't help but feel like an asshole for it. I hope to take my brother's advice to heart tonight, to let loose a little, and to show Dani that I'm more than just another spoiled rich man.

As we pull up in front of her building, I step out and make my way up the stairs to her apartment. It still shocks me that she lives here; her roommate's family owns the Italiana Hotel, and I pay Dani more than the average assistant makes. Why, then, are they living in such a tiny dump? I can't shake the worry that it isn't safe enough for her. I knock on the door, and soon I hear the click of heels against the floor. In less than a second, the door swings open.

"Hey."

"Hi." I try to find the words, but I'm momentarily speechless. Standing before me is the most beautiful woman I've ever seen. Dani's hair cascades in loose curls, and her makeup is simple and natural. Her long, red, silky dress clings to her like a glove, with thin straps and a flirty dip at the front that remains professional, complemented by a slit that rises to her mid-thigh. At that moment, all I want is to forget the gala and take her back to her bedroom to rip that dress off her.

"Um. Is this okay?" Dani asks quietly. Damn this girl. As if she weren't beautiful enough, her lack of awareness only makes her even more alluring.

"You look stunning." Her smile lights up the room.

"Really? I look fine?"

"More than fine. There's no way you'll stay unnoticed in that dress." Her eyes widen, and I can't help but laugh. "You ready?"

"I guess so. Oh! Wait." She steps over and grabs a bag off the counter.

"What's in the bag?" I question.

"Notepad and pens. You know, to take notes."

I smile softly as I reach for the bag, sliding it off her shoulder with care. I place it back in its original spot, my voice gentle. "You don't need that." I extend my arm, and she takes it.

As we begin our descent down the steps, suddenly Dani stumbles forward. I quickly grab her arm and pull her close to prevent her from falling. Before I release her, I breathe in her familiar scent—coconut.

"Thanks," she says, her cheeks flush with embarrassment. "I don't usually wear heels this high."

"It's quite alright." I chuckle, captivated by her. This woman is trouble—delicious trouble.

21.

Dani

Stunning. He called me stunning. I couldn't tell if he was just being polite, but the way he looked at me made me believe he was sincere. I've never felt particularly pretty, perhaps because I heard the word "ugly" echo in my ears throughout my childhood. So, when this incredibly sexy man called me stunning, it made all the hassle of the evening worth it. And believe me, it was a major hassle.

I absolutely hate shopping. While I might have decent clothes for work, Izzy usually picks them out. When we go shopping, I stand there, slurping down a drink while she shops for both of us. This time was no different. We ventured into Saks Fifth Avenue, and I was immediately overwhelmed. But Izzy was in her element, so I let her do her thing.

Eventually, we stumbled upon a silky, sleeveless red gown with a scoop neck. It was Ralph Lauren and nearly $3,000. I silently thanked my lucky stars for giving Izzy the credit card—there was no way I could have handed it over for that amount. And that didn't even include the accessories! But after Dean's compliment, I thought it was totally worth the expense, even if it was on his card. Somehow, I didn't think he'd mind the price. The evening was off to a promising start.

And then I go and fall. Who does that?! Why does this keep happening in front of my boss? But his laugh —oh, that laugh. It is a sound I rarely hear, and it sends shivers through me. I was so shocked about our interaction that my body betrays me when I slipped off one of the steps and went down. Suddenly, I find myself flung upward, realizing I am pressed against Dean. All I can think about is how good he smells—sandalwood I think—and how hard his chest feels against me.

I freeze for a moment, so incredibly close to him, and quickly straighten myself out, muttering an apology.

As we step outside, I catch sight of a limo. A limo! I can almost picture my mother's face, green with envy, if she could see me tonight.

"What was that?" Dean asks, holding my door open for me. Oh no, did I say that out loud?

"I was just saying that my mom would be so envious if she saw me tonight. Between the fancy party, the gown, the limo, and the handsome guy next to me."

"Handsome, huh?" I roll my eyes.

"Don't act like you don't know how hot you are. Just don't let it go to your head too much. We all know how big your ego is, and you need to fit through the door to get into the gala." He smiles, and I can't help but feel my heart flutter. His smile is rare, making it feel all the more special when it appears.

"Is your mother typically jealous?" Crap. I didn't want to ruin this night by bringing up my mom.

"To be honest, I can't even tell you. I haven't talked

to her since I graduated high school."

"I'm sorry." His expression turns genuine. Maybe that is why I feel compelled to share. At that moment, I feel like I could trust him—like I could tell him anything. Well, maybe not everything, but I open up a little.

"I'm not. She wasn't a good mom. She wasn't even a good person. I often wondered if she ever truly loved me. To her, I felt more like an inconvenience than a child. She seemed to endure my presence rather than embrace it, casting the blame on me for the disappointments in her own life. Always on the lookout for a wealthy man who could swoop in and transform our existence, she instead attracted men looking to use her. I couldn't wait to get away from that suffocating atmosphere."

"Is that why you have a thing against rich men?" I manage a smile.

"Partly, I guess. I never want to be anything like my mother. But that's not the main reason." I glance out the window, avoiding his gaze.

"What about your father?"

"Prison. I never had any kind of relationship with him." I didn't want to hear another apology for my shitty upbringing, so I quickly turned the conversation back to him.

"What about you? Are you close with your parents?"

"My mom and I are very close, intertwined in a way that feels almost instinctual. My father, however, was a different story. We often clashed, our heads butting like stubborn rams. I think it was our similarities that fueled our conflicts; both of us were fiercely determined and resolutely serious. Jay, on the other hand, embodies my mother's easygoing spirit. They both embrace life. My father and I were driven by a relentless pursuit of perfection, tirelessly striving for our goals. Now, with my father gone, the distance between my mother and I have grown. I find myself wanting to have more time together but it isn't very easy.

"Why is that?" He sighed.

"The atmosphere between us had shifted after my father's death, as if an unseen weight hung in the air. She seems more melancholic in my presence, a shadow of the person I once knew. I couldn't shake the feeling that I was a constant reminder of her loss, a truth she would never voice aloud, but one I sensed regardless."

I place my hand gently on his arm, and he meets my gaze, searching for understanding.

"If you have a good relationship with your mom, you should reach out to her," I urge. "Express how you truly feel. It may be difficult, but you'll never find closure if you keep it all bottled up inside."

A soft laugh escapes me, tinged with irony. I should heed my own advice, yet I knew it was far easier to say than to do.

"You're right. Maybe I will." His lips curve into a faint half-smile, and I can't help but consider it a victory. For the first time, I see Dean in a new light. He often seems so guarded, using a tough exterior to keep others at bay. I understand that instinct all too well. This is why I had managed to keep him from getting under my skin. Mostly. But tonight feels different. I catch a glimpse of the real

Dean, and a flutter of realization hits me—I am in trouble. It won't take much for me to fall for him.

****

Entering the Stonebrook Gala is an experience unlike any I have ever encountered. It is breathtaking. As I step inside, I take in several rooms, each filled with its own unique ambiance. One room features a collection of dark gray plush chairs, where waiters glide by, balancing trays of appetizers and glasses of champagne. Another room houses a small bar, complete with high-top tables and bar stools, illuminated by black lights that cast a captivating purple glow.

The much larger room unfolds before me, dotted with tables adorned with flickering candles that create a soft, inviting light. A large bar sprawls across one side, while a dance floor beckons in the center. Although we weren't late, a crowd of several hundred people had already gathered, filling the space with laughter and conversation. I had yet to explore the entirety of the place, yet I find myself wanting to pat my own back for the role I played in bringing it all together.

"You okay?" Dean smirks, glancing at me.

"Fine. Why?" I reply, suddenly aware of how tightly I'm gripping his arm. My cheeks flush as I release my hold. "This is just very different from my typical Saturday nights." He chuckles, his amusement evident.

"You want a drink?" he asks.

"Please." I watch as he makes his way to the bar,

shaking hands and nodding at a few familiar faces along the way.

"You hate to say goodbye, but you love to watch him walk away." The unexpected voice startled me, and I turned to find Carla standing beside me. She looks incredible; her hair and makeup are undoubtedly done by a professional. Gone was her usual poof; instead, her hair was styled in a sophisticated bun that accentuated her flawless complexion. The emerald green of her dress makes her green eyes pop and highlights the vibrancy of her red hair. She resembles a queen.

"Carla! Who knew you had such a naughty side?" I laugh.

"I'm old, not blind, dear," she replies, a playful glint in her eye.

"You look beautiful," I compliment her.

"Thank you! You look divine yourself," she returns. "If you're trying to win brownie points, it's working," she teases.

"I don't need brownie points, Carla. You loved me the moment we met, with all my poise and grace." She laughs but then sighs, glancing over at Dean, still engaged in conversation with the bartender. "I can see why he likes you. Be good to him, dear. He's been hurt before. It's nice to finally see him smile." She squeezes my arm gently and offers me a small, encouraging smile before drifting off toward an older couple.

I find myself pondering her words. He's been hurt before. Was she referring to that Gabby girl? Did she cause his pain? Is that why he acts like such an asshole? But is he really an asshole all the time? Not necessarily.

Right now, his mood swings are giving me whiplash, yet I sense there's something deeper beneath the surface. My thoughts swirl as I question if I've completely misjudged him.

"Your drink," he says, handing me a glass before taking a sip of his own. Carla is wrong—there's no way he could possibly like me. Not in that way.

"Thank you," I reply, taking a sip and realizing it's a sweet wine. I glance at him, surprised. "How did you know?"

He shrugs nonchalantly. "From that night at your place."

"You noticed what I was drinking?" I ask, still taken aback by his attention. He shrugs again.

"As much as I'd love to stand here and discuss how I know your drink preferences, I have some mingling to do," he says with a smirk. I roll my eyes.

"I also have some mingling to do—specifically with the bruschetta and arancini," I retort playfully. He shakes his head, a smile spreading across his face.

"Mingle away." I turn to leave, but his large hand catches my elbow, and I feel his warm breath against my ear. "I'll come find you in a bit," he whispers in that low, gravelly voice that sends a rush of heat through me. It's both thrilling and embarrassing.

As we part ways, I search for appetizers to distract myself, though I know no amount of food can quell the yearning that simmers within me.

"Delicious." I spin around, startled by the male voice behind me.

"Excuse me?"

"The fritto misto. It's delicious," he repeats, reaching past me to grab more. He's cute—tall and lean, styled blonde hair, and dressed in a perfectly fitted navy suit. Any other woman might be swooning over his attention, but all I can think about is what Dean is doing. I don't want to be rude, so I respond.

"It is." He flashes a smile that reveals perfect teeth. How can they be that white?

"What brings you to the gala tonight? Are you a client of Stonebrook?"

"No, I'm actually an employee."

"Beautiful and smart." This is the moment I should blush and flirt back, but I can't bring myself to do it. I offer a polite smile and scan the room until I spot my target. But all I see is a stunning woman, model-like in her beauty, all over Dean. I mean absolutely flawless. I bet she doesn't even know what it's like to wake up with bedhead or ugly cry. I do. I'm sure she looks classy as hell even when she cries. She's laughing at whatever he's saying, standing too close, and touching his arm. What's worse is that he's laughing with her! Laughing! I barely get a smile from him. I feel like such an idiot. How often have I heard his rule about not mixing business with pleasure? He's just being polite to me.

I finish my drink and glance back at Mr. Perfect in front of me. It's like choosing a scoop of vanilla ice cream when all I really want is triple chocolate cake—still sweet, but far from satisfying.

"What's your story?" I ask.

"I own a restaurant. I've been a client of Stonebrook for several years now."

"Wow. That explains your enthusiasm for the food." He chuckles.

"I'm Blake."

"Dani."

"Well, it's a pleasure to meet you, Dani. Maybe we can have dinner sometime?"

"Oh. Um...."

"She's busy." I glance over at Dean, who looks furious.

"Dean!" Blake turns to extend his hand. "Good to see you."

"Blake. How's business?" Dean asks, his eyes filled with irritation as they dart to me.

"It's great. Better than ever. Your suggestions were spot on."

"Good to hear. Now, if you'll excuse me, I'm going to steal Miss Cliff away." Blake looks at me, then back at Dean, nodding.

"Of course. Dani, it was nice meeting you."

"Same here." I offer a small wave as Dean grips my hand and pulls me away. Once we're far enough, I stop and tug my hand free.

"What the hell?" Dean furrows his brow at my outburst. "What? We were just talking about the fritto misto! Not that it's any of your business." He continues to glare, jaw clenched. I throw my hands in the air and sigh. "What if I wanted to keep talking to him?"

"You don't."

"You have no idea what I want!" I retort, crossing my arms.

"Don't I?" A slight smirk lifts the corner of his mouth as he leans in slightly. He's trying to play dirty, but I won't let him. I can't. How can he be all over some woman and then think he can just charm me?

"I don't know what game you're playing, Mr. Anderson, but I won't be part of it. Why don't you go after the woman who's clearly been giving you all the signals? She doesn't even wake up with bedhead. Me? My hair is a disaster in the morning, and when I cry, it's an ugly sight. I bet she looks classy as shit when she sheds tears. I need to leave."

I turn on my heel and walk away, hearing him call my name, but I don't stop. A part of me wants him to chase after me, to prove that my doubts about him are unfounded. But then I hear someone call his name, and I realize that what I truly want tonight will remain out of reach. My eyes begin to well with tears, and I know I must escape. I cannot cry in public!

I turn the corner toward the elevators and run straight into something solid. A large pair of hands grips my arms, steadying me. I go to thank them when I see his face. Tommy.

"I, I, I'm sorry." I start to sidestep him, hoping he doesn't recognize me, but he grabs my wrist, holding me in place. Fuck.

"It's been a while, Dani." His eyes roam over my body, and I suddenly feel nauseous, struggling to breathe.

"Let go of me, Tommy." His smile feels menacing.

"Tommy," I whisper, trying to pull my arm away.

"Don't ruin this deal for me. Just one word from you, and I'll ruin you." Ruin me? He's already done that. I part my lips, desperate to speak, but the words remain lodged in my throat. He must notice the bewilderment in my eyes because he continues.

"I doubt Dean would be pleased to learn he hired a money-hungry whore. A user, just like your mother." He smirks, his gaze icy. "I'll see you around... babe." With that, he releases his grip and strides away, disappearing around the corner. I stand there, frozen, staring at the empty space he once occupied. Nothing he said made any sense. I'm not any of those things. I'm nothing like my mother. I have to get out of here. In mere seconds, all my progress over the years has been erased. In mere seconds, I'm back to being that girl left alone in that filthy motel room. Weak. Scared. Alone.

22.

Dean

I want to pursue her, and I start to, until a booming voice calls my name. As much as I yearn to follow her, I can't ignore Frank Bugatti. She is probably just in the restroom.

"Dean, my boy! How are you?" he asks, shaking my hand with a firm grip.

"I'm well. How about you, Frank?"

"Just wonderful."

"And Virginia?"

"Still as beautiful and full of life as the day I met her." Frank and Virginia have been together for nearly fifty years. Since I've known them, their love has never faltered. My thoughts drift back to Dani. If she wants to leave, I won't stop her. But that doesn't keep her from occupying my mind. All night, I craved conversation with her, the warmth of her touch, the closeness we had shared on the ride here. Yet this party was crucial for checking in with existing clients and attracting new ones. When I spotted Blake Johnson chatting with her, I felt a surge of anger. I couldn't escape Maria, another client, fast enough. Jealousy wasn't my usual sentiment; I had never felt so out of control when it came to my emotions as I did around Dani. But then I remembered how her breasts pushed up when she crossed her arms, how captivating she looked when she was angry, and how adorably she rambled about her bedhead. I assumed she was referring to Maria Estevez. While Maria was stunning and playful, she was happily married with four children; I had always seen her strictly as a client. Dani accused me of being jealous, but the truth was, she was jealous too.

"Dean?" My thoughts are interrupted, and I realize I haven't heard a word Frank had said.

"Yes, Frank?" I force a smile.

"Who is she?"

"Who is who?"

"The woman. You have the look of a man in love. For that reason, I'll forgive you for not listening to a word I've said."

"My apologies, Frank. I don't typically get distracted, but I assure you, I am not in love. Now, fill me in. I heard your nephew might be taking over?"

Frank began to excitedly share his plans for retirement and the new possibilities that await him once his nephew takes the reins of the company. Love. I'm not even sure if that was in the cards for me. But one thing I know for certain: I have no room for distractions. And Dani is a distraction. Her anger toward me might actually be for the best.

****

Frank and I wrap up our discussion just as I catch

sight of Tom Hansen approaching.

"Hey, Dean," he greets, extending his hand.

"Tom," I reply, shaking his hand firmly. My brother's concerns echo in my mind, and although Tom has given me no reason to distrust him, a lingering wariness hangs in the air.

"This is quite the party," he remarks, glancing around.

"Thank you. I must admit, it was all my assistant's doing," I respond, trying to keep the conversation light.

"The pretty brunette, right?" His words strike a nerve, igniting an urge to strike him.

"Have you and your grandfather had a chance to review our marketing plan yet?" I ask, sidestepping his comment.

"About that... I'd love to arrange a meeting to discuss it further."

"I can definitely set up a meeting with you and the marketing team," I say, keeping my tone professional.

"I'd actually prefer if you could be there as well," he replies, a hint of insistence in his voice.

"I can see what I can do," I say cautiously.

"I appreciate that," he nods, his expression unreadable.

"Alright, I need to speak with a few more clients but enjoy the party. I'll make sure to get back to you this week about the meeting," I say, stepping back.

"Sounds good," he responds, though I walk away with a knot of unease in my stomach. Typically, I handle initial meetings with clients, but my marketing team is more than capable of managing things without my presence unless there's an issue. I'm more of a behind-the-scenes guy, so Tom's insistence on my involvement puzzles me.

As I glance back, I catch Tom staring intently at me. His expression shifts abruptly as he offers a quick wave, leaving me to wonder if the intensity I felt was merely a figment of my imagination.

****

After mingling with various clients, I suddenly realize that it had been over an hour and a half since I'd last seen Dani. A sense of unease creeps in as I scan the room, hoping I might have merely overlooked her. I search high and low, but it soon becomes clear: she had left. Had I pissed her off that much?

I pull out my phone, my fingers trembling slightly.

Me: Where are you?

There's a pause, a moment that feels like an eternity. Finally, a response comes through.

Dani: Home.

A sinking feeling settles in my stomach. She really had gone.

Me: I'm sorry.

I'm not one to apologize lightly, but this feels different. If our earlier conversation had driven her away, then I owe her this much.

Dani: For what?

Me: Being an ass.

Dani: I didn't leave because of you. I was just tired.

Me: I'm not sure I believe you.

Dani: That's your prerogative.

I find myself at a loss for how to navigate this conversation. It's clear she's upset about something—whether it's me or some other issue, I'm uncertain. I know I should probably let it go, but I can't resist the urge to keep pushing.

Me: Are you okay?

Dani: Dean, why do you care?

That's a fair question. Why do I care? Why does the sudden shift in the tone of our evening gnaw at me so intensely? I can't simply remain silent, so I resort to my usual defense mechanism: asshole remarks.

Me: I don't typically have my dates walk out on me.

Dani: First time for everything.

Damn her sharp tongue. Despite the tension, I can't help but smile at the fire she throws my way.

Me: Goodnight, Dani.

Dani: Goodnight, Dean.

23.
Dani

I open the door, and the moment I close it behind me, a rush of relief washes over me. I lean against the sturdy wood, closing my eyes as I slide down to the floor, the weight of the world pressing down on my shoulders.

In those fleeting moments when I thought I saw Tommy, I convinced myself it was merely a figment of my imagination. But now, faced with the undeniable truth, I yearn for the comfort of insanity. Perhaps I could dismiss this as mere coincidence—that his sudden need for marketing assistance and his presence in New York have nothing to do with me.

Yet, deep down, I know better. Tommy is a master of manipulation, a calculating strategist. I can't shake the feeling that his true motives for being here are far more sinister than the polished businessman persona he so expertly projects.

"Dani? You're home early."

Izzy rounds the corner, her expression shifting from casual curiosity to alarm as she takes in my presence. "Oh Dani, what happened? Did he hurt you? I'll kill him. He probably has tight security, but I can work around that. We'll have to drive out of the city to bury the body. We don't have the necessary equipment, so we'll need to go shopping—using cash, of course."

"Izzy?"

"Hmm?" she replied half-heartedly, likely still plotting the details of my boss's demise.

"Izzy. While I'm not thrilled with Dean at the moment, it's not him." Her brows knit together in confusion.

"Then what is it?" My gaze drops to the floor as Izzy settles beside me, her patience unwavering.

"Tommy."

"Tommy? You saw him again? It's not that I don't believe you, Dani, but are you sure it's not your anxiety playing tricks on you?" I meet her eyes, my own filled with dread.

"I wish it were. I ran into him. Literally." Her eyes widen in horror.

"Did he hurt you? Because I'll kill him. If it were Dean, I'd make it quick, but Tommy? I'd make sure he's properly tortured before I end his life." The fervor in her voice is both alarming and oddly comforting, a testament to her loyalty. I recount the evening, starting with my desperate flight from the party and Tom's chilling threat to ruin me if I utter a word.

"You have to tell him, Dani. You have to tell Dean. He should know. He would want to know," Izzy presses, her concern evident. Deep down, I know she is right; Dean needs to understand the type of man he is dealing with. Despite his Jekyll and Hyde persona, I know he cares about my safety. But the thought of revealing everything makes my stomach twist.

"I can't, Iz. I just can't. I'm going to quit."

"Quit? You know I love you and will always support you, but do you really believe that walking away and quitting is a wiser choice than confronting your boss with the truth - that his client raped you in high school and is now threatening you?"

"It's taken me years to come to terms with what happened. Opening myself up again would feel like reliving it, and I just can't. I can't go back there."

"And what makes you think that if you quit, he'll leave you alone?"

"I'm tired. Goodnight, Izzy." I rise, which is no easy feat, but I manage to walk away from her. I step into my bedroom and slam the door behind me, the finality echoing in the silence.

As I make my way over to my bed, my phone dings.

Dean: Where are you?

I was genuinely taken aback that he had even noticed my absence.

Me: Home.

Dean: I'm sorry.

Well, I didn't expect that.

Me: For what?

Dean: Being an ass.

He can actually acknowledge when he's being an ass. Quite impressive, really. While part of me would relish letting him believe he's the cause of my departure,

I'm not in the mood to play. Instead, I choose to be as honest as I can muster.

Me: I didn't leave because of you. I was just tired.

Dean: I'm not sure I believe you.

Me: That's your prerogative.

Dean: Are you okay?

His text leaves me confused by his unexpected kindness. It leaves me uncertain of how to react, and instinctively, I retreat into my familiar armor of defensiveness.

Me: Dean, why do you care?

Dean: I don't typically have my dates walk out on me.

I can't help but let out a soft laugh, rolling my eyes in amusement. Whether he was teasing me or genuinely shocked, it didn't matter. At that moment, I decided to give him a taste of his own medicine.

Me: First time for everything.

Dean: Goodnight, Dani.

Me: Goodnight, Dean.

Exhausted, I collapse onto my bed, too drained to even undress, left alone with my haunting memories.

****

I find myself awake at an uncharacteristically early hour, a shocking realization for someone who typically cherishes sleep. Despite the exhaustion that clings to me,

I tossed and turned throughout the night.

Finally, I decided to prepare for work, planning to arrive early to submit my resignation. Did I really want to quit? Absolutely not. Even with my frustrations toward Dean, I genuinely enjoyed my job. Carla and I were starting to build a friendship, and I even learned the name of the front desk receptionist, Nicole, who I now greet as I slowly make my way to the elevator. She nods in my direction, likely puzzled by my early arrival. A nod! We've made real progress. Yet, I can't shake the thought that I might never discover if Nicole could become my potential best friend replacement after Izzy's impending arrest for murder.

As I step off the elevator, I arrive at the office before even Carla. While I'm unsure of Dean's exact arrival time, I know him well enough to predict he's already there. His office door is closed, so I knock twice.

"Come in." I take a deep breath and enter.

"Mr. Anderson?" He glances up from some contracts, momentarily startled by my presence.

"Dani. What are you doing here this early? Everything okay?" He sits up straighter, as if bracing for whatever news I'm about to deliver.

"Actually, no. I quit. I apologize for not providing proper notice, but I can't work here any longer." I notice his jaw tense and his grip tighten on the armrests of his chair. For a moment, I brace myself for a tirade about my lack of notice, but instead, he exhales deeply, rubbing his forehead as he closes his eyes.

"Is this about what happened at the party?" I could easily fabricate a story. I could tell him he's a complete ass hat and that I can't work for someone so indecisive. I could confess that this is because he is too attractive, and I can't keep my promise to keep things professional. I could even tell him the truth—that he evokes feelings in me I've never experienced before, but I'm stuck because his client is targeting me. Yet, I can't bring myself to voice any of that.

"I'm not leaving because of you."

"Why do I feel like you're not being entirely honest with me?" Because I'm not. I'd almost prefer him to yell at me and send me packing than face this emotionally complex moment.

"I'm sorry. Goodbye, Mr. Anderson." I turn, reaching for the door handle.

"Come away with me." I pause and turn back, my heart racing.

"Uh, what?"

"Come away with me. I have a business meeting a few hours from here this weekend. Join me." What the hell is happening? As if this situation isn't complicated enough, he's inviting me to go away with him? I can't give in; I just can't, no matter how tempting the offer sounds.

"I can't. You should probably ask that woman from the party to accompany you." To my surprise, he laughs.

"I don't want Maria to go with me. I want you to come. Besides, I doubt her husband and children would approve." Husband? Children? I completely misread that situation. Can I plead temporary insanity due to my attraction to the most handsome man I've ever met? Mortification washes over me. Play it cool. Just play it cool.

"Well, fuck me." Oh no! That is the opposite of playing it cool! I want to face palm myself right now, but instead, I shut my eyes, praying I didn't just say that out loud. I open my eyes to find the heat in his gaze. Yep, definitely said that aloud. His eyes darken with desire, and I'm sure I could come just from the way he is looking at me right now.

"Yes."

"Yes?" he whispers, almost incredulously.

"I'll go." He leans back, a smile spreading across his face.

"Great. I'll make the arrangements."

"Great."

"Good."

"Wonderful."

"You can get to work now, Ms. Cliff."

"Right." I turn and walk out of his office, feeling as if I'm on autopilot. What just happened? I was supposed to quit! Instead, I agreed to go away with him for the weekend! Even worse, what do I pack? I slam my head against my desk. "What is wrong with me?"

"I haven't figured that out yet, but I'll let you know when I do," Carla replies, setting her purse down.

"Please do. What do you call it when you consciously make choices you know are completely bad for you?"

"I believe that's called masochism. Are you a masochist, dear?"

"I haven't figured that out yet, but I'll let you know when I do."

"Touche." I lift my head and turn my computer on, preparing to research masochism. It's going to be a long week.

24.

Dean

This week has stretched on longer than any I can recall. As I sit in my office on Thursday evening, the clock ticks closer to 9 p.m., and my mind turns to the early morning ahead. Tomorrow, I will be leaving, and she will accompany me—a decision I never intended to make. That's precisely why I hadn't pursued her at the party; I felt the weight of crossing a line with an employee, breaking my most sacred rule.

I've traveled this road before, and it only led to distrust and the shutting down of my heart to any semblance of love. Love is a double-edged sword, leaving you exposed and vulnerable. I've witnessed the fallout of letting someone in, and I refuse to find myself in that position again.

Amid this turmoil, I found myself needing to postpone a meeting with Tom and some clients until next week. A potential new client, an old friend of mine, reached out, eager to discuss opening another chain in Burlington. He values my insight and has asked me to assess the space and the area for its investment potential. Taking time away from work is rare for me, but I owe him this favor—after all, he was there to pull me from the depths of embarrassment when Gabby and I ended things.

I hadn't planned on bringing Dani along, but panic set in when she announced her decision to quit. I can't keep her, yet I'm not ready to let her go, and deep down, I know I'm being unfair. We've already established that I'm a selfish asshole. Even though she insists that her decision has nothing to do with me, I can sense that she's hiding something.

Is it my attraction to her or just plain curiosity? Most likely both. I need to uncover the reason behind her sudden desire to leave. If it isn't me, then what is it? As the CEO, I feel like I should know if there is something or someone within my company that is making her want to leave. My thoughts drift away from work and settle on her, as I wrestle with the idea of texting her.

Fuck it.

Me: Are you asleep?

Dani: Of course, I am. My overly needy boss has me waking up at the crack of dawn to drag me away for the weekend.

Me: Sounds awful.

Dani: Doesn't it?

A smile creeps across my face. I admire her unapologetic honesty and the courage she has to speak her mind. Most of my employees—well, all except Carla and Jay—can hardly meet my gaze, let alone express their opinions. It's always "Yes, Sir," "Right away, Sir," and "Let me kiss your ass, Sir." Her candor is a breath of fresh air.

I realized I hadn't replied to her when another message pings my phone.

Dani: Is there a reason you texted me so late at night?

Shit. Why did I reach out? I can't let her think this is anything more than professional.

Me: It's 9:15. And you call me old? I just wanted to confirm you'll actually be ready on time for me to pick you up at 5 a.m.

Dani: Are you implying that I'll be late without your help?

Me: Yes.

Dani: Fine. That's a fair assumption. But you should bring coffee. For your safety.

Me: Duly noted.

Dani: And a banana nut muffin wouldn't hurt.

Me: Now, who's needy?

Dani: Fine. It's your funeral.

As difficult as it is, I force myself to text her goodnight and set my phone down. Yep, I'm definitely in trouble.

****

We arrive outside Dani's apartment at 4:55 a.m. Uncertain whether to go up and offer help, I hesitate, but just as I decide to open the door, she bursts out. Her hair is thrown into a messy bun, with stray strands framing her face. Black-rimmed glasses perched on her nose, and she did not don any makeup—just a hint of lip gloss. Dressing in well-worn dark gray sweatpants and an oversized red

Giants sweatshirt, she clearly hadn't put much thought into her appearance this morning. Yet, at that moment, she had never looked more beautiful.

I stand up and take her bag as she slides over to make room in the seat. Handing the bag to my driver, I climb back into the car. "Good morning," I greet her.

"Is it?" she replies, sinking deeper into her seat, her head resting against the headrest.

"Coffee and a banana nut muffin," I announce, holding up an extra-large cup and a small bag. Her eyes widened with delight as she quickly snatched them from me, taking a generous sip of her iced coffee.

"Thank you," she says, her voice warm.

"I did it for my own personal safety," I tease.

"Mmmm," she moans, her eyes fluttering shut in enjoyment. A rush of heat courses through me, a teenage-like response I can't control. Watching her savor her breakfast stirs something primal; the way her lips wrap around the straw ignites vivid thoughts of what it would feel like to have those lips wrapped around my cock.

Opening one eye, she gives me a curious glance. "Why are you staring at me?"

"Should I give you and your coffee some alone time?" I quip, but she shoots me a glare that makes it clear she is definitely not a morning person.

I spent the rest of the car ride trying to focus on critical emails, trying to ignore the tantalizing distraction sitting beside me.

****

We arrived at the terminal, and I noticed that Dani had gone quiet.

"You okay?" I ask, glancing at her. She looks pale.

"Yeah. Of course. I'm great. Why wouldn't I be?" She answers, keeping her head down. I nod slowly. She's a terrible liar.

Once we are on the plane, she quickly tries to stow her bag in the overhead compartment but she has a difficult time pushing it all the way in. I reach up behind her and I can feel her body stiffen against me. I can't help but smile, noticing how being this close to me affects her. I push her bag the rest of the way in for her, brushing against her arms as I do. She pulls her arms away like she was burned and whispers a quick thank you. Dani makes her way into her seat, leans her head back, and closes her eyes.

"Are you sure you're okay?" I press.

"Mm-hmm," she mumbles, her jaw clenches and her hands grip the armrests tightly.

"Are you afraid of flying?"

"I might have done some research on how to survive a plane crash. Did you know that most crashes happen in the first eight minutes after takeoff and the last eight before landing?"

"It's going to be fine," I reassure her.

"Famous last words."

The announcement comes over the intercom, instructing passengers to fasten their seatbelts. Minutes later, we are taking off. Dani has her eyes squeezed shut, her knuckles white as she grips the armrests.

"Just breathe," I whisper, leaning closer.

"Breathing won't matter if we crash," she retorts with a hint of humor, making me chuckle.

"Just take a deep breath in and exhale slowly." She inhales but lets it out in a rush. "Slower." This time, she takes a deeper breath, allowing herself to exhale at a measured pace. The plane picks up speed, and we are officially airborne. Her hand shoots out, grasping my arm. I let it slide this time, continuing to guide her through her breathing. By the time we reach cruising altitude, she begins to relax, though her grip remains unchanged.

"Are you trying to cut off my blood supply?" I joke, glancing at her hand still clutched around my arm. Realizing what she is doing, she quickly releases it.

"Sorry."

"It's fine. Feeling any better?"

"For now," she replies, turning on her phone. I pull out my own phone, responding to important emails, trying to distract myself from the anxious woman seated beside me.

****

Even though the flight is just over an hour long, it isn't long before Dani succumbs to sleep. Thankfully, there are only about twenty minutes left, because as she shifts, her head nestles against my shoulder, enveloping me in her scent. It's a sweet, tropical aroma, likely from that damn coconut shampoo, and it takes every ounce of self-control not to lean down and inhale deeply like some creep.

She remains blissfully unaware during the flight announcements, so I move quietly to fasten her seatbelt. She stirs slightly, but as soon as the click of the belt echoes in the cabin, she settles back into her slumber. I can't help but watch her as we begin our descent. A few strands of hair fall across her face, and I instinctively brush them behind her ear. My gaze lingers on her lips, and I find myself wondering what it would be like to kiss her. Just then, the plane jolts during landing, and she shoots up in alarm.

"Are we crashing?" Panic laces her voice as she grabs my arm again, and a laugh escapes me, surprising even myself. It seems I have been laughing more lately, and I welcome the feeling.

"We've landed," I reassure her, watching her eyes dart around as she registers her surroundings and the seatbelt snug against her.

"You put my seatbelt on?" she asks, a hint of disbelief in her tone.

"I didn't want to wake you, and for good reason. At first, I thought it was a fluke, but now it seems you're actually attempting to eliminate my limb through lack of blood flow," I reply, a teasing smile playing on my lips.

"Oh my God. Did Dean Anderson just make a joke? We should be more concerned about a plane crash than Hell freezing over," she retorts, deadpan. "Now, can we get off this damn plane?"

25.

Dani

As we journey through Burlington, my gaze is glued to the car window, captivated by the sights unfolding outside. Moving to the city was my only experience of travel, making this expedition a delightful novelty, though I wouldn't dare admit that to Mr. Anderson.

Burlington is a stunning city, and while I hold a special place in my heart for New York City, there's something inherently different about Burlington. It feels warmer, and more inviting. I did some research before arriving, and it's clear there's a wealth of activities to explore, from art galleries and museums to outdoor adventures like biking and kayaking.

Navigating through Church Place Marketplace, I'm surrounded by an array of shops and restaurants. Just two minutes later, we arrive at Hotel Vermont. Despite being accustomed to towering buildings, I find myself in awe of the architecture. Stepping inside, I'm struck by the beauty of the interior. With only the weekend ahead of us, I hope our schedule allows for exploration. I'm grateful I packed my heavier coat, as the Autumn air is already chilly, and Burlington feels a touch cooler than home.

"Are you coming, Miss Cliff?" Dean's voice cuts

through my reverie.

"This is amazing," I reply, turning to follow him.

"I'm glad you approve." We head toward our rooms on the top floor, where he hands me my key. "This is yours. I'm right next door. We need to meet Casey for dinner at 6 p.m."

"What's the plan for the weekend?" I inquire, watching him casually tuck his hands into his pockets.

"This evening, we'll discuss his expansion over dinner. Tomorrow morning, we'll visit the building he's considering purchasing and explore the area to determine if the investment is worthwhile. Our flight home is on Sunday, early afternoon. Remember—6 p.m."

"What will you do until then?"

"I've got some work to catch up on." I nod. It's only 10 in the morning, which gives me a solid six hours before I need to prepare for dinner. That should allow ample time for some exploration, not to mention there will be plenty of time for activities the rest of the weekend outside of the time allotted for work. I should be thrilled. So why does a sense of disappointment wash over me when Dean's door clicks shut behind him?

****

I don't even change my outfit since I'll be out exploring, fully embracing my role as a tourist. A short walk from Church Street leads me to Burlington Waterfront Park, where I stroll along the path, soaking in the sights and sounds of the people around me while admiring the breathtaking view of the lake.

As I gaze out at the water, thoughts of Tommy and my job flood my mind. How can I work here knowing that Tommy has access? I had spent my senior year enduring the sight of him being worshipped by our peers while I faded back into the shadows as the so-called "trashy scholarship student." The only person who stood by me was Izzy. She was always kind, and even when I tried to push her away, she refused to let go. I kept my struggles to myself until after graduation. She urged me to call the cops and press charges, but I had spent enough time with those people to know the harsh truth: the word of some "trash rat" would never hold weight against the rich boy who ruled the school. I survived all of that, and now, I was determined not to let him win. *Fuck him,* I thought. "I'm not quitting!" I yell, letting my voice ring out.

"Good for you, dear," says an elderly lady who has been walking behind me, causing me to jump. A few wary stares from passersby followed.

"Yes," I whisper to myself, feeling a surge of determination. "Good for me."

I snap a series of pictures to send to Izzy before heading back to explore the shops. One store catches my eye: Ecco Clothing. I step inside and begin browsing. Although I had packed for tonight's dinner, I found myself frozen in front of a stunning dress that I knew I had to have. It's a beautiful lavender tie-front gather dress with a daring slit up the front. It's sexy yet classy enough for a business dinner. Perhaps it is the sense of liberation from my pep talk at the lake, but at that moment, I feel brave and confident—I need this dress.

When I glance at the price tag, my eyes nearly bulge. I shouldn't be spending this much on a dress! Shutting my eyes, I realize I have already mentally committed to it. It better be worth it. After leaving the store with the dress in hand, I strut back to the hotel to prepare for the evening ahead.

Two hours later, I'm finally ready for dinner, with twenty minutes to spare. I FaceTime Izzy. "Hey bi—holy shit!" I panic as I see her reaction.

"What? What's wrong?" I ask.

"Nothing. You just look... hot as fuck!" I roll my eyes at her compliment.

"Shut up."

"Seriously, girl. You look flawless. That dress is killer. New?"

"Yep. I found it while wandering around town today."

"I'm so glad you channeled your inner Izzy and bought it. Your boss is going to lose his mind when he sees you in it."

"I'm not so sure about that."

"Well, I am sure. Every man's eyes are going to be on you tonight," Izzy teases, noticing my wide eyes. "Oh, stop it! You won't even notice because you'll be too busy staring at your hot boss." I open my mouth to argue but shrug instead.

"I decided I'm not going to quit."

"You're going to tell him?" Izzy asks.

"No. But I'm not going to let Tommy take anything

else from me. I'm not really sure what his end goal is but I have to believe that it's all coincidence and he just is trying to help his grandfather's business."

"I hope that's all it is to, Dani, but you can't let your guard down. Especially if you aren't going to fill Dean in on the situation."

"Trust me, walls are up. I don't trust him at all but I can't go back to living the way I did seven years ago. I actually enjoy this job. Maybe if I just keep my head down, he'll eventually just disappear." Izzy looks unsure and I'm sure it mirrors my own, despite my words.

"You know I support you no matter what you choose, but please be careful. Stay close to Mr. Hottie. I mean really close. Like on top. Or under. Either is fine." I roll my eyes but can't help but laugh. She is the most ridiculous person I know. We chat for a few more minutes before hanging up, and I check the mirror one last time.

A knock sounds on the door. I take a deep breath, grab my purse, and open it. There stands Dean, looking impeccable in black pants, a black shirt, and a black blazer.

"Hey," I greet breathlessly.

"H… Hi. Hey," he stammers, his eyes scanning my body. "You look beautiful."

"Thank you," I respond, a blush creeping onto my cheeks. In that moment, I know it was all worth it. I doubt a man like Dean Anderson stutters often.

26.

Dean

I can hardly tear my gaze away from her as we head to the restaurant. Dani is always beautiful, but tonight - she radiated an almost ethereal glow. For a moment, I consider suggesting we skip dinner and spend the evening in my hotel room, but the animated recounting of her afternoon holds me captive.

We arrive at Hen of the Wood far too quickly. As I open the door for her, I catch a glimpse of the wonder in her eyes as she takes in the restaurant. Once inside, we are swiftly seated at a secluded table in the corner. I take her coat and pull out a chair for her. Dani shoots me a suspicious look.

"I can be a gentleman when I choose to be," I reply with a smirk.

After ordering drinks, we exchange stories, and I fill her in on my friendship with Casey. Just as our conversation reaches a natural pause, I look up to see Casey approaching us. I stand and extend my hand in greeting.

"Hey man, how's it going? Thanks for meeting me," Casey says.

"Of course. I'm eager to hear more about what has

you so excited about this place."

"Be prepared to be here all night; he won't stop talking about it," a familiar female jokes. My heart sinks. I know that voice all too well. My gaze shifts toward her, and I feel my jaw tighten.

"What the hell are you doing here?" I demand, noticing Dani's startled expression as she glances between Gabby and me.

"Didn't Casey tell you? We're dating," Gabby declares, her smirk twisting the knife in my back deeper.

"No. He didn't," I manage through gritted teeth, locking eyes with Casey, who looks guilty as fuck.

"Sorry man, I wanted to tell you, but I figured you'd be cool with it since it's been so long." The urge to flip the table and confront my so-called friend surges within me, but then I feel Dani's hand on my leg. She's watching the two of them, her support grounding me even as confusion clouds her expression. It's keeping me sane enough that the motherfucker across from me may live to see another day.

"I came here as a favor to you; rearranged my work schedule and took time off I don't have to fly here and help you with your potential investment. And you have the audacity to bring her here? If you want a gold-digging lying bitch to keep you warm at night, that's your prerogative, but I won't sit here and pretend I'm okay with it." I throw down enough cash to cover our drinks and storm out.

As I reach the door, a hand grasps my arm.

"Dean, please stop." I pause, inhaling deeply

before turning around. Gabby stands there, the bitch's expression unreadable.

"Trying to get with my brother wasn't enough? Now you had to go for my friend?" I spit, but she remains unfazed.

"Stop being dramatic, Dean. I'm sorry we didn't tell you, but neither of us thought you would throw a tantrum and storm out."

"A tantrum?" I let out a bitter laugh. "I'm not throwing a tantrum. I'm furious. He betrayed me, and you knew precisely what showing up here would do."

"Dean, baby," she coos, stepping closer. "I heard about your new plaything. I wanted to see for myself if you had actually moved on." She places her hand on my cheek, pulling me closer to her lips. "Guess not."

"Still the same manipulative bitch," I retort, pulling away. She looks shocked, as if my rejection has caught her off guard. While she is still the gorgeous woman I remembered, I could see the ugliness within her. I have a million things I want to say, but I know that walking away would sting her the most. So, I turn on my heel and leave without saying another word.

27.

Dani

"I came here as a favor to you," he says, frustration boiling in his voice. "I rearranged my work schedule and took time off I don't have to fly here and help you with your potential investment. And you have the audacity to bring her here? If you want a gold-digging lying bitch to keep you warm at night, that's your prerogative, but I won't sit here and pretend I'm okay with it." With a flick of his wrist, Dean tosses his napkin onto the table, accompanied by a few bills, and begins to walk away.

Before I can even shift my chair to follow him, Gabby stands up and moves in his direction. I stare after her, then turn to Casey, bewildered.

"What the hell just happened?" I ask, unsure if I'd actually get a response. Casey looks down, raking his hands through his hair.

"Gabby is his ex. It didn't end well."

"And you thought bringing her here was a good idea?"

"I love her. I consider Dean a good friend. I thought he'd be over it by now."

"A good friend? A good friend wouldn't date his 'good' friend's ex-girlfriend, ask him to take time off work for a potential investment, and then bring that ex to dinner. Maybe instead of investing in an expansion, you should invest in therapy because there's no way you're in your right mind." I throw my napkin on the table, standing up in frustration. I start to move but pause, turning to face him. "You thought he'd be over it, but is she? Shouldn't your girlfriend be consoling you instead of chasing down her ex-boyfriend?" Without waiting for a response, I grab my coat and walk away in search of Dean.

I push through the door and step outside, scanning the area but catching no sight of him.

"He left." Gabby is leaning against the wall, a cigarette in hand, smoke curling lazily from her lips. Despite her questionable habit, she looks stunning —thick, curly dark hair cascading just beneath her shoulders, golden skin, petite yet curvy. And those large, dark brown eyes paired with full lips reminiscent of Angelina Jolie. That was what Dean had. This woman, exuding waves of sex appeal, had once been his. Why would I ever think he'd be interested in me? Just plain Dani. Mediocre Mary. Average Alice. A regular Rachel. An ordinary Olga. God. I was so uncool that I made up names to describe how common I felt. *Focus, Dani.*

"He left?" I ask, trying to sound unfazed.

"Get used to it, sweetheart. He's a selfish bastard who only thinks of himself," she replies, taking another drag of her cigarette. Despite his faults, something inside me urges me to defend Dean. Yes, he can be a bastard, but I'd seen glimpses of kindness beneath that hard exterior. Perhaps my jealousy was getting the better of me, driving me to want to knock this near-perfect woman down a few pegs.

"Apparently, he's not all that bad; otherwise, you wouldn't be chasing him down, leaving your boyfriend sitting at the table alone."

"I don't chase anyone, sweetheart," she shoots back with a smirk.

"No. Just their money." My smirk replaces hers, as anger flickers across her face. I don't have time to listen to this bitch, so I turn away, searching for any sign of Dean.

****

With no idea where Dean might have gone, I called an Uber and headed back to the hotel. Fortunately, the driver is the silent type, as I can't hold a conversation even if I wanted to—my mind is racing with thoughts. I hope Dean is back in his room. As I walk toward the elevators, I notice the Juniper Bar and Restaurant and pause. I approach the entrance when a girl, likely a few years younger than me, stops me.

"Hi. Welcome to Juniper. Are you interested in being seated?"

"Actually, I was hoping to take a quick look and see if my friend is here. Tall, dark, and…"

"Broody? Yes, he's sitting at the bar," she says, pointing in his direction.

"Thank you," I reply, a quick sigh of relief escaping my lips. I make my way to the bar and take a seat next to him. The bartender approaches, but I wave him off. We sit in silence for what feels like an eternity before Dean finally speaks.

"He's supposed to be my friend," he slurs. How much has he had to drink already?

"Some people get so caught up in their own world that they don't realize how it affects those around them." Dean gulps down the last of his drink and waves down the bartender for another.

"I don't love her anymore."

"You really don't have to explain anything to me," I say, although I was relieved to hear that confession. He grabs the drink in front of him and takes a large sip.

"I thought we were going to get married. She and this guy were business partners," he begins. "I was ready to give her everything she needed to launch her business venture. As far as I knew, she didn't have any family to support her, and all I wanted was to see her happy. My brother kept trying to warn me, but I didn't listen. I came home early on our second anniversary, planning to propose later that evening. That is, until I found her in bed with her so-called business partner. It was a punch to the gut. I later discovered that her family had disowned her, and to make matters worse, she had made advances on my brother, who turned her down because he wasn't a piece of shit. Fucking Casey."

"I'm sorry you went through that. And I'm sorry you feel betrayed. If it makes you feel any better, I doubt that she and he will actually work out. Women like Gabby always believe the grass is greener on the other side and spend their lives crossing bridges rather than stopping to see what's right in front of them. Casey is just another pitstop before the next bridge, and I'm sure he will realize how much he fucked up when he gets left behind."

Dean nods and finishes the last of his drink. I can see he is about to order another, so I stand and move his glass away. "I think you have had enough. Let's get you upstairs." At first, I'm not sure he hears me, but after a deep breath, he turns to get up. He's sluggish, so I wrap my arms around him to keep him upright. To my surprise, he doesn't resist; instead, he throws his arm around me, leaning against me.

I hadn't considered that helping him upstairs would mean being in such close proximity to him. I try to focus on the task at hand, reminding myself that he is upset and drunk, but my brain selfishly notes the hard muscles beneath his shirt and the intoxicating scent that envelopes me. *Focus, Dani!* We managed to reach our rooms, and I thank God he was able to retrieve his key; there was no way I could handle a body search. As the door swings open, I pull him towards the bed, both of us tumbling onto it in the process.

"I'm sorry," he mumbles as we both lay side by side.

"Sorry for what?" I ask, confusion clouding my thoughts.

"For making a scene. Storming out," he exhales deeply before whispering, "and for leaving you."

"The situation was unexpected. You clearly loved her and felt betrayed. There's nothing to apologize for. I'm a big girl. I can handle myself." I sit up, and he follows, turning to face me. He's so close that I can feel the warmth of his breath on my face. His hand gently caresses my cheek.

"I shouldn't have left you."

"Really, you don't have to—" Before I can finish, his

lips meet mine. The kiss starts light and soft but quickly morphs into something more passionate. I'm caught off guard, instinctively opening up to let his tongue slip in. I can taste the scotch on his breath, but at this moment, I don't care. This feels right. My hands reach the back of his neck, fingers lightly grasping his hair. He moans softly, pushing me back onto the bed, his lips trailing over my jaw and down my neck. I close my eyes, surrendering to the sensations.

The smell of alcohol, the dimly lit hotel room.

Suddenly, I'm jolted back to a night I desperately want to forget. Panic surges through me, and I gasp for air. "Stop," I whisper.

"Hmmm?" he mumbles, nibbling my collarbone.

"I said stop." I push him away gently. He sits up abruptly, as if snapping out of a trance. "Did I do something wrong?"

"No. I just need to go to bed - so do you." I scramble to my feet, hastily fixing my appearance before rushing toward the door. I hear him calling my name, but I don't stop. *Suffocating. I can't breathe.*

In less than a minute, I'm in my own room. I kick off my shoes and quickly get rid of my dress before collapsing onto the bed. I squeeze my eyes shut, but the tears still flow. I pull the covers over my head, trying to hide from the nightmares that await me tonight.

28.

Dean

I wake up the next morning, still clad in the clothes from the night before. A groggy haze envelopes me, but as I shake off the remnants of sleep, the memories of the previous night come flooding back. Dinner. Gabby. The bar. Dani. The kiss. Holy hell, I kissed her. And then she ran away.

I rub my hands down my face, cursing my own foolishness. What was I thinking? I wasn't thinking at all. The alcohol had dulled my senses, and with her body pressed so close to mine, that damn coconut shampoo clouded my judgment, stripping away all my inhibitions.

Glancing around for my cell phone, I spot it on the floor. I check the time. Damn. It was already past eight. I never sleep in this late. My first instinct is to reach out to Dani, but something holds me back. This entire weekend has gone to shit.

Taking a seat at the desk, I open my laptop, quickly booking the first tickets home I can find. I shoot Dani a text, letting her know when to be ready. I know I should probably go to her and face the music, but I feel like such a piece of shit. We'd have time to talk on the flight home. Maybe by then, I'll come up with an apology that is worth hearing.

****

After my shower, I packed everything away. Our flight is scheduled to leave at 2 p.m., and the clock is ticking close to 11:30 AM, urging us to check out and get moving. As I step out the door, I bump into Dani.

"Hi," I say, a little awkwardly.

"Hi," she replies softly, giving me a soft nod.

"Ready to go?" I ask. She nods again, and we head downstairs to check out. Once we are in the car, the ride to the airport is quiet. The hour-long drive feels like an eternity, the weight of last night still hanging between us.

When we finally arrive, we make our way through the terminal, each step feeling heavier than the last. We find our seats at the gate, and I try to occupy myself with my phone, but my stomach growls loudly, cutting through the silence. I glance at Dani, embarrassed.

"I'm hungry too," she admits, a small smile tugging at the corners of her mouth.

"Let's find some food then." We grab our bags and head to a cozy little restaurant, where we find a table to drop our luggage and walk up to the counter to order. Burgers and fries seem the perfect choice, and we return to our table with our meals.

"This is so freaking good!" Dani exclaims between bites of her burger. She catches me staring and raises an eyebrow. "What? What's so funny?"

"You look like a stray dog that found a chicken wing that missed the dumpster, with just a bit of meat left on it," I laugh.

She smirks. "I'm hungry! Need I remind you that I didn't get to eat dinner last night?"

Her comment stings, though I know she doesn't mean it that way. I sigh, deciding it was time to clear the air. "I am really sorry about last night, Dani."

She starts to shake her head, about to speak, but I raise a hand to stop her. "No. Please, hear me out." She nods, so I press on. "I was a jerk last night. I stormed out, leaving you alone to drink away my frustrations, and I took advantage of you. You were there for me, and all I wanted was to forget the evening. I... I made a mistake." For a brief moment, I think I see hurt flicker across her face, quickly masked by a forced smile.

"A mistake? I thought you never made mistakes," she asks, her voice soft but tinged with something unreadable.

"Rarely," I smirk, trying to lighten the mood.

"Well, when a man of your caliber apologizes and admits to making a mistake, how can I not accept?" Her expression is calm yet serious. I brace myself, sensing this won't be as easy as I hoped. But then she takes a breath and continues, "You were going through a lot. I get it. But there's no need for an apology. I kissed you back. But you're my boss..." Her voice trails off, leaving an unspoken tension in the air.

"Exactly," I chime in. "It was unprofessional, and that's on me."

"It's forgotten," she states, picking up her burger once more and diving back in. "No harm, no foul."

It's forgotten. I should feel relief, but instead, disappointment settles in my chest.

****

We settle into our seats on the plane, the hum of anticipation filling the air as we approach takeoff. I can see the nerves creeping back into her, tightening their grip. My instinct urges me to reach for her hand, to offer comfort, but the weight of our recent conversation holds me back. Dani squeezes her eyes shut, her breaths coming in quick bursts, a silent battle waging within her.

"How much did I tell you last night?" I avoid looking at her, but I can feel Dani's gaze piercing through me.

"Just that you were going to marry her and she cheated on you with her business partner."

"Great. So everything."

"I doubt that what you told me was everything. You gave me facts. But you didn't really say how it all affected you, though I can make my own assumptions." I finally look at her, watching her run her hands through her hair, combing it out. I'm not sure I want her to make her own assumptions.

"I really did think she was the one." I'm not one to open up willingly but I push onward, even though I've only shared this with my brother. "I've never had much luck with relationships. It became clear that the women I dated were often more interested in what I could provide —money, status, perks—than in me. Eventually, I decided to step back from dating and focus on having fun during the rare moments I escaped the office. Gabby was one of my employees. One night, we went out, and what I intended to be a one-time fling turned into something more. We kept crossing paths, and I found myself looking forward to seeing her, thinking about her when she wasn't around. She didn't seem interested in what I could do for her—at least, not outside of the bedroom."

I glance over and catch Dani rolling her eyes, which makes me chuckle. "I fell in love with her, and I believed she felt the same way. She moved in, and I opened my bank accounts and credit cards to her. I envisioned a future together. I knew she had dreams of starting her own business, and I was ready to support her in every way possible. Finding out that she was using me just as everyone else before her was like a knife to my chest. That's why I'm so closed off. That's why I don't mix business with pleasure. The few times I've let my guard down, I've been fucked over and I know that I can act like a huge asshole sometimes," I explain when she lets out a sarcastic laugh. "Okay, I can act like a huge asshole all the time."

"Well, maybe not all of the time."

"I really am sorry about last night Dani. I dragged you into all of this and that's not fair to you."

"I told you there was no need for an apology. Besides, it's nice to know that you're human and actually have feelings."

"Please don't tell anyone. I've worked hard for my intimidating reputation." She laughs and rolls her eyes.

"Don't worry. Your secret is safe with me."

"I appreciate that," I respond, laying my head against my seat.

"I'm so sorry, Dean," Dani says, reaching out to rest her hand on my arm. "Last night must have been incredibly hard for you. It must have brought up so many feelings." She opens her mouth as if to say more, then hesitates.

"What?" I prompt.

"Nothing," she replies quickly, tucking her hair behind her ear.

"What were you going to say?" I press. She sighs.

"You told me last night that you weren't in love with her. Was that the truth?"

"Yes," I say quickly, my teeth clenching. "I'll admit that last night caught me off guard, and I dislike surprises. But I don't love her. It just dredged up memories I wished to leave buried."

"Thank you," she murmurs softly.

"For what?"

"For trusting me enough to share this." I lean my head back again and close my eyes, letting silence envelop us. Trust had been shattered when I gave it to Gabby, but as I sit here, drowning in memories, a realization strikes me—one that terrifies me. I do trust Dani. With my eyes still closed, I finally respond, "You're welcome. I might just fall asleep now. You aren't planning anything after I pass out, are you?"

She laughs softly. "So much for trust, huh? No. Necrophilia really isn't my thing."

I laugh too, but as the plane continues to glide through the sky, I realize something more terrifying than trusting her - I might just love her.

29.
Dani

Surprisingly, the days following the business trip have been remarkably uneventful. I thought everything was fine between Dean and me, but it seems he's been avoiding me. He hides in his office, and aside from bringing him coffee and files, we hardly see each other. To be honest, I'm uncertain about how I feel. It's as if I miss him, but that's impossible. I don't really like him. Not at all. Sure, he's attractive, makes me feel safe, and occasionally makes me laugh, but there's no way I actually like him. So why am I sitting at my desk, concocting excuses to go in and talk to him?

Because that kiss nearly unraveled me. We agreed to forget it, but I can't shake it off. Despite my instinct to run away like a frightened child due to my PTSD, it was the first time in ages I felt truly alive—terrifying yet liberating. My mind races with thoughts of what might have happened if I hadn't fled. Would he have continued to touch me, exploring every inch of my body? My legs instinctively squeeze together at the thought of how he would tease me with his tongue before piercing me with his large...

"Dani!" I jump at the sound of my name, desperately hoping Carla doesn't notice the flush of embarrassment on my cheeks.

"Yea? Yes?" I stammer, trying to pull myself away from those inappropriate thoughts. Carla stares at me longer than necessary, her brows raised, I have hope in God she can't read my mind. I'm relieved when she doesn't question it.

"Mr. Anderson would like to see you in his office, dear."

"Oh. Why didn't he just call me?" She rolls her eyes.

"He did." My eyes widen in surprise, wondering how I missed that. "Must have been one hell of a daydream," she smirks. I glare at her playfully as I make my way toward his office, taking a deep breath to mask my earlier thoughts. I lightly knock on the door before letting myself in.

"Yes, Mr. Anderson?" I ask, striving for normalcy while trying not to let my eyes linger on him as he leans back in his chair, looking effortlessly casual. He furrows his brows, and I panic. *Shit. Does he know? He knows. Please don't fire me for my unintentional eye fucking. Could that be considered sexual assault? Unwanted eye fucking? It must be frowned upon in most workplaces. Crap. He's still staring.*

"Why didn't you answer your phone?"

"Oh, I, uh... I didn't hear it. I was thinking about someone... I mean, something." I mentally scolded myself for the slip-up, hoping he didn't catch it. I notice his jaw clench, realizing he did. My face feels like it's on fire—I can practically fry an egg on my cheeks at this point. He sits up straight and glances at his computer.

"Set up a meeting with Alice Dupont for next

week."

"Okay. Sure." I linger for a moment before realizing I've been dismissed. As I turn to leave, he calls me back.

"Yes?"

"Next time you choose to ignore my call because you think you have better things… to do, you're fired." Ouch. As much as I want to flip him off, I nod and quickly exit his office, confused by the sudden shift in his demeanor. I don't understand how he could have been so sweet two weekends ago—more vulnerable than I've ever seen him—and yet, today he's cold and standoffish. What could I have possibly done to upset him? He seemed apologetic about what happened that weekend, but is he actually angry that I didn't just throw myself at him? Is that why he's avoiding me? Out of anger? For what, exactly? For saying no? What a pompous jerk!

Shame for my earlier thoughts begins to creep in, quickly morphing into anger. I storm to my desk, completing my tasks as quickly and efficiently as possible, and speed out before I run into him again. I know I said that I wanted to continue working here but not if my job would constantly be held over my head every time he was in a pissy mood. Maybe it's time I start looking for another job.

****

I want to forget today. With each passing mile toward home, my excitement grows to sink into the couch, indulge in mindless television, and savor some comfort food. Though, I might have to hold off on the food; Izzy has an uncanny ability to detect my stress relief habits. She's like a predator, honing in on my negative emotions and compelling me to confront them. While I value her concern, there are moments when I simply wish to pretend everything is fine. Today is one of those days.

As I enter the apartment, I kick off my shoes and toss my purse onto the table.

"Hey, D!"

"Hey, Iz." I catch a glimpse of Izzy rushing into the bathroom as I round the corner into the living room. I can't help but chuckle at her frantic preparations. She had messaged me earlier, letting me know she had to go to the hotel for a few hours. We're polar opposites, which is likely why we're best friends. Opposites attract, after all. While I dash about because I'm nearly always late, she scurries in a frenzy out of fear of tardiness, even though she consistently arrives at least fifteen minutes early, no matter the occasion.

After Izzy leaves, I grab the remote and press play, settling in to watch a reality show overflowing with drama—definitely not my preference, but a welcome distraction. Just a few minutes in, a loud banging on the door makes me jump. Assuming it's Izzy who has forgotten her keys, I stride over and swing the door open without checking the peephole.

My jaw drops as I freeze, my mind struggling to comprehend the sight before me. As the shock gradually fades, I finally manage to find my voice.

"What the hell are you doing here, Mom?"

She smiles, lightly taps my cheek, and breezes past

me into my apartment.

"I'm in town. Thought I'd say hi."

No way. My mom is not the type to drop by just for a casual visit. She hasn't reached out once since I left. If she's here, there's definitely a reason—and it's probably one that's going to infuriate me.

"What do you want?" My tone is sharper than I intended, but she never seemed to care about my absence during the years we spent apart. She scoffs, her expression unreadable.

"Can't a mother just stop by to see her daughter?" she asks, drifting around the room, her gaze lingering on the pictures that crowd the walls. I narrow my eyes, taking in her haggard appearance. Despite my feelings toward her, I've always thought she was beautiful—long, thick blond hair framing her thin, oval face, large blue eyes sparkling with mischief, a small nose, and full lips that concealed perfectly straight teeth. She was petite, her small frame accentuated by the push-up bras and tight clothes she wore. But now, as I look at her, she appears aged. Her hair is graying and thinning, her teeth stained, and wrinkles etch lines around her eyes and mouth. She seems too thin. When she turns to face me, her eyes are dull, devoid of any emotion.

"What do you want?" I ask again, my voice steady but cold. She sighs.

"I need money." I roll my eyes.

"What makes you think I have any money to give you?" I cross my arms over my chest, bracing myself.

"Oh, come on, dear. Your little friend can help, can't

she? With all the money her family has. And I know you have a decent job. I just need a little."

"How much is a little?" I inquire, skepticism lacing my tone.

"Only $7,000," she replies, shrugging as if she'd asked for seven dollars instead of a small fortune.

"$7,000?!" I exclaim; the disbelief evident in my voice.

"Well, I actually need $23,000, but seven would do for now."

"Tw-Twenty-three thousand dollars?" I stutter, my heart racing. "For what?"

"I may have gotten into a little pickle with some debts I have."

"Some debts?" I throw my hands in the air, frustration bubbling over. "If it's just some debts, why can't you talk to the bank or file for bankruptcy?"

"It's not exactly those kinds of debts, darling." I shut my eyes, rubbing my forehead in a futile attempt to alleviate the headache forming. I have no idea what kind of trouble my mother has gotten herself into, but I know I want no part of it.

"You need to leave," I whisper, the words heavy with finality.

"What?"

"Leave. Get out!" I yell, the volume of my voice echoing in the quiet room.

"Oh, stop being so dramatic, Danielle. Just give me the money, and I'll leave you alone."

A surprising wave of hurt washes over me. I realize I've never stopped wishing I could be enough for her—that one day, she would finally pull her head out of her ass and want to be a good mother, to truly know me. Anger simmers within me, fueled by the longing for her love and approval, driving the rest of our conversation forward.

"I don't have that kind of money, and even if I did, I wouldn't give it to you. I'm not some damn ATM. Why don't you go back home and find a man to solve all your problems like you always do? Or better yet, instead of spending your days chasing after men and spreading your legs, why don't you get a job?" I spit at her, the words escaping with a mixture of anger and relief. I see a flicker of emotion in her eyes for the first time. She opens her mouth as if to respond but then falls silent.

As a child, I never dared to speak to her like this. But I'm not a child anymore, and she doesn't deserve my respect. We stand frozen, locked in a tense stare, neither willing to break the silence. Finally, she nods and turns toward the door. I watch her walk away, a nagging uncertainty creeping in. How did she even find me?

"How did you find me?" I call out, my voice steady but laced with curiosity. She pauses, her head turning just enough for me to catch her reply.

"I ran into that charming Tommy Hansen. Still handsome as ever." It's a final jab, a reminder of the past. She knows all too well what he did to me. To this day, she believes I fabricated the story to mask my embarrassment over being dumped.

I stride over and slam the door behind her, letting

out a frustrated growl. It dawns on me, as I lock up and grab a gallon of rocky road, that if he led her here, then he knows exactly where I live.

****

"Oh no. Dani?"

"Hmmm?" I groan, feeling fingers brush the hair away from my face. It takes a moment to register that Izzy must be home. *Great. I fell asleep.* I lift my head slightly and catch sight of the empty ice cream carton and the nearly empty vodka bottle.

"Want to tell me what happened?" Izzy asks as she settles beside me.

"My mother was here." I don't need to look at her to know the expression on her face.

"What. The. Fuck. How? Why?" I slowly sit up, surprised that I haven't thrown up yet.

"She wanted money," I explain, recounting every detail of our conversation, including how she found my address through Tommy.

"I'll kill him. I'll seriously kill him. I'll rip his intestines out and choke him with them." I turn to her; she's dead serious. I chuckle and lean my head on her shoulder.

"I appreciate your enthusiasm for murder, but it's complicated." She whips her head toward me, confusion etched on her face. Izzy is my best friend and the only person I can count on. "Please tell me all of this is a coincidence."

"Dani! That can't be a coincidence. He's stalking you! That piece of shit," she rants.

"Stonebrook is one of the top marketing firms on the East Coast. What if it's just a coincidence?" Izzy stares at the ceiling, taking a deep breath—a sure sign of her frustration.

"I'm going to say it again. This isn't a coincidence, Dani. He knows where you live. He sent your mom here. He wants you to know that he knows. He wants you scared! What if he doesn't stop here? What if he tries to hurt you again?" she asks quietly. I see the worry etched on her face, but what can I do? He hasn't technically done anything warranting a call to the police. "Does Dean know what he's done to you yet?"

"Of course not!" I snap back.

"Maybe he should. You really think he'd keep Tommy as a client if he knew what he did to you?" I shrug, pondering her question.

"It doesn't matter what he would do. I'm not going to jeopardize a deal for him. It's not like he and I are an item. He's my boss; he doesn't need to know about my past with Tommy." Izzy looks at me, her brow furrowed.

"I disagree. But you know I'll support you no matter what, even if I don't agree. Just... please be safe?"

"I know. Thank you. I will. Tommy has a meeting there tomorrow. I'll just call off. I have a feeling I'm going to have a rough night anyway." After today's events, making that decision feels easy. Izzy nods, glancing at the mess on the floor.

"Let me whip you up something that will help." I

nod, accepting what I suspect is just aspirin and a bottle of water. *I might as well text him now.* I search for my phone, finding it wedged between the couch cushions, and type a quick message.

Me: Won't be in tomorrow. Need a personal day.

I don't expect a response. It's nearly midnight, and while I know he works late, he wakes up early; this is probably past his bedtime.

Dean: Why?

Me: I just need a personal day.

Dean: No.

Me: No?

Dean: Tell me why you need off or your ass better be at work.

Me: It's none of your business, and I won't be there. Figure it out for one day or fire me. Either way you can fuck all the way off.

I brace myself for an asshole remark, but nothing comes. The nerve of that guy! How dare he demand to know anything after treating me like garbage this past week? I take the aspirin, gulp down the whole bottle of water, and start cleaning up my mess. I grab my phone and take it to the bedroom with me. Perhaps I shouldn't have told him to fuck off but the audacity of his response! He can really bring out the bitch in me. Despite finding him infuriating, I can't shake the disappointment when I see no new messages waiting for me.

****

Izzy has the luxury of a late start at work, allowing her to spend the entire day with me. We indulge in Chinese takeout for lunch and cram in as many romantic comedies as possible before she gets ready. When Izzy finally leaves, the apartment falls into an unsettling silence. I've never felt uneasy being alone here before, but the thought of him knowing my whereabouts sends a chill down my spine.

I pull myself up and head for the shower, having skipped one since the morning before. Even I can't ignore the stale scent of myself any longer. Stepping into the shower, I turn the water to the hottest setting I can tolerate, scrubbing my skin until it feels raw.

After what feels like an eternity, I finally emerge from the steam and throw on a pair of pajama shorts and a tank top. I sink into the couch, draping a light blanket —an ever-present companion on the back of our sofa— over my legs as I flip through the channels. I'm not in the mood for television, especially after a day filled with movies, but honestly, I lack the energy for anything else. Just as I contemplate surrendering to sleep, a sharp knock echoes through the apartment. I freeze, uncertainty gripping me. I can't even recall if the door is locked. With trepidation, I tiptoe toward the sound when another knock follows, deepening my unease.

"Dani, open the door."

I exhale deeply, unlocking the bolt and swinging the door wide open.

"What are you doing here, Mr. Anderson?" I ask, bewildered to find him standing at my threshold. His gaze slides over me, lingering until it finally meets my eyes.

"Who is he?" The moment those words escape his lips, panic surges through me. How could he possibly know? My heart races, pounding unhealthily against my chest. I am acutely aware of how people perceive you once they learn your history—like you're shattered, fragile. I guess I am. If I weren't, would I be here, hyperventilating because my boss uncovered a part of my past that I know, deep down, wasn't my fault? Yes, I am broken.

"What?" I manage to whisper.

"Who are you dating?" he asks again. Processing his question, laughter bubbles up from somewhere deep inside me. It's absurd; he isn't asking about what I thought he was. Relief and disbelief intermingle, and I open the door wider, inviting him in, which he accepts.

"You can't be serious. You came all this way just to ask if I'm dating someone? Couldn't you have just texted?"

"You haven't answered my question." I roll my eyes.

"No. I'm not dating anyone. Not that it's any of your business." I retort, crossing my arms. Despite my irritation, I notice confusion etched across his face, his brows furrowed.

"So you weren't out late last night with someone else?"

"Um. No."

"Then who were you busy thinking about yesterday when you ignored my call?" My heart sinks. I feel my cheeks flame as panic rises within me. I can't tell him. I can't make this moment any more awkward than it already is.

"You!" The words blurt out before I can stop myself. I close my eyes, mentally scolding myself. His hand finds my chin, tilting my face up so he can meet my gaze.

"Dani." The softness of his voice compels me to open my eyes. "You were thinking of me?" I nod, feeling a rush of vulnerability. "What about me?"

I swallow hard before answering, "What would've happened if I hadn't run from you?"

"Mmhmm. What else?" He steps closer, invading my space, stealing the breath from my lungs.

"Just, um, how it would feel."

"How what would feel?"

"You touching me. Tasting me."

Before I can think twice, his lips crash onto mine. Our kiss ignites with an urgency I didn't expect, all teeth and tongue, a stark contrast to our first kiss at the hotel. This kiss is fueled by hunger and need. I know I should stop this, but I can't. He's steel, and I'm the magnet—irresistibly drawn together, unable to break free from the electrifying attraction we've fought for too long.

30.

Dean

I sit at my desk, immersed in my work as always, but lately, it feels different. Ever since my trip to Vermont just shy of two weeks ago, I've found myself retreating into my office, trying to avoid the beautiful woman just outside my door. I wonder if she even noticed my absence. If she does, she hasn't mentioned it.

I've always prided myself on understanding women, yet Dani utterly confounds me. The way she looks at me, and how her body responds to my presence suggests she finds me attractive and is interested. But then, after I kissed her, she fled and insisted we forget it ever happened. I can't wrap my head around it. It seems clear she doesn't want to take our relationship beyond employer and employee, which is the rational perspective. But it's hard to maintain that mindset when her pouty lips invade my thoughts throughout the day.

I feel the strain against my pants as I picture those pouty lips around my cock. I shift uncomfortably in my chair, torn between the urge to relieve myself and the reality that I have work to focus on. If I'm going to indulge, it will be with her, not alone. I try to redirect my thoughts to upcoming meetings and realize I need to set some up. I picked up the phone to call Dani about some tasks. It rings, but there's no answer. Annoyed, I dial Carla, and she answers promptly.

"Yes, Mr. Anderson?"

"Is Ms. Cliff at her desk?"

"Yes, Mr. Anderson."

"Could you send her to my office, please?"

"Of course, Mr. Anderson." I hang up, trying to understand why she's ignoring me. I know I've been distant, but she continues to execute her tasks flawlessly. A light knock interrupts my thoughts, and she lets herself in.

"Yes, Mr. Anderson?" she asks, but I'm momentarily speechless. Her cheeks are flushed, as if she's just had a quick fuck. I know for a fact she hasn't; Carla would have informed me if she had company. Is it wrong to use Carla as my eyes and ears? Probably, but I can't bring myself to care. Unbeknownst to her, she belongs to me. I study her, trying to decipher her embarrassment, and decide to break the silence.

"Why didn't you answer your phone?"

"Oh, I, uh... I didn't hear it. I was thinking about someone, I mean something."

She recovers quickly, but I catch her slip. Who could she be thinking about? The pink flush of her cheeks and her nervous fidgeting suggest her thoughts are far from innocent. I strive to appear unaffected, but I clench my jaw, sitting up straighter and focusing on my computer screen, desperate to divert my attention.

"Set up a meeting with Alice Dupont for next week," I instruct.

"Okay. Sure." She hesitates for a moment, as if realizing she's overstayed her welcome. Just as she turns to leave, I call out.

"Next time you decide to ignore my call because you think you have better things...to do, you're fired."

The surprise on her face is fleeting, quickly replaced by a mask of neutrality as she exits without another word. Perhaps my remark was unnecessary, but I couldn't help myself. I'm grappling with emotions I can't quite articulate. It's more than just being pissed; I think I might actually be feeling jealousy. Damn. She might very well be my undoing.

****

I spent the entire afternoon making phone calls and leading meetings. After my last meeting of the day, I walk back into my office, but before I can close the door, my brother seizes it and waltzes right in.

"What do you need, Jay?"

"Must you always act like I'm such a bother? I might have some really important news for you."

"And do you?"

"Do I what?"

"Have important news?"

"Nope," he replies, popping the p. "I just came to see what's been going on with my big brother." He plops down in the chair across from me, getting comfortable.

"Nothing's been going on."

"Mmhmm."

"What?"

"Okay. How do I put this nicely?" He asks himself, tapping his chin.

"What has crawled up your ass?"

"Excuse me?"

"For a few weeks, you seemed like you were actually enjoying life a little bit. Then all of a sudden, you're all about work and piling on an even larger workload. Today, I could tell you were distracted during the meetings—not because it was blatantly obvious but because I'm your damn brother, and I know you. So why don't you tell me what the hell has crawled up your ass?" We lock eyes. I know he is expecting me to spill all my problems like he's my fucking therapist. While I'd rather tell him to get the hell out, I know he won't let this go.

"I kissed her."

"You kissed her. You kissed her." I wait for Jay to process what I'm telling him, and I see the lightbulb go off when his eyes widen. "Holy shit, man, you kissed Dani?! About time you took my advice."

"I was not taking your advice; it just happened." I recount that weekend and everything that followed. "But now I think I fucked everything up because I believe she's into someone else."

"What?" Jay scoffs. "No way."

"She ignored my call today because she was thinking of someone. I don't think she meant to say that and tried to cover it up, but I know what I heard."

"You like her?" Jay leans his elbows on the edge of my desk. I hesitate for a moment, even though I already know my answer.

"Yes."

"Fight for her. Tomorrow's Friday. Ask her to go for drinks or something."

"You don't think I'd be making a mistake? This could turn into another Gabby situation."

"Maybe," he shrugs.

"That's not encouraging." He laughs.

"Sorry, man, but I can't predict what's going to happen if you ask her out. But I can tell you that for a little while, you were happy, and I haven't seen that in a long time. She might not be the one for you, or maybe she is, and you'll end up together with 2.5 kids and a house with a white picket fence. I have zero interest in that, but I know you do. I think you'll regret not trying."

"And if this all goes wrong?"

"Then I guess I'll have to announce that we're looking for another secretary. Maybe I'll handle the hiring next time." I roll my eyes as he smirks at me. He pushes back from the chair and stands up, running his hands through his hair. He turns to leave, but just as he opens the door, he turns back. "If it goes wrong, I'll be here for you. Just like I've always been." He closes the door, and I know I should head home because there is no way I can focus on work with my thoughts completely consumed by a certain brown-eyed brunette.

****

On nights when I manage to return home at a reasonable hour, I usually find myself in bed before midnight. Yet, settling down eludes me. This evening, after working out in my gym and taking a refreshing shower, I prepared myself a simple dinner. With a glass of bourbon in hand, I retreat to my office, where I begin reviewing the files for tomorrow's meetings. After an hour, I feel my eyelids growing heavy, prompting me to close everything up and head to bed. Just as I am about to turn off the light, my phone pings.

Dani: Won't be in tomorrow. Need a personal day.

Me: Why?

Dani: I just need a personal day.

Me: No.

Dani: No?

Me: Tell me why you need off or your ass better be at work.

Dani: It's none of your business. I won't be there. Figure it out for one day or fire me. Either way you can fuck all the way off.

I hold back my response for two reasons, knowing that she's absolutely right and I need to win her over, not provoke her further. I admire her sharp tongue and the fierce spirit she displays when challenging me, yet I realize that pushing her buttons would not serve my purpose. As her employer, I understand that her reasons for taking a personal day were none of my concern, but as someone utterly infatuated, I crave the truth. Was she seeing someone? Was that the reason for her absence tomorrow?

The thought of another man in her bed, touching her, whispering her name as he held her, sent a chill through me. No, I can't allow myself to go there. I can't bear to think of another man claiming what I feel is mine. And while my possessive thoughts should have taken me aback, I'm not. She belongs to me—the moment she stumbled into my office, she had captured my heart.

****

It is halfway through the day when I prepare for my meeting with Mr. Hanson. We have a few ideas to pitch, and I hope he will be more than satisfied. While I can't fully grasp his reasons for traveling all this way for his grandfather's small business, it's clear he has no qualms about spending any amount of money to get what he desires.

I have kept myself busy, yet I still feel the void left by her absence on the floor. I long to reach out to her, but I can't afford the distraction of her response—or the sting of rejection if she chooses not to reply. So, I gather my files and make my way to the conference room, ensuring everything is in order. Once satisfied with the setup, I position myself by the elevator to await my client.

Tom steps off the elevator, exuding a confident swagger I have cultivated over the years. It is the kind of confidence that comes from understanding one's high stature. While I have earned the right to walk with such arrogance, I doubt he had, other than harboring a sense of entitlement. But if his entitlement translates into a substantial payout for the company, I will sit back and tolerate whatever presumptuous nonsense he feels compelled to share.

"Tom. Good to see you again," I say, extending my hand for a shake.

"Dean. Likewise. I'm surprised to find you here. I expected to be greeted by that charming secretary of yours. Where is she, anyway?" he asks, scanning the floor. I feel a muscle twitch in annoyance at his fascination with Dani, but I maintain my smile.

"She has another obligation today. Why don't we head back to the conference room? I have some ideas I think you're going to love." An expression flickers across his face so swiftly I almost think I had imagined it. Before I could analyze it further, a smile replaced it as he nodded, gesturing for me to lead the way.

****

"Dani, open the door."

I stand here, uncertain of my purpose, driven to madness by the silence and absence of her presence today. I know she's mine, and I'm ready to claim her. No more pretending I don't feel anything; this girl makes me feel everything. The door swings open.

"What are you doing here, Mr. Anderson?" Dani asks, surprise etched across her face. That makes two of us. She stands before me in shorts that barely covers her ass and a tank top that accentuates her breasts. I swallow hard, my gaze taking in every inch of her beauty. It wouldn't surprise me if a line of men were waiting for a chance with her, and that's exactly why I need to be here. I can't afford to lose her because I can't get my head out of my ass.

"Who is he?" Her eyes widen, and her breath quickens, revealing that she didn't expect me to know. As her boss, I might not be her number one confidant, but I can't shake the unease at the thought of her hiding something from me.

"What?" she whispers.

"Who are you dating?" I press, watching her closely. I see her body relax, and then she laughs—she actually laughs at me. I'm confused and surprised by the action. She opens the door wider, inviting me in, and I step inside.

"You can't seriously have come all the way over here just to ask if I was dating someone? How about a text?"

"You haven't answered my question," I reply through gritted teeth. She rolls her eyes at me, a gesture that makes my hand twitch with the urge to punish her.

"No. I'm not dating anybody. Not that it's any of your business if I was." She crosses her arms, and I furrow my brows, trying to decipher how I misread this entire situation. Unless she's lying. But why would she need to? She looked nervous when I first asked, so if she's not dating anyone, what's behind her jittery demeanor?

"So you weren't out late last night with someone else?"

"Um. No."

"Then who were you busy thinking about yesterday when you ignored my call?" Her cheeks flush pink, and silence falls as she seems to grapple with an internal struggle.

"You!" The admission spills from her lips, her eyes closing in what looks like shame. I'm surprised by her response, but it's exactly what I want to hear. I want her to know there's nothing to be embarrassed about. I gently lift her chin, making her meet my gaze.

"Dani," I say softly. She opens her eyes. "You were thinking of me?" I smirk. She nods, and I press further. "What about me?"

I can hear her swallow hard before she answers, "What would have happened if I didn't run from you?" Holy hell. My dick springs to life at her admission, desire coursing through me. I'm not delusional, and these feelings aren't just one-sided. With that added confidence, I continue.

"Mmhmm. What else?" I take a step closer, closing the distance.

"Just, um, how it would feel." I step in again, trapping her against the wall, leaving her no escape.

"How what would feel?"

"You touching me. Tasting me."

Before I know it, my lips crash against hers, igniting a kiss that is both wild and fervent. Although I had kissed her before, this moment transcended anything I'd experienced previously. I hadn't intended to take it this far, but now that I had a taste of her, there was no way I could walk away. My thoughts are consumed by the way she eagerly welcomes my tongue, and though I sense there is something she isn't revealing, I push that thought aside for another time. At this moment, all I want is to claim every inch of her and make her wholly mine.

I lean in, pressing soft kisses down her neck and along the curve of her collarbone. She tilts her head back, granting me even greater access, an unspoken invitation that deepens the moment. My hands roam her body, making their way to her perky tits and she releases a soft moan as I pinch her nipple. I gently lift her into my arms and make my way to her bedroom. With a careful push, I opened the door and, in one fluid motion, lay her down on the bed.

"Get naked," I demand. She seems hesitant but does as I ask. "Good girl," I say as my eyes trace her body, taking in the beautifully sculpted work of art in front of me. I push her legs open and place myself in between as I take her nipple into my mouth, sucking and nipping, ensuring that I take turns, paying attention to both. She begins wriggling beneath me as my hand cups her pussy. "You are so fucking wet, baby." I head down south as I lick and kiss my way down her stomach and along her thighs, teasing her.

"Please," I hear her beg. My dick twitches at how much she wants this.

"Please, what, baby? I want to hear it," I command as my fingers tease her entrance.

"I need you to touch me," she breathes heavily. "I...I want you to make me cum." That's all I need to hear before I slip my fingers into her tight cunt and finger fuck her as I lap up her juices with my tongue. I can feel her begin to clench around my fingers and I suck on her clit as my fingers continue to pound into her. "Fuck! Dean!" She cries out as she releases her orgasm. I lift my finger to her mouth.

"Taste yourself. You taste so damn good." Never taking her eyes off of me, she opens her mouth and sucks my finger clean. I'm so fucking hard that the strain against my pants is painful and I know that I need to be inside of her right now. I lift my shirt off and start on my pants as I notice her enjoying the view, biting down on her bottom lip. I get undressed in record time. As I pull myself free, her eyes widen.

"Will that fit?" she asks, genuinely concerned. I chuckle as I lean over her, kissing her as I line up my cock and push myself in. She cries out in pleasure.

"Perfect fit," I whisper. I feel her nails dig into my back, which only encourages me to pump in and out of her harder. "You're so fucking tight, baby." Her moans carry through the room as she gets louder, climbing closer to her climax. "Don't cum until I tell you, or you'll have to be punished." I swear, I feel her get even wetter at my words, and fuck, if that doesn't push me even closer to the edge. I pull out, and she whimpers at the loss, but just as quickly, I flip her over onto her stomach, pulling her ass towards me.

I give it a slap and rub the spot, stealing another moan from her. I re-enter her from behind. I grab her hair and pull her face up to me as I pound into her. She's looking at me with hooded eyes, and I kiss her hard. With one hand, I give her a tug on her nipple as I rub her clit with my other. "Now," I growl. She screams my name at her release, and I follow—both of us going over the edge together.

She sinks onto the bed, her exhaustion palpable, and I make my way to the bathroom to fetch a warm, damp cloth. With tender care, I wipe her skin, erasing the remnants of what we had done. Once we are both settled beneath the covers, I find myself enveloping her in my arms, despite my usual aversion to cuddling. As I close my eyes, a profound sense of peace washes over me, and I surrender to the most restful sleep I have experienced in ages.

31.

Dani

I awaken the following morning, alone in my bed, grappling with the uncertainty of whether last night had been a mere dream. The lingering, pleasant soreness in my lower regions suggests otherwise; yet, waking up alone stirs a sense of unease about what lies ahead. Last night had been nothing short of incredible, a moment where I finally relinquished control and placed my trust entirely in him. I am grateful I let my defenses down, for I have never had an experience that hot, where I actually felt alive and not on autopilot. In light of my past encounters, this one felt like my first.

However, this incredible night unfolded with my boss, who is now inexplicably missing. My mind races with thoughts of how we will navigate the aftermath. What does this mean for us? A noise from the kitchen jolts me from my reverie. Assuming it's Izzy bustling about, I reluctantly roll out of bed. I open my door, only to be surprised by the sound of voices. As I round the corner, I come to an abrupt halt at the sight of Dean standing at the stove, while Izzy sits casually at our island.

"Hey girl. Look at what I found this morning," Izzy exclaims, her eyes sparkling with excitement. I can see she's eager to hear the story behind this moment, but I choose to ignore her, shifting my focus to Dean, who is busy plating something. The tantalizing aroma wafting from his direction makes my stomach growl loudly as I make my way to the bar stool next to Izzy.

"You made breakfast?" I ask, the obvious question escaping my lips.

Dean turns around, sliding two plates in front of us. A stack of chocolate chip pancakes, generously topped with extra chocolate chips, sat invitingly on the plates. My absolute favorite. I glance at Izzy, silently inquiring if she had mentioned my preference to him, but she simply shrugs and begins pouring syrup over her pancakes. Dean takes a seat across from me, his own plate in hand. As I finish pouring syrup onto my pancakes and pass the bottle to him, our fingers brush against each other. A jolt of electricity shoots through my hand, causing me to pull back quickly, unsure what to say. I focus on my pancakes, diving in with a soft moan of delight.

"Mmmmm. Oh my God," I savor the taste.

"I bet you were saying that last night too," Izzy chimes in mischievously.

Dean coughs, clearly caught off guard by her boldness, while my cheeks flush a deep crimson. Izzy laughs, grabbing her plate.

"I'll leave you two to chat. I need to start getting ready for work anyway. Thanks for breakfast, Dean." He nods in acknowledgment, but his gaze remains fixed on me. I can't fathom why I had allowed myself to be so vulnerable last night, but this morning, I feel nothing but awkwardness and insecurity.

"Why chocolate chip pancakes?" I venture,

breaking the silence.

He shrugs. "You look like someone who would enjoy chocolate chip pancakes." I raise an eyebrow at him. "It may also be one of the few things I can actually cook from scratch."

"Well, it happens to be my favorite breakfast, and it's delicious."

"Thank you." The silence that follows is thick, almost suffocating.

"What are we doing here, Dean?" I finally confront the elephant in the room. "This morning, when I woke up and you weren't there, I thought I had my answer. But this"—I gesture to our plates—"I can't put my trust in you not to break my heart if you aren't all in. I can't do that again."

"Again?" he asks, curiosity lacing his tone.

"You aren't the only one who has pictured a future with someone and ended up hurt, Dean." He continues to look at me, and it feels as if he were gazing straight through to my soul. My heart races, and I feel as though I can barely breathe as I await his response. He pushes himself up from his seat, and I squeeze my eyes shut, willing myself not to cry. *Don't cry, Dani. Don't cry. Hold your shit together.* Suddenly, I feel hands gently grasping my face.

"Look at me, Dani." I open my eyes to find him leaning in close. "I'm in. I'm all in."

He closes the distance between us, and as our lips meet, it is more than just a kiss. It's a promise.

****

Dean had to head to the office to take care of a few matters, leaving me with several hours to fill since Izzy was at work. I decided it was the perfect opportunity to dive into a book I had bought months ago. Settling on the couch, I embarked on my thrilling journey through the pages in my hands.

Just as I reached the halfway point of the story, my phone buzzed, interrupting my immersion.

Dean: Get ready. I'll pick you up at 6.

Me: Ready for what?

Dean: Our date. Wear the purple dress.

I bristle at being bossed around, yet there was something undeniably hot when he took charge.

I place my bookmark against the last page I read and set it on the coffee table. Making my way into my bedroom, my mind bustles with ideas on where we might be going. I spend the next hour perfecting my hair and makeup, singing along to the tunes streaming from my phone. I just so happened to be really getting into the groove when another text chimed in. I eagerly tapped the screen to see the message assuming it's Dean again.

Unknown: Avoiding me now?

I drop my phone as if it has just burned me. There's only one person this could be. How the fuck did he get my number? A whirlwind of questions races through my mind, and if I were braver, perhaps I would confront him or hell, I would just tell him to fuck off. Instead, I block the number and retreat to my bedroom to slip into the dress Dean insisted I wear. I try to push aside the fear that is creeping in but it flows through my veins, seeping into every nook and cranny of my mind and body. I refuse to let him spoil my night because for the first time in a long time, I actually feel happy.

As another text comes through, I glance at my phone—my heart racing. I exhale, not realizing how tightly I had been holding my breath until I see Dean's name on the screen. I reach for my purse and open the door, eager to head downstairs when I suddenly collide with something solid. My senses heighten as a pair of strong hands grip my hips, steadying me, while the warm, earthy scent of sandalwood envelops me.

"Keep looking at me like that Miss Cliff and we won't make it past this hallway."

I swallow hard, imagining all the ways I want him to touch me. His gaze follows the movement, and I can sense he's reconsidering this whole date. It's as if I have lost the ability to form a coherent thought. He chuckles softly, takes my hand, and gently tugs me toward the stairs, leading us to the car.

"So, are you going to tell me where we are going?" I ask as the car begins to move.

"No." I've never been good at handling surprises. While some women may thrive on the thrill of the unknown, I find it unsettling. The unpredictability leaves me feeling unprepared, a state I always strive to avoid. Dean must sense my unease because he squeezes my hand and offers me a reassuring smile.

"It's not too far. I think you'll enjoy it."

"No other hints?"

"You don't like surprises, do you?"

"Not really my favorite."

"Alright, just one hint then. It'll definitely get your creative juices flowing."

"Hmm. Maybe that's not the kind of juices I want flowing tonight," I reply, crossing my legs and letting the hem of my dress slide up my thigh. His gaze darkens, following the movement. Clearing his throat, he sidesteps my suggestion.

"Good thing we have all night." I roll my eyes, catching the slight twitch at the corner of his mouth. "Keep rolling those eyes, and I might have to punish you later."

"Promise?" His eyebrows raise in surprise at my boldness. I'm quite surprised myself. Typically, I hold the reins, but when it comes to intimacy, I've never felt this confident before, and I certainly have never had any kind of sexual verbal sparring beforehand, like some form of foreplay. The playful banter feels new yet exhilarating.

As our conversation dwindles, the car glides to a halt. Dean steps out first, and just as I reach for the handle to open my door, it swings wide, revealing him on the other side. I can't recall ever having a date who opened the door for me. It strikes me that Dean might be a rare breed—or perhaps I simply haven't been discerning enough in my choices of men.

"Wait. You're taking me to the art museum?" I peer up at Dean, utterly astonished.

"That is my plan, but if you'd rather be somewhere

else, we can go," he replies, a hint of uncertainty in his voice. I've never seen this man waver in his convictions; his certainty has always been a defining trait. Yet, it fills me with gratitude to know that my thoughts hold significance for him.

"Absolutely not," I retort, narrowing my eyes at him. "Of course I want to be here. How did you know?"

"I may or may not have spotted some brochures in your bedroom," he admits with a sly grin.

"Ah, so you were snooping?" I tease, raising an eyebrow. Dean feigns shock.

"I was not snooping. I don't snoop." He insists, though I can't help but laugh. I grab his arm to pull him forward, but he stands his ground, drawing me closer to him.

"You're different, Dani. I've never felt the need to think so much about a date—until now," he confesses. His piercing blue eyes seem to look straight into my soul, and my breath catches in my throat as he leans in, wrapping me in his embrace.

When our lips finally meet, it's a kiss so soft and sweet, a surprising contrast to the hard-edged masculinity that is Dean. He pulls away, a smirk playing on his lips, fully aware of the effect he has on me. Nodding toward the entrance, he takes my hand and leads me through the doors.

****

"I can't believe you took me here!" I exclaim,

bubbling with excitement as we begin our walkthrough.

"Have you ever been?" he asks.

"No. Izzy and I have been trying to carve out some time to come together, but our schedules just don't align these days."

"Will she be upset that you came without her?"

"Not at all. She would have joined me, but art isn't really her thing."

"But it's yours?" I glance away from the art to look at him. He generally looks interested in my response.

"Kind of. I took art classes in high school, and I even continued with a few after graduation. It was more of an outlet for me than a hobby. My interest deepened after taking a field trip to the National Gallery of Art in D.C. Just wandering around, trying to grasp what the artist felt or experienced while creating their masterpiece—it made me think it could be a way to escape when I needed to forget."

"Forget what?" Dean asks, shifting his focus from the sculpture in front of us to me.

"My childhood. It wasn't the greatest," I reply with a sigh, fleeting memories washing over me. I realize I've already shared too much, yet Dean's patient silence encourages me to continue. "I don't know my dad. He went to jail during my first year of life and never reached out or tried to know me. It felt like I was erased from his existence. To be honest, I don't even know if he's out of prison or if he's even still alive."

"Do you ever think about finding out?"

"Nope. He's dead to me, regardless. I'd much rather

invest my energy in the people who matter to me, and who I matter to." I glance at Dean, his expression a mix of curiosity and understanding.

"And your mom?"

"We were never close. She was always bringing home boyfriends, trying to use them for money, sex, or both. If they could help her in some way, she was in love with them. They never lasted long though."

"That couldn't have been easy."

"No. I didn't really understand it all until I was older, but she wasn't the greatest role model."

"So how did you turn out so great then?" I laugh, feeling my cheeks redden.

"Not all of her boyfriends were terrible. A few genuinely seemed to care for me, treating me as if I were their own during their brief time with my mom. They imparted some valuable life skills and encouraged me to contemplate my future and what I truly want out of it. There was one guy in particular. His name was Jack. He was my favorite. Jack opened my eyes to the idea that life had so much more to offer than what I was experiencing. He encouraged me to break free from my mother's shadow, instilling in me the belief that I could achieve anything on my own."

"Sounds like a good guy."

"He was. He even kept in touch with me after he left my mom, until one day he just didn't. Later, I discovered he had died in a car accident." My mind drifts back to the day I tried to find him. I asked my mom, but all she said was that he had probably moved on, that he was done with me just like he was with her. At first, her words hurt, and I believed them. But deep down, I knew he would never abandon me, so I began my own search. When I finally uncovered the truth behind his silence, I experienced grief for the first time in my life.

"That must have been difficult to find out." I'm grateful he doesn't just offer me a hollow apology like most people do. Reflecting on my initial impressions of him, I realize how wrong I was. I never imagined that he had the ability to be sensitive to anyone's needs or feelings, especially my own.

"It was. I felt sad for myself and for all the people who would miss out on the chance to know him. Yet, there was also a sense of relief—not because of his death, but because my mom was mistaken; he hadn't left me behind by choice."

"I understand that. There is nothing wrong with feeling that way," he says, offering reassurance and validation. Before I can succumb to a wave of mixed emotions, overwhelmed with declarations of love for this man, I begin to walk into the next room.

"Come on. Let me show you my favorite painting."

32.

Dean

I possess only a fleeting knowledge of art, never having taken the time to stand before a painting and attempt to fathom the artist's intent at the moment of its creation. Watching Dani as she navigates the museum, deeply analyzing each piece, fills me with a sense of longing; I wish I had invested time in studying art beforehand. Typically, I take pride in impressing others, but in this moment, it is she who captivates and astounds me with her insights.

We find ourselves in front of a piece titled "The Scream." "What do you see?" she asks. I understand that art is subjective, yet at this moment, I'm feeling insecure and want to give a response that will impress her. I study the figure on the bridge, seemingly screaming, hence the name.

"I see a man on a bridge. He looks distraught, maybe yelling for help. Perhaps he just witnessed someone jump off the bridge." I brace myself for her laughter, too anxious to meet her gaze.

"You're not too far off," she replies.

"I'm not?" I ask, stealing a glance at her.

"No," she smiles. "Munch is expressing his own

dark emotions. The figure didn't witness a jump; he is, in a way, screaming for help himself. This painting conveys themes of fear and loneliness."

"And this is your favorite painting?" I inquire, raising my eyebrows in disbelief. She laughs.

"One of them," she responds, still chuckling. "I know it's a bit unconventional, but I was drawn to it when I first saw it in high school. In a way, it made me feel less alone."

"And now?" I ask, pulling her closer to me.

"Now it feels like a memory. Like the girl I used to be." She smiles, wrapping her arms around my neck and pulling me in for a kiss. Damn, I'm utterly lost for this woman.

****

We begin our stroll toward Central Park when Dani suddenly halts.

"Oh my God!" she exclaims, darting across the street.

"Where are you going? What's wrong?" I call out, hurriedly following her.

"A Halal food truck! It has the best food ever! I'm in love with their gyros!"

"Hungry?" I ask.

"Starving," she replies. We approach the cart, and I order two lamb gyros. As we wait, I can't resist the urge to ask more questions. I need to know everything about this woman. "You graduated from a private school."

"I did," she says, narrowing her eyes and stretching out her words, clearly curious about my comment.

"I'm just trying to understand how you ended up here."

"Well, when a man and a woman…" she starts, but I cut her off.

"Smart ass," I chuckle, amused by her teasing.

Our gyros are ready, and we grab them, resuming our walk toward Central Park. I watch her take a large bite, my dick responding to the sounds she makes as she chews. She glances at me with raised eyebrows.

"What?"

I smirk, leaning closer to her, inhaling the sweet scent of coconut from her shampoo as my lips hover near her ear. "Just thinking about how I'm going to hear those sounds come from that pretty little mouth when it's wrapped around my cock." Her eyes widen at my words, and despite her innocent facade, I know she revels in my dirty talk. I pull back, taking a bite of my food, and I'm pleasantly surprised. "Wow. This is delicious."

"Seriously, you've never had this before?"

"I don't really eat at food trucks."

"Why not?" She looks appalled at my confession. I shrug.

"Usually, I'm so caught up with work that I don't take much time to enjoy the city. It's just easier to have food delivered."

"I grew up in a pretty small town. I never thought I

would have the chance to leave. That's why I applied for a scholarship to get into that particular high school. There was no way my mom could afford it, but I had the grades and the determination." She pauses, and a flicker of shame crosses her face—though I can't quite understand what she has to be ashamed about. "While I once loved the quiet of the town, after high school, I just needed a change. Izzy is from here, and when she returned, I went with her. It was a lot to adjust to at first—the bright lights, the constant noise, the bustling activity at all hours. But now, I've come to love it. After standing out for so long, it feels good to blend in." Blend in. She's deceiving herself if she thinks she can truly blend in and go unnoticed by the world.

"I don't doubt you stood out. You're smart, funny, and beautiful—there's no way you weren't noticed," I say. She smiles but it doesn't reach her eyes.

"I wish that's why I stood out. High school was anything but easy. I didn't have the money that the other kids did, which made me a target. The only reason I had any friends at all was because I dated one of the popular guys, and that didn't end well. After that, I found myself ostracized." I want to know more about her story—who the asshole was that broke her heart, what he did, the names of everyone who made her feel alone. But I don't press her. I can tell she rarely opens up, especially about her past, and I don't want to jeopardize the connection we have, the fact that she's choosing to talk to me. I don't want to push her away because I'm being fucking greedy. "Izzy stayed by my side through it all," she continues. "Even during my darkest moment."

"Your darkest moment?" I ask, surprise lacing my

tone. This woman shines so brightly that I can't fathom what could ever possibly dim her light.

"One night, I swallowed a bunch of pills, driven by a desperate search for peace. I'm still not sure if I genuinely wanted to die that night or if I just needed to silence the chaotic thoughts swirling around in my head for a little while. I was young, not fully aware of the consequences or how it would affect those around me. Maybe that wasn't the core issue, though. Honestly, I just didn't think anyone would care. Izzy was furious with me, but she didn't leave my side the entire time I was in the hospital. It was in that stark, sterile room that I realized I actually had someone in my corner."

"Well," I begin, halting our walk to face her directly. "I'm glad you didn't succeed. This world needs you in it, Dani. I need you in it." Her gaze lifts to meet mine, her eyes glimmering with unshed tears. I catch her glance at my lips, and I take that as my invitation. Leaning down, I kiss her gently at first, nudging her lips with my tongue. She parts them, deepening the kiss.

There we stand, in the heart of Central Park, lost in each other like two lovesick teens. I pull away slowly, noticing her eyes remain closed, savoring the moment. With a soft kiss on her forehead, I embrace her, feeling her melt into me as though my touch could erase all her worries. We linger in that embrace, time slipping away as the world around us fades.

Noticing her shiver, I take off my coat and drape it around her shoulders. She looks up, and I find myself lost in those big brown eyes.

"Thanks," she whispers. Taking her hand, I pull her

along as we head back to the street.

"Where are we going now?" she asks.

"Time for dessert."

33.

Dani

Of course, he lives in a fucking penthouse—a luxurious haven for a rich asshole. A very rich, sexy asshole.

As we ascend in the private elevator, the air thickens with sexual tension, heightening with each floor that we pass. When the elevator doors slide open directly into his unit, I momentarily forget the alluring view beside me and drift toward the window, captivated by the breathtaking panorama of the city.

"This view is stunning."

"Yes. It is." I glance over and catch him watching me intently. A blush creeps up my cheeks as I feel his gaze pierce through me. He strides toward me, his eyes never leaving mine. I swallow hard, and I could swear I see them darken with desire.

His fingers graze my hand, trailing up my wrist and along my arm. The light touch sends a thrill through me, nearly unraveling me. He continues his way up my neck before cupping my face in his hands, as he leans in, kissing me feverishly.

Just like our first time, we are desperate for each other. Our tongues intertwine, and our bodies close the distance that separates us. I feel him, hard and ready, pressing against my stomach. My hand instinctively moves down, stroking his length through his slacks, eliciting a low moan from deep within him.

He pushes me against the window and slides down to his knees. His hands creep up my thighs, fisting the small scrap of fabric that acts as a barrier. He pulls and rips my panties off, throwing them off to the side, while lifting my leg up over his shoulder. He looks up at me, smirking. "My favorite dessert," he mumbles before his tongue flicks and sucks my clit. I grab his hair as my hips start to move with need, riding his face as he fucks me with his tongue. I'm not sure if he's just that damn good or if it's the feeling of empowerment that I can bring a man like Dean Anderson to his knees, but it doesn't take long before I'm screaming his name, coming so hard, my vision darkens. Dean places my leg down, his mouth glistening with my juices. He stands up and kisses me, forcing me to taste myself.

He grabs under my ass and picks me up, my legs wrapping around his hips. He carries me over to his couch and sits with me straddling him. I begin moving my hips, rubbing myself against his cock. He pulls my dress over my head, reaches behind me and unclips my bra with one hand. I pull it the rest of the way off of me and Dean immediately pinches my left nipple between his fingers while licking and biting down on my right. I gasp, a thin line between pleasure and pain.

As good as it all feels, I find it unfair that he's still fully dressed while I'm completely bare. I slide off his lap, falling to my knees in front of him. My hands glide down his hard chest, feeling the lines of his muscles as they

A.M. ROBERTS

make their way to his zipper. I unbutton his pants and pull his cock through, his tip slick with excitement. I lick the length of his cock before kissing the tip. I stare up at him, noticing his breaths getting quicker and heavier. I slide him into my mouth, sucking and licking as I work the bottom of his shaft with my hand. He's so large, it's difficult for me to take him all in. He grabs onto the back of my hair and starts fucking my mouth.

Normally I would hate this, never allowing a guy to take control of me in this way, but with Dean, I just find it hot as hell. "I'm going to fucking claim your mouth, baby," I hear him say just before I feel the warm and salty liquid hit the back of my throat before I swallow it all down. "Such a good fucking girl," he says as he pulls out.

I lean in, our lips meeting in a breathless kiss. My fingers tangle in the hair at the nape of his neck while his strong arms encircle my waist, lifting me effortlessly to my feet. He pulls back slightly, tucking a loose strand of hair behind my ear. "Stay with me tonight," he murmurs, his forehead resting gently against mine.

The hour is late, and the idea of disentangling myself from this perfect specimen to sleep alone fills me with reluctance. I can already imagine the dreams of missed pleasure haunting my night.

"You begging?"

"I don't beg."

"No. You just tell me what to do," I reply, my fingers deftly undoing the top button of his shirt.

"I am your boss," he states, a smirk playing on his lips.

"You just enjoy being bossy," I tease back.

"And you fucking love it," he counters, his fingers slipping between my thighs, a testament to my body's betrayal of his commands. My head reclines, a soft moan escaping my lips as he continues his tantalizing play. He's already hard again, and both of us are desperate for more. With a gentle but firm lift, he carries me into his bedroom, where he lays me down with careful grace. As he lets his shirt fall away, my gaze is irresistibly drawn to the masterpiece before me—every muscle of his body sculpted to perfection. In a swift motion, he sheds his pants and underwear, revealing a figure reminiscent of Adonis himself.

He lifts me further up on the bed and climbs on top. I can feel his hard cock gliding along my slit. I tip my head back, feeling the friction against my clit. "Dean," I moan.

"Tell me what you want Dani," he demands, his voice low and husky.

"I need you inside me. Fuck me Dean."

He lines himself up and thrusts hard inside of me. I yell out in pleasure as he pushes my legs up and hits me deeper. "Fuck, baby, I love that your tight cunt chokes my cock." I feel myself climbing higher at his filthy mouth.

"Harder, Dean. Fuck me harder." His hips begin to move at a faster pace, hitting me harder. His thumb moves in a circular motion over my clit, eliciting loud moans out of me. He pinches my nub and I scream out as my body shakes, exploding into my orgasm. Dean groans, following me with his release as I feel his hot cum filling me up.

He pulls out, slipping off the bed, and strides into

the adjoining bathroom, leaving me with a moment to explore his expansive bedroom. The space speaks of minimalism, with its sparse decor and simple design. The cool gray and blue hues create a calming atmosphere that seems to resonate with him. Moments later, he returns, a damp cloth in hand, attempting to clean me up, though I know it's a futile effort. Our hands are drawn to each other, igniting passion once more, and we lose ourselves in each other's embrace, surrendering to the waves of pleasure that wash over us two more times before finally succumbing to a blissful, orgasm-induced sleep. Nestled in Dean's arms, I feel a sense of safety enveloping me; here, the nightmares cannot reach me.

****

I wake early, Dean still asleep beside me. I take a moment to study his beautiful face, noting how different he looks in slumber. His features soften, free from the tension of pinched brows and a clenched jaw. He's so damn handsome and before he wakes, I try to commit this version of him to memory. Deciding to rise, I set out in search of my phone, realizing I never texted Izzy to let her know I wouldn't be coming home. I hope she isn't too worried.

I slip into one of Dean's T-shirts and continue my search. Spotting my purse on the floor by the window, I pause to take in the scene before me. The sun begins to rise, its rays wrapping the city in the promise that a new day always brings. Last night was incredible, and the happiness I feel is both exhilarating and terrifying. I have never been able to hold on to joy for long; it's only a matter of time before loss creeps back in.

Before my thoughts can spiral, I bend down and retrieve my phone from the bag. As I scroll through the screen, I notice multiple missed messages. Clicking on Izzy's, I can't help but chuckle.

Izzy: How is the date going?

Izzy: You aren't tied up and currently being murdered, are you?

Izzy: Or sold to sex traffickers?

Izzy: Bitch, the only acceptable reason for ignoring me is that you better be getting some hella good dick.

Izzy: If you come home able to comfortably sit, I'll be highly disappointed in you.

She is probably still asleep, but I quickly text her to share that I'm experiencing a level of soreness that would make her proud.

After sending the message, I exit our conversation and notice another notification from an unknown number.

Unknown: Ignoring me won't save you.

My jaw tightens, and my grip on my phone becomes firmer. Anger surges through me. I can only assume this is Tom again, and I have no idea what twisted game he's trying to play, but I refuse to let him disrupt my life again. With a decisive tap, I block the number, hoping he'll just give up. Beneath the surface, a truth gnaws at me—a truth that demands to be shared with Dean. I should tell him about the darkness that had shadowed my childhood, about the man who had once wielded power over me, and how he had resurfaced to taunt me with memories of the chaos he had become. Yet, an invisible weight holds me back. Dean was already aware of a portion of my past, some of the many scars I carried, and I fear this revelation would only cement his belief that I am a burden, unworthy of the complications I will undoubtedly bring into his life.

I hear footsteps behind me. "Damn that is a beautiful sight." I turn to face him, noticing his eyes traveling down my body, a smirk playing on his lips.

"Oh come on, I look a mess," I protest.

"You're walking around my place in nothing but my T-shirt. You're a fucking wet dream, Dani," he replies, pressing a soft kiss to my neck. Just then, his phone rings from the other room.

"Aren't you going to get that?" I ask, closing my eyes as his lips trail toward my jaw.

"Nope," he responds, playfully biting my bottom lip. The phone rings again, and he sighs, leaning his forehead against mine.

"Go ahead. Answer it." As he retreats to the bedroom, I head into the kitchen, searching for coffee. The space is stunning, with white cabinets and sleek black appliances, just as tidy as the rest of his home. Spotting a coffee machine on the counter, I gather what I need and start brewing a pot. When Dean emerges from the bedroom, the coffee is ready and poured into two mugs. He takes the one I offer, sipping carefully.

"Something came up with one of the marketing projects. I have to meet with Chris and his team."

"Oh. Okay," I say, trying to mask my

disappointment.

"You can stay here if you want."

"Thanks, but I have some things to take care of. Do you mind dropping me off at my place first?"

"Of course. But first, shower," he insists, setting our mugs down on the counter. He lifts me effortlessly, carrying me into the bathroom, once again proving just how magical his dick is.

****

Dean drops me off in front of my apartment building, stepping out to give me a goodbye kiss that leaves me wishing we never left his bed. As we part, a sense of emptiness washes over me, but I muster a smile and wave goodbye, heading toward the door.

Upon entering my apartment, I gently close the door, hoping not to disturb Izzy if she's still asleep.

"Well, look what the cat dragged in," a voice calls out, startling me. I turn to find Chad and Izzy lounging on the couch, each holding a mimosa.

"You scared the shit out of me," I scold Chad, still catching my breath.

"And you look freshly fucked," he retorts with a mischievous grin.

"Mimosa?" Izzy offers, extending a glass toward me. I take it and settle between the two of them, bracing myself for the inevitable interrogation.

"So, did you have a good time?" Izzy probes, her

eyes sparkling with curiosity.

"I had a great time," I reply, a smile creeping onto my lips.

"Okay, spill the details. We need every last bit," Chad insists, leaning in closer.

"You are definitely not getting all the details."

"Oh come on! You have to give us something!" Chad chimes in, his voice filling with excitement. "We have seen you after countless nights out, and you never glowed like this before."

Izzy leans closer, smirking. "Well, having multiple orgasms will do that to you, won't it, Dani?" A flush creeps across my cheeks.

"Oh my God! You little slut!" Izzy laughs, playfully tossing a couch pillow in my direction. I can't help but laugh along with her.

"Okay, okay!" I raise my hands in surrender before taking a long sip of the ice-cold drink in my hand. "He was amazing, truly the best sex I've ever had."

"To be expected," Chad interjects, his tone dripping with sarcasm. "You tend to date men who are way beneath you."

"Thanks, Chad," I reply, rolling my eyes.

Izzy continues, "Oh come on, you know you've never dated anyone with the idea that it would lead to something more. You picked mediocre guys because you didn't want the sex to be so good that it would trap you." I down the last of my drink, feeling the truth in her words.

"You're right," I admit, a sigh escaping my lips. "I

never thought that being happy was in the cards for me."

"Babe," Chad chastises, "You never believed you were destined for happiness, which is completely crazy because you deserve it more than anyone."

"How long until it's all ripped away from me?" I reply, my voice barely above a whisper.

"What makes you think it will be taken from you?" Izzy questions, her brow furrowing with concern. I simply shrug in response.

"Is this about Tom?" I glance at Izzy; she always had an uncanny ability to read between the lines of my thoughts.

"Wait. Does he not know?" Chad interjects, his expression shifting to one of surprise. I shake my head. "Don't you think that's something you should share with him?"

"I just don't want to scare him off. Tom hasn't technically done anything other than being in the same city as me and maybe a few texts."

"First of all, he's a client at your workplace, and you've seen him outside our apartment. Secondly, what do you mean by a few texts? He's texting you now?" Izzy presses, her concern evident.

"Only a couple of times. It's from an unknown number, but I can't think of anyone else it could be. I keep blocking the numbers, hoping it will all just stop if I don't react."

"Danielle Elizabeth Cliff," Chad groans, wiping his hands over his face in frustration. "Let me get this straight. The man who assaulted you is a client where you work, knows where you live, and is texting you? And you don't think this is something you need to tell Dean or, hell, the police?"

"Well, I—" I start to explain, but he cuts me off.

"No," Chad states firmly. "Do you really think Dean would be glad to learn he's been helping the man who assaulted his girlfriend? Absolutely not, Dani!"

"Listen, sweetie, we love you. Even though we all thought Dean was a gigantic asshole at first—"

"A very hot asshole," Chad interjects, earning glares from both of us.

"I don't think he would want you to deal with this on your own. He would want to know. He would want to protect you."

"I don't want him to feel like he has to protect me. I want a partner, not a babysitter. He already has enough stress in his life; I don't want to add to the weight he carries." I avoid looking at either of them, knowing they wouldn't agree with me. I can't bear to see any judgment or disappointment on their faces.

"You know we have your back, no matter what you choose. Just think about it, okay?"

"Okay."

"And let us know if that bastard texts you again. If I have to move in here for a while to make sure that piece of shit doesn't come near you, I absolutely will," Chad says, determination etched on his face. I smile at him. Chad's offer to stay with us speaks volumes about the depth of our friendship. Known for his strong desire for personal space, he often expresses doubts about ever settling down, unable to bear the thought of being mindful of another's presence in his home. This gesture, then, is not just a simple invitation; it is a testament to the bond we share, one that transcends his usual reservations.

"Thanks, Chad." I say, placing my hand over his.

"Although you'll owe me, because that would mean I'd have to abstain from hot men and could potentially miss out on meeting my soulmate," Chad continues, giving my hand a squeeze.

"And there he is," I tease. "For a second, I was worried a decent human being had overtaken your body." He chuckles, but his expression quickly turns serious.

"You know we've got your back, right?" Izzy tells me, placing her hand on my leg to nab my attention. I grab Izzy's hand and lean my head on Chad's shoulder.

"Yeah. Yeah, I do."

34.

Tom

For months, I have been a silent observer, weaving myself into the fabric of her life, revealing myself only when I desired her gaze. I have played with her mind, pulling the strings of her emotions like a puppeteer. She remains blissfully unaware of the countless hours I spend watching her, studying her every move. Every action of mine is meticulously calculated. I once believed she would be wise enough not to indulge in a game of pretend with her boss, yet I vastly underestimated the man's allure.

Weeks have passed, and their connection seems to grow deeper, leaving scant opportunity for me to reach out. I have been patient, but my tolerance is waning.

I'm rather astonished that she hasn't replied to my messages. Curiosity has always been a challenge for her to suppress. Yet, it seems she is entirely absorbed in him.

She believes she can cast me aside, erase me as if I were merely a figment of her imagination. She thinks she can pretend that she doesn't hold my soul hostage. Danielle has belonged to me since the moment she entered my school; the chains that bind us may be thin, but they are far from broken. She is mine, and I will do whatever it takes to ensure she understands the depth of that claim.

35.

Dani

The past few weeks have been nothing short of extraordinary. Initially, I feared that embarking on a relationship with my boss would be a grave mistake, yet the ease with which we connected has left me questioning my instincts. Despite these thoughts, my focus remains solely on my happiness. With the surge of clients at Stonebrook, work has become overwhelmingly busy, granting us little time together at the office.

Of course, there were those moments—like the time I gave him a blowjob at his desk after a grueling meeting, or our quick fuck between phone calls. Despite the immense pressure he and his brother are under, Dean always carves out time for us during the week. I've even begun to leave some of my belongings at his place for convenience, and surprisingly, rather than complain about his space being invaded, he seems to embrace it.

Our routine has become comfortable, allowing me to momentarily forget about Tom and the threatening messages that once haunted me. Since confiding in Izzy and Chad about those threats, I haven't received any further communications, though they still check on me regularly. Slowly, I find myself lowering my defenses, letting the walls around my heart crumble. I had always believed that happiness was not meant for me, yet I allowed myself to trust, to hope that perhaps I was mistaken.

Having been trapped, tied up in a dark void for so long, I had not realized how desperate I was for light— only to discover that I was never truly free, merely misled by the loosening of the ropes that bound me.

****

I walk into work alone today, having enjoyed a restful night in my own bed. Knowing that Dean had a crucial meeting to prepare for with Jay this morning, I insisted he take the time he needed to rest and focus. Carla was also out this morning for an appointment, leaving me to manage everything on my own.

I set my coffee on my desk and settled into my seat, ready to tackle my list of tasks. After making several phone calls to arrange meetings and sorting through a mountain of emails, I decide it is time to stretch my legs. I walk over to the printer to grab some important documents that Dean would need later in the week.

But as I round my desk, my arm inadvertently knocked my coffee cup to the floor. "Damn it!" I exclaim, frustration bubbling up as I hurry to the bathroom for paper towels. Fortunately, the floor was luxury vinyl tile rather than carpet, making it easier to clean up the spill. I hope the dark gray hue of the flooring will disguise any lingering stains.

With my back turned to the elevators, I hear the familiar sound of the doors opening. "Sorry, Carla! I promise I'll get it all cleaned up," I call out, assuming it is her. But when silence meets my words, I sense something is off. The sound of footsteps is different, and an unsettling chill creeps up my arms. I turn around slowly, my heart racing, and find Tom standing just a few feet away, his presence transforming the atmosphere in the room.

"You always were clumsy," he points out, a hint of amusement in his tone.

"You don't have an appointment," I reply, hoping he can't detect the tremor in my voice.

"I don't need one."

"Then why are you here?"

"Isn't it obvious?" he questions, a smirk playing on his lips. I realize he's not here for business. The way he's cornering me in this office, with no one else around, confirms my worst fears about his presence in my city. I take a deep breath, trying to mask the fear that grips my body, determined not to show any weakness. He thrives on my vulnerability.

"If you want to see Mr. Anderson, you'll need to make an appointment," I suggest, moving toward my computer.

"I don't need an appointment. And drop the 'Mr. Anderson' act—it sounds ridiculous when you're fucking him." My eyes widen in shock, but I shouldn't be surprised. I knew he was out there, and if he was watching me, he'd certainly know about us.

He steps closer, and I instinctively back away, continuing to retreat until my back presses against the wall.

"What do you want from me, Tommy?" I whisper, feeling my strength wane.

"What do I want?" he echoes, his voice low and intense. "What do I want? I want what's mine!" His voice rises as he closes in, trapping me with his arms on either side of my head. Leaning down, he buries his face in my hair, inhaling deeply. I close my eyes, struggling to keep my breath steady and the panic at bay.

I know someone is bound to arrive shortly, and I aim to maintain control of the situation until then. I lock eyes with him, those same dark pools that I have gazed into countless times before. Only back then, I was blissfully naive, too wrapped up in love to notice the emptiness lurking within. Yet now, as I peer into those depths once more, the truth is undeniable: a chilling void resides there, a malevolence that sends shivers down my spine.

"And what is yours?" I ask, trying to understand his intentions. He laughs, a sound filled with disdain.

"Still playing fucking games."

"I'm not playing games. I genuinely want to help you." He straightens, his presence suddenly more imposing as he slams his hands against the wall, causing me to flinch.

"You don't want to fucking help me!" he accuses, raking a hand through his hair. I recall how often I used to run my fingers through that thick mane, and how I adored the mess it created. In those moments, he seemed even more handsome, rugged in his disarray. Yet now, despite his physical allure, the darkness within him seeps outward, revealing the ugliness of his soul and twisting my stomach in knots.

"You messed up, Dani," he continues, his voice low and dangerous. "You're mine, and you've strayed. But I'll remind you of what you've forgotten. I was your first, and I'll be your last. You belong to me, and I won't stop until you make the right choice."

Before I can react, he pushes his body against mine, capturing my chin and kissing me with a roughness that sends panic coursing through my veins. My mind spirals, thoughts muddled as his tongue demands entry. My fight-or-flight instinct kicks in, and with no room to flee, I choose to fight. I thrust my arms between us, pushing him away just enough to create some space.

As he smirks and lunges at me once more, I seize the moment. My hand rises, connecting sharply with the left side of his cheek. For a fleeting second, he's stunned, and I dart around him, desperate for escape. Just as I think I've broken free, his hand snaps around my wrist, halting my flight.

I turn, meeting the fury radiating from him, but before he can retaliate, the sound of the elevator interrupts us. He pulls me close, his breath hot against my ear.

"You say one word, and I'll destroy him."

"Leave him out of this," I retort, my voice steady despite the fear coursing through me.

"One. Fucking. Word."

The elevator doors slide open, and Carla steps through, almost reaching her desk before she catches sight of us. Tom kneels down, retrieving the paper towels that lay scattered on the floor.

"Oh. Everything okay here?" Carla asks, her gaze narrowing with suspicion as she scrutinizes both of us. I can sense her curiosity about Tom's presence, especially since she had Dean and Jay's schedules and knew he hadn't arranged a meeting. A part of me wants to confide in her, to lay bare the weight of everything Tom had inflicted upon me—both past and present. I long for liberation, yet I am acutely aware of Dean's hard-won position. I can't fathom the extent of Tom's potential to hurt him, but I know that the devil recognizes no boundaries. I refuse to let Tommy destroy Dean the way he had shattered me.

Perhaps it is foolish to prioritize Dean's well-being over my own, but perhaps that was love. At that moment, a realization washes over me: I am in love with Dean. He reignited a spark that was still deep within me, and I will do anything for him, even if it means that I will get burned in the process.

"Oh, uh, yeah, Carla," I reply, praying my expression doesn't betray my distress. "Mr. Hansen came by hoping to see Mr. Anderson, and I told him he needed to set up a meeting. When I reached for my coffee, I accidentally spilled it. He was just helping me clean up. Actually, I'll grab some more paper towels."

As I walk toward the bathroom, I close the door behind me and lean over the sink, taking deep breaths. My reflection in the mirror reveals an 18-year-old girl staring back at me—a broken soul, stripped of innocence and battered by lies and manipulation. I inhale deeply once more before grabbing a handful of fresh paper towels.

Stepping out of the bathroom, I spot Tom and Carla engaging in conversation. Tom is leaning in closely, his charm in full effect, and she seems to fall for it. I bend down to clean up the remnants of the spill just as I feel him come beside me.

"Let me help you finish cleaning this," he says, his voice loud enough for Carla to hear, as he takes half of the towels from my hand. My body tenses at his touch, wishing he would simply leave, but he always needed to assert his dominance. As he swipes the remaining liquid from the floor, he leans in closer, whispering just loud enough for me to catch his words: "You're going to regret that."

He stands up, tossing the paper towels into the trash can behind Carla's desk, wishing her a good day before disappearing through the elevator doors. Finally, I stand up and return to my desk, only to notice a slip of paper resting under the keyboard. The message was clear: *You made the wrong choice.*

36.

Dean

Tom Hansen had once again called to request a meeting with me. I found myself tempted to explain that I had multiple teams to manage and clients to nurture after our initial meetings. However, Carla had mentioned that he seemed quite adamant about this meeting, and my curiosity ultimately overruled my usual approach to client interactions. Our meeting was imminent, yet I had no clue how to prepare, as Tom had given me no indication of what to expect.

Lately, whenever I felt overwhelmed, I would call Dani into my office. She had a knack for relieving my stress, whether it was by climbing into my lap, spreading her legs on top of my desk, or just getting down on her knees.

Unfortunately, today, she is out running errands, leaving me to find coping mechanisms that don't require a sexy brunette within reach. Unsure of what Tom would bring to the table, I decided to overprepare, ensuring I was ready for any scenario. A few minutes before his arrival, I make my way to the conference room and settle in, waiting for him to arrive.

The door swings open precisely at our scheduled time, and Tom walks in, his expression unreadable. He takes a moment to get comfortable before launching into his reason for being here without so much a greeting.

"Listen, Dean, I need to be honest with you. Danielle isn't who you think she is." Confusion flickers across my face as I glance up sharply.

"What the hell are you talking about?"

"I should have said something sooner, but I didn't want my past with Danielle to interfere with our business —and by extension, my grandfather's."

"Your past with Danielle?"

"Yes. Danielle and I used to date. I thought we were in love, but it turns out she's just an exceptional actress. We both attended a prestigious high school; my family was wealthy, while Dani was a scholarship student. Even though she came from a humble background, her beauty and intelligence captivated me. Her lack of wealth never deterred my interest. When she agreed to go out with me, I was excited. She seemed different from the other girls who were obsessed with status and money. But I was wrong. Her mother always used men as stepping stones for social advancement and financial security, and Dani apparently adopted the same approach. I was merely a bank account to her, not someone worthy of loyalty. I truly believe that the two of them may have been collaborating all along."

"You're mistaken," I reply, my voice steady. "She confided in me about her mother. She wouldn't betray my trust like that."

"But if that's the case," he presses, an eyebrow arched in disbelief, "then why was her mother in her apartment not too long ago? Did she mention that visit to you?"

A wave of anger washes over me, rigidifying my entire body as I realize I may have unwittingly given my heart to another gold-digging liar.

"Why are you telling me this?"

"We've done quite a bit of business together, Dean. I'd like to think of us as friends. I see how close you two have grown, and I don't want you to experience what I did. It took a toll on me. She consumed every corner of my mind, and it took years to move on. I would hate to see you in the same situation. When you hold a high status like we do, it's crucial to have people in our corner looking out for each other."

"You should go, Tom." He nods, pushing himself up from his chair. Just before he heads for the door, he slides an envelope across the table toward me.

"What's this?" I ask, curiosity piqued.

"Something you need to see. We'll talk soon, Dean." With that, he exits the room, leaving me alone with the proof and chilling realization that I've made yet another heart-wrenching mistake.

****

With a reluctant sigh, I reach for the envelope and tear it open. Inside, I find photographs of a woman entering and exiting Dani's building. A sinking feeling settles in my stomach—this must be her mother, confirming that Tom hadn't lied after all. My breath quickens, and a tightness grips my chest as the bitter truth dawns on me: I've been fucked over once again.

I pace anxiously in my office, contemplating my next move. Should I wait to speak with Dani, delve deeper into this, and uncover the truth? Yet, I've never been one to shy away from difficult conversations. Just weeks ago, Dani confided in me about the torment she endured at the hands of her mother, revealing the fractured relationship between them. Yet, here I was, staring at photographs of her mother entering Dani's apartment building. Tom had warned me, recounting similar manipulations from her. Given how Dani portrayed her mother, it wouldn't be far-fetched to believe that this woman could twist her daughter's loyalty to further her own schemes, using Dani as a pawn in her twisted game.

Despite her being forced into her mother's schemes at a young age, now an adult, she faced a choice: to continue living under her mother's shadow or to forge her own path. She was acutely aware of the pain Gabriela had caused me; the deep scars that made trust a fragile thing. Yet, even with this understanding, Dani had the audacity to attempt to strip me of my hard-earned money. It had always been about the money for her. A tumult of emotions surged within me—hurt giving way to anger, directed at Dani for her lies and deceit, and at myself for being ensnared by them. I summoned her in, knowing that she was back from this morning's errands.

I hear the soft click of the door as it swings open, and she greets me with a small smile as she steps inside.

"Hey. What's up?"

Her casual demeanor, both in appearance and tone, contrasts sharply with the chaos swirling in my mind.

She has no idea that my world has just flipped upside down, nor is she prepared for the interrogation that is about to unfold.

"Was your mother at your apartment?" I ask, watching her eyebrows knit together in confusion.

"How do you know that?"

"Why?"

"Why?" she echoes, caught off guard.

"Why was she there?" I press, my tone firm.

"She wanted money, but I told her no." My eyebrows shoot up in surprise. It seems she isn't going to outright lie, but she's definitely omitting key details.

"Why did you tell her no? Was it because, at that moment, you hadn't gotten me where you wanted me yet?" The look on her face is as if I've just slapped her. Even now, despite her betrayal, I ache to reach out and comfort her, but I know I can't.

"What are you talking about?" she replies, frustration creeping into her voice.

"I know you're a smart girl, Dani, so please don't play dumb right now."

"Dean, what is this about?" She stands with her hip cocked; arms folded defensively across her chest.

"This is about you using me for my money, continuing the same bullshit you pulled in high school with Tom."

"Tom?" she gasps, stepping back. Her eyes widen, and I can see the moment she realizes that I know everything. She's caught.

"There's no point in lying to me, Dani. Tom told me what happened back then—how you tried to manipulate him, too."

"But—" she begins, shaking her head, but I won't let her interrupt. I need to speak my truth, and I can't give her the chance to manipulate me again.

"I honestly don't want to hear anything you have to say. You're no different than Gabriela."

"Dean," she argues, desperation creeping into her voice.

"And to think I started to—"

"Started to what?"

"Nothing. Get out. You're fired."

"Dean," her voice trembles, and I see her eyes glisten with unshed tears. I remind myself those tears are not for me, but for her own failures.

"Get out!" I shout. She stands there, mouth opening as if to argue, but something in my expression must convey that it's futile. Her lips close, and she turns away, leaving the room with a heavy slam of the door behind her.

Perhaps I had overreacted, my emotions surging high. Some might call me irrational, but I refuse to let anyone trample over me or treat me like a fool. I am a God damn billionaire, the CEO of the largest marketing firm in New York City. I will not be outsmarted by a pretty brunette who thinks she can con me with a flutter of her beautiful eyes and sweet whispers in my ear.

I realize, with a sinking feeling, that I almost made a confession I would have regretted. Before I can process this revelation, the door swings open, and my brother steps inside.

"Lover's quarrel?" he teases, but his playful smirk disappears when he sees my face. A long sigh escapes him. "What happened, Dean?"

I hand him the photographs.

"What is this?" he asks, confusion etched on his features.

"That's Dani's mom," I reply.

"You'll need to give me more than that. I'm not sure how Dani's mom relates to your girlfriend storming out of here in tears."

"Tom came by this morning. He gave me these photos and told me he dated Dani in high school. Said her mom used her to get Tom's family money. They were scheming against me, apparently."

"Wait. Tom? That Hansen guy?"

"Yeah."

"He dated Dani? In high school?"

"Yep."

"And he's only telling you this now?" His tone is incredulous, and I can only shrug.

"Dani told me she hated her mother and her upbringing, but now her mom is visiting her in her apartment?"

"You can hate your parents, Dean. That doesn't mean they just disappear from your life."

"Why does it sound like you're defending her?"

"Dean," he begins, settling into a chair in front of my desk, "you know I'm always on your side. I just can't see Dani being anything like Gabriela. I actually like Dani. Gabby was always a bitch; you were just too pussy whipped to see it."

"And I refuse to make that mistake again," I snap, frustrated that he's trying to reason with me.

"Not to mention, I've always gotten weird vibes from this Tom guy. Why wait until now to bring this up? Doesn't that seem strange?"

"I don't know, Jay, but what I do know is that she never told me she knew him, let alone dated him. Why keep that hidden? What could he possibly gain by telling me any of this? I've been trying to piece it all together for the last two hours, and it just doesn't make sense."

"Why does he even have pictures of her mom entering her apartment building? Don't you find any of this suspicious?"

"He clearly knew what she was up to and was just trying to gather proof because he knew I would need it," I counter, halting in front of him.

"Really, Dean? You know what I think? I think you're so blinded by Gabby's betrayal that you can't think straight right now," Jay retorts, jabbing a finger into my chest. He must have a fucking death wish, but before I can react, he presses on. "So, you have no fucking clue what's going on, and you called her in here to what? Break up with her?"

"Technically, I fired her."

"Oh. So you have no idea what the actual truth is,

and you just called her in here to fire her?" He shakes his head in disbelief. "Please tell me you at least heard her out first."

My silence answers him.

"Oh for fuck's sake, Dean. You didn't even let her explain?"

"I thought you were on my side."

"I am, but as your brother, it's my job to let you know when you're being a complete idiot. This is me telling you that you're being a complete idiot."

I lean forward, resting my elbows on the desk as I drag my hands over my face, tugging at my hair in frustration. Perhaps he has a point. I hadn't given her the opportunity to explain herself at all.

"Listen, man, I'm here for you. If she did what you think she did, then I fully support whatever choices you make moving forward. But you should find out the actual truth. If she's innocent in this, then you just fucked up a really good thing you had."

He stands, giving my shoulder a reassuring clap before walking out and leaving me to stew in my own misery.

However, as the adrenaline fades and I take a moment to breathe, the pain intensifies. I can pretend to be glad that I uncovered the truth, that I should be relieved she's gone, yet reality sinks in as I gaze out at the city skyline, recalling Dani's awe at the breathtaking view from my penthouse. I am falling for her. What if Jay is right? What if my anger has blinded me, the echoes of my past failures reverberating within me, leading me to jeopardize my relationship? I understand that there's no turning back from the events that have transpired. Even if I came to discover that my accusations were unfounded, there would be no return to the way things were. The damage is done, and the weight of my actions looms heavy over me. Love is a peculiar force; it has the power to unveil our greatest strengths, yet it can also expose our deepest flaws. And in this intricate game of love, I find I have now lost twice.

37.

Dani

I burst through the doors of Stonebrook, my heart racing as I sprint into the shadowy alley, desperate for solitude before the dam breaks. In a city that never sleeps, I find solace in the anonymity it offers—a place where no one will notice the girl crumpled against the cold brick, tears streaming down her face. I sink to the ground, burying my hands in my hair as I struggle to process the whirlwind of emotions that has left me reeling. Just this morning, we shared laughter and made plans for dinner, our future bright and full of promise. But now, the reality hits hard: it's over. We are over.

I should have taken Tom more seriously. He has always been indifferent to anyone's feelings, driven solely by his own desires and whims. I often wonder why I didn't confide in Dean weeks ago or why I hesitated to reveal my relationship with Tom when his family name appeared in my email that fateful day. I had countless chances to be honest, and while I never outright lied about my past, I concealed a significant part of myself from him. How did I expect our relationship to flourish when he remained oblivious to the shadows that lurked within me?

He doesn't know that he's the first person I've ever

allowed to take control during sex—how vulnerable that makes me feel. I still wake up from nightmares, but somehow, I've never experienced one while nestled in his arms. Every single day since prom night, I've battled with the reflection in the mirror, grappling with self-acceptance. Yet, with him, I find a new version of myself emerging, one that feels more authentic and alive.

He bared his soul to me, revealing a vulnerability I knew was rare for him. Trust did not come easily, especially after the betrayal by Gabriela. Yet, I found myself holding back, unable to fully embrace the depths of his being. I may have made mistakes, but Dean never granted me the chance to defend myself against the venomous lies that Tommy must have unleashed. In his eyes, betrayal painted me guilty without a second thought. Our relationship resembled a delicate snow globe—idyllic yet precarious. When left undisturbed, it radiated beauty and tranquility, but with just a single shake, it spiraled into chaos and confusion.

I'm unsure how long I linger in this frigid air, but a chill seeps into my bones. Despite the numbness gnawing at my insides, I know I can't remain outside much longer. Thankfully, I remembered to grab my purse before rushing out, and now I pull out my phone to call an Uber. Luck is on my side as one is nearby, and within minutes it arrives.

As I slide into the backseat, I provide my address, feeling the weight of my phone in my hand. I stare at the screen, half-expecting him to call or text, to tell me that this is all a mistake. My fingers itch to reach out, to explain everything, but he's made it abundantly clear that he has no interest in what I have to say.

I refuse to be that pathetic, heartbroken woman, begging for scraps of affection. No, I'll save that version of myself for the solitude of closed doors, where the echoes of my heartache can rest unseen.

****

As I unlock my apartment door, I'm surprised to find Izzy already home. She's lounging on the couch, legs crossed, a bag of chips resting in her lap, engrossed in some reality television. Her gaze flicks up, surprise etched on her features as well.

"What are you doing home so early?" she asks, a hint of curiosity in her voice. "Unless you've come to join me for lunch today. Though, I would have made something a bit more substantial than chips."

"Chips sound perfect," I reply, the corners of my mouth lifting slightly. "Ice cream, chocolate, and maybe a bit of alcohol would also hit the spot right now." I notice her expression soften.

"Oh, sweetheart. What happened?" she says, her voice warm as she pats the space beside her. I shuffle over to the couch, curling my legs up and wrapping my arms around my knees. I took a moment to steady myself, fighting back tears before I could find the words.

"I messed up, Iz. You were right. I should have just told him everything when Tommy showed up."

"Do you want to talk about it?"

"I can't explain how, but somehow, Tommy managed to get to Dean. He must have spun some tale about me trying to swindle him for his money."

"And Dean believed him?" Izzy exclaims; her outrage palpable at the very thought that anyone could think so poorly of me. I nod, pressing on with the story.

"He called me into his office, asking about my mother's visit. It took me a moment to grasp what he was on about, and when I finally tried to explain, he just kept cutting me off. He was furious, completely unwilling to listen. And then... he fired me."

"What a fucking prick," Izzy responds, shaking her head in disbelief. "To think I actually liked the guy. So that lowlife reached out to Dean and fabricated lies about you? What the hell is his problem? Why would he do this?"

I avert my gaze, staring at the floor.

"Dani?" she asks softly.

"Last week," I begin to explain, "Tommy came into the office when I was alone and without warning, he kissed me. Obviously, on instinct, I pushed him off. I'm not sure what would have happened if Carla hadn't walked in a minute later. Tommy continued to rant about how I belonged to him and how I had made the wrong choice. I honestly had no idea what he was talking about."

"Why on earth didn't you tell anyone about that, Dani?"

"Because I was protecting Dean!" I shout, my emotions spilling over. I squeeze my eyes shut and inhale deeply. "I couldn't let him ruin Dean's career, which is what he threatened if I told anyone."

"And who's protecting you?" The question seems straightforward, yet it digs deep. I had always faced life alone. Growing up, I was left to navigate everything by myself. My father was absent, leaving repairs and problems to me, and my mother was not the kind of person I could turn to for guidance. I learned early on to rely solely on myself, tackling every challenge, big or small. The shame of my home life kept me from making friends, and it wasn't until I started dating Tommy that I finally began to break free from my shell. Izzy became my first true best friend, but even with her support, I struggled to voice my internal battles. Despite allowing Izzy into my life more than anyone else, asking for help remained a daunting task, even when I knew I couldn't bear the weight alone.

Despite my silence, I sense that Izzy understands me clearly. "What do you need from me?" she asks, taking my hand. "I have no problem going down to that office and kicking his little bitch ass. I'll make it my mission to ruin Tom's life if that's what you want. Whatever you need, I'm here for you." Her unwavering support brings a smile to my face, even amidst my despair.

"Can you just sit here with me for a little while?" I request softly.

"Absolutely, hun," she replies, wrapping her arm around me. I rest my head on her shoulder, focusing on the television's current drama, finding it easier to immerse myself in someone else's heartache than to confront my own.

****

The early Saturday morning light filters through

the curtains, casting shadows on the wall as I sit there, nursing a cup of coffee. Sleep had eluded me for the past few nights, more than usual, and now I find myself staring into space, lost in thought. I know I have to gather the rest of my belongings and return my keys, but the thought of facing Dean makes me hesitate.

With a sigh, I resolve to email Jay about when I could come in, but just as I'm about to draft my message, an email from Carla catches my eye.

Subject: *Personal Items Collection*

Dear Miss Cliff,

I hope this message finds you well. I wanted to inform you that you are welcome to collect any personal items this Saturday morning before 10 a.m. Please note that no one will be in the office during that time. Kindly return your keys or any other items belonging to Stonebrook to Steven, who will be there to let you into the building.

Best regards,

Carla Albright
Executive Secretary
Stonebrook Marketing

I read the email twice, processing the details. Today would be the day, I think, as I prepare to face whatever awaits me at Stonebrook.

I suppose that settles any lingering questions I have about going there. Glancing at the clock, I see it's nearly 8 a.m. Izzy is still lost in sleep, likely not to stir for a while since she worked late last night. With a sense of resolve,

I decide it's time to get dressed and head out. There's no more procrastinating, especially since I know I won't be running into him while I'm there. I gather a few tote bags to carry my belongings. Even though I'll probably be back before she wakes, I jot down a quick note for Izzy, letting her know where I'm headed and that I'll return in an hour, just in case she does wake up.

Once I'm ready, I order an Uber. By the time I step outside, the driver is already pulling up. I slide into the backseat, placing my totes and purse beside me. As I stare out the window, familiar sights pass by, reminding me of the last couple of months. A wave of reality washes over me: this journey will soon come to an end. Setting aside my complicated feelings about our relationship, I realize I genuinely enjoyed my job. Once I got the hang of things, I found joy in leaving the office to run errands, the satisfying feeling of checking tasks off my list, and engaging with new, interesting people who were passionate about building and expanding their businesses.

When I arrive, I step out of the Uber and stand frozen, staring at the doors ahead. A wave of fear washes over me as I contemplate what comes next. I gather my belongings, but then what? Once again, I'll be alone and without a job. I know Izzy will inevitably offer to cover the rent until I find something new or suggest a position at the hotel, which I'll likely accept. After all, as someone who refuses to see others as mere ATMs, I can't allow her to shoulder my financial burdens completely.

Surrounded by a bustling crowd that brushes past me, oblivious to my inner turmoil, I feel myself slipping back into the dark thoughts I thought I'd left behind. I'm insignificant. I'm pathetic. I'm worthless. The weight of despair settles heavily on my chest, and I wonder if I have anything left to give. Traffic flies by behind me. The temptation to take a step back, to end it all, flickers in my mind—a longing for an escape from shame, heartbreak, and sadness, replaced only by the promise of peace.

Suddenly, a teenager jostles me as they push through the crowd, snapping me out of my reverie. I shake my head, forcing myself to clear those haunting thoughts, and force my feet to move toward the doors. When I finally reach them, I lift my hand and knock, the sound echoing my uncertain resolve.

Steven, one of the security guards I've grown familiar with, approaches the door and unlocks it for me. He gives a nod, his expression tinged with pity, yet he remains silent, loyal to his boss. A few minutes later, I found myself at my desk, packing my totes with an assortment of pens, highlighters, notepads, and other office supplies I'd purchased for myself. As I sort through my belongings, my gaze lands on a slip of paper protruding from one of my notebooks. Curiosity piqued, I pull it out and recognize Carla's handwriting.

Dani,

I'm so sorry about everything. I overheard what happened, and I know you would never do anything you were accused of. I truly hope everything works out for you, whatever that may be. Please don't hesitate to reach out. You're family.

With love,

Carla

I tuck the note into my tote, fighting back tears.

Uncertainty gnawed at me regarding how I was perceived after our fight; her previous email felt so distant and impersonal, leading me to believe she had sided with Dean. Yet, here was proof that she was just remaining professional and, more importantly, she was supportive. It felt good to know that someone besides my best friend believed in my innocence. Despite the weight of the totes filled with supplies, I leave feeling inexplicably lighter.

I step out of the elevator, keys clutched tightly in my hand, ready to pass them to Steven. My eyes scan the lobby, but he is nowhere in sight. As I walk past the front desk, something catches my attention—a pair of feet, toes pointed upward. My heart races, and I gasp, dropping my totes to the ground with a thud.

"Steven!" I call, rushing toward him. I shake him gently. "Wake up!" Relief washes over me as I check for a pulse and see the faint rise and fall of his chest. But that relief quickly turns to horror as I notice the blood trickling from his head. He must have struck it against something, but looking around, I can't find the cause.

I fish my phone from my pocket, ready to call 911. But just as I am about to dial, a strong arm wraps around my chest, and a cloth presses over my mouth. I kick and struggle, but my limbs grow heavy, and darkness begins to close in around me.

****

As my eyes flutter open, a heavy veil of fatigue clings to them, making an effort to see feel monumental. Confusion envelops me like a thick fog as I attempt to orient myself in this unfamiliar space. It takes precious moments before coherent thoughts begin to crystallize, and I regain a measure of control over my body.

My gaze sweeps across the room, shrouded in darkness, devoid of windows. Time is an enigma here; I have no way of knowing how long I've been trapped in this place. I instinctively attempt to move my arms, but they feel uncomfortably numb. Panic surges within me as I discover they are bound tightly behind my back. My legs are similarly restrained to the chair, adding to my growing sense of dread.

With my heart pounding in my chest, I struggle against my bonds, but the ropes remain unyielding. The last memory that flickers in my mind is of Steven sprawled on the ground. At the time, I thought he had merely hit his head, but now, I fear that he was rendered unconscious by whoever has taken me. The urgency of the moment washes over me; I never had the chance to call 911, and all I can think about is the hope that he is okay.

I strain to catch any sounds that might reveal my location, but the silence envelopes me, unnerving in its intensity. After what feels like an eternity, the faint echo of footsteps breaks through the stillness. Just as my eyes begin to acclimate to the darkness, the door swings open, flooding the room with blinding light.

"Oh good. You're awake."

Though I can't see him immediately, that voice is unmistakable. As my vision slowly adjusts to the harsh brightness, clarity comes; it's Tommy. My mind races with a torrent of questions, yet one looms above the rest, demanding an answer.

"Why, Tommy?"

He chuckles, a sound dripping with arrogance. "Because you're fucking mine, and I'm tired of waiting for you to figure it out."

"I don't understand," I reply, confusion washing over me.

He snickers, as if my words are absurd. "You don't understand," he echoes, his tone dripping with condescension. "Let me clarify: I chose you. You walked into my school, and I chose you." His voice drops to a whisper. "But then you left."

"You left!" he suddenly yells, slamming his hand against the wall, causing me to flinch. "You weren't meant to leave."

"Tommy. You. Raped. Me." I can't contain the outrage that surges within me at his audacity to think I would stay near him after everything he did. "You took something that wasn't yours to take."

"Not mine to take? You were mine!" He leans closer, his voice a venomous whisper. "This is mine!" His hand cups between my legs, and I try to squeeze them shut, but the ropes binding me render it impossible.

"You left me alone in that hotel room. You went out of your way to dismantle every friendship I had managed to build and bullying me until death felt like a preferable option to enduring another day with you. You treated me like shit on the bottom of your fucking shoe, and you dare to say you wanted me to be yours?"

"You are mine. I had to break you. I needed you to

depend on me, to understand that you had no one else but me."

"But that didn't happen, did it? You may have shattered a part of me, but not all of me. I had Izzy. I didn't need you." I exclaim, my eyes fixed on his clenched jaw and narrowed gaze.

"Shut the hell up!" he shouted, causing me to startle.

"Please, Tommy. Just let me go," I plead, desperation lacing my words.

"I'll never let you go," he replies, his fingers trailing up my arm before seizing my jaw. "If I can't have you, no one will."

I spit in his face. He recoils just enough to gather the force to strike me. The impact is so fierce that my entire head snaps to the side. "Bitch," he mutters, lifting the hem of his shirt to wipe his face clean.

"Tommy, just let me go. I swear I won't tell a soul. No one needs to know this ever happened. Please, Tommy." My pleas are abruptly silenced as his hand closes tightly around my throat, cutting off my air.

"Shut the fuck up," he demands, his grip tightening. Memories flood my mind like scenes from an old film reel: Izzy and I, laughing uncontrollably on the couch, tears streaming down our faces as we improvised dialogue to a black-and-white movie playing on mute. Chad and I, pretending to be marathon runners in Central Park, and chasing after a group of cute guys only to end up vomiting and nearly passing out from exhaustion. Dean and I cooking breakfast together, our nearly naked bodies distracting us until the smoke alarms blared, and the bacon burnt to a crisp. Earlier today, I had contemplated death, but now, facing it, all I want is to live. Just as my vision begins to blur, he releases his grip, and I gasp for air. I want to survive, and that means doing whatever it takes.

"I'm going to kill you. But not yet. I'm not finished playing with you," he says, completely unfazed, as if he were merely postponing a mundane chore rather than deciding the fate of someone's life.

"Tommy, you don't have to do this. If you want me to be yours, fine. I'll be yours. I'm yours."

"Are you really mine?" he asks, challenging me. "Prove it." I open my mouth to question what that means when, with a swift motion, he draws a knife and slices through the rope binding my legs. He then moves behind me, cutting the restraints from my wrists. My shoulders scream in protest as they are freed, but with him looming behind me, I attempt to rise quickly, eyes darting toward the exit. A sharp tug on my hair halts my movement, pulling me back.

"Don't even think about it. You claim to be mine? You can't be truly mine if you haven't surrendered all of yourself to me."

He drags me through the door into a dimly lit hallway. We traverse the corridor and enter a room that appears to have been hastily converted into a makeshift bedroom.

"Why have we come here?" I ask, my voice trembling with uncertainty.

"I told you before," he begins, the intensity in his gaze unwavering. "I was your first, and I damn well intend to be your last."

As I enter the room, memories of my teenage-self flood back—a time when I sobbed in the bathroom after my assault, feeling utterly trapped. The walls seem to close in around me, suffocating in their proximity. I struggle to recall the self-defense moves I had learned years ago, but all I can focus on is the desperate need to escape.

With determination, I lift my foot and bring it down hard onto his. The impact causes him to release his grip, and in that fleeting moment of distraction, I bend forward, driving my shoulder into his gut. We both tumble to the ground, and I scramble to get away quickly, racing toward the door.

Just as I reach the threshold, I feel his hands shove me from behind, propelling me into the opposite wall. He seizes my upper arms, forcing me down onto the floor, his weight pressing heavily on top of me. I fight against him, but he lands a punch to the left side of my face, followed by another blow to my jaw. The pain is unbearable, and I instinctively cross my arms over my face, trying to shield myself from further strikes.

He grips my shoulders, hoisting me up before slamming me back down onto the ground. My head bounces off the hard floor, and my vision blurs. I open my mouth to plead for mercy, but he silences me with yet another brutal slam. As my head strikes the ground once more, a familiar darkness envelops me, pulling me under.

38.

Dean

In the solitude of my home office, I immerse myself in work, desperately trying to distract my mind from the lingering ache of missing her. Despite everything Dani has done, a part of me still longs for her presence. I understand that Jay remains skeptical, unable to fathom that she could be capable of such betrayal, but I was also blind to Gabriela's true nature. Deceit has many faces, and it often lurks in the shadows, waiting to ensnare the unsuspecting.

Carla, ever the silent observer, does not share her thoughts on the matter, though I can sense her disapproval simmering beneath the surface. Perhaps I am hastily drawing conclusions, rushing to judgments without gathering all the necessary pieces to see the full picture. Yet, how do I reconcile my actions? If Dani is truly innocent, I have not only wrongfully accused her of being a gold digger but, in a fit of selfish anger, I severed our ties and dismissed her from her position. The weight of my decisions bear down on me, leaving me to wonder if redemption is even possible.

I'm considering calling Jay to see if he's free for lunch when my phone suddenly rings. An unknown number flashes on the screen, but I decide to answer anyway.

"Hello?" I answer.

"Where is she?" a demanding female voice pierces through the line.

"Who are you asking about? And who is this?"

A frustrated sigh responds, revealing the speaker. "It's Izzy. I need to know where Dani is."

"Why would I know where Dani is?" I reply, confusion creeping into my voice.

"She went to your office to pick up her things since some asshole fired her. She said she'd be back around nine. It's after ten and she's not back. She isn't answering her phone either."

"I'm not at the office. My security guard is there, and I'm sure he would have told me if something was wrong. Maybe she just took a walk."

"No. She wouldn't leave without telling me. She wrote that she would be back, and I haven't heard anything since. I wouldn't have called you unless it was important. This is serious. Something's not right. I suggest you meet me at Stonebrook because I'm getting into that building, and if you're not there with the key, I'm breaking the damn door down. I'm leaving now."

I open my mouth to reply, but the line goes dead. Great, just what I need—a headache. Even though Izzy can be a handful, I know she wouldn't reach out unless she was truly concerned. I grab my coat and dial Jay.

"Hey man. What's up?" he answers.

"Glad you picked up. I need you to meet me at the

office."

"Damn it, Dean. Why? You know I hate working on weekends."

"I know, but this isn't about work," I explain. "Izzy called. Dani went to the office to grab her things and she's been gone longer than expected. She's not answering her phone. I'm going to meet her there, but I'd rather not go alone."

He bursts out laughing. "You scared of this girl or something?"

"No, it's not that. I just don't want her making up some crazy story to get back at me for—"

"Breaking up with and firing her best friend?" he finishes for me.

"Yeah," I admit. "Will you meet me there? I'm heading out now." I step into the elevator, the doors sliding shut behind me.

"Sure, I'll be there," he replies before I hang up. I text my driver, who quickly responds that he's already parked outside.

****

I arrive at the office swiftly, scanning the area for Isabella and Jay. Neither in sight, but that's understandable; they both live a bit farther away. As I retrieve my key and unlock the door, my heart sinks at the sight of Steven sprawled on the floor. I rush to his side and notice a gash on his head. Panic surges through me as I pull out my phone, dialing 911 and relaying every detail I can muster. Just as I hang up, I feel a presence behind me.

"What the hell?" Izzy calls out, her voice laced with shock. I gently tap and shake Steven, urging him to wake, but he only stirs, still lost in unconsciousness.

Glancing at Izzy, I see her bent down, picking something up before she approaches the bags abandoned on the ground.

"What are those?" I ask, my voice trembling. She meets my gaze, fear flickering in her eyes.

"They're Dani's. And her phone was on the floor."

My heart races. "So where the hell did she go?"

"I told you I had a bad feeling," Isabella murmurs, her voice barely above a whisper. Just then, a groan pulls my attention back to Steven, who is beginning to regain consciousness.

"Steven," I say, sliding closer to him.

"Damn," he groans, pressing his hand to his head, the weight of the situation settling heavily around us.

"I've already called for an ambulance. They should arrive any moment now. Do you remember what happened?" I press gently.

"All I recall is letting Miss Cliff into the building," Steven responds, his voice shaky. "I was waiting for her to come back down, but I can't remember seeing her. Then I heard footsteps behind me, and before I could turn around, I was hit. After that, everything just went black."

The doors swing open, and the paramedics rush in with a stretcher, followed closely by two officers and Jay. I turn back to Steven, my heart racing, desperate for answers.

"Do you know who hit you? You don't think it was Dani...?" I ask, trailing off, the weight of my own suggestion hanging heavily in the air.

"No," Steven insists, shaking his head. "Dani would never do something like this. Whoever attacked me was taller and stronger—it was definitely a man." I step aside to allow the paramedics to assist Steven and lift him onto the stretcher. Just then, Jay approaches and places a reassuring hand on my shoulder.

"What happened?" he asks, concern etched across his face.

"That's what we'd like to know," interjects one of the officers. I turn to face him; he was an older man in his fifties, tall and broad-shouldered, with dark skin and short-cropped black hair. Some might find him intimidating, but I just see a man who can help us find Dani.

"I am Officer Dixon," he states, his voice steady and authoritative. "This is my partner, Officer Grant," he adds, gesturing towards his companion. "Could you share with us what transpired here?"

"Steven, my security guard, was attacked. He came here to let a former employee in to collect her belongings." I sense a sarcastic chuckle from behind me, likely Izzy disapproving of how I described Dani.

"And where is this former employee?" asks the second officer, a younger woman probably in her mid-twenties. She is tall and slim, with strawberry-blonde hair pulled into a tight bun, her blue eyes fix on me, awaiting my response.

"We don't know. When we arrived, her belongings were scattered on the floor, including her phone."

"But you believe a man is responsible for this?" she presses, clearly having overheard my conversation with Steven.

"Dani would never do this," Isabella interjects, her frustration boiling over. "Something must have happened to her. She wouldn't just leave her things behind, especially not her phone."

"We're going to need a description of this employee, We will also need to take a look around the building. Do you have security cameras?" the older officer asks, his tone businesslike, as the gravity of the situation settles in.

Jay steps in, a determined look on his face. "I can give you everything you need." He leans closer, whispering for me to check the office to see if Dani is still in the building. Grateful for his support, I pivot towards the elevator that leads to my office. Just as I step inside the open doors, I hear footsteps trailing behind me.

"What are you doing?" I ask, glancing back.

"Following you," Isabella replies with a casual shrug. "What about you? We should be out looking for her right now." The doors close, enveloping us in a thick tension.

"We can't search all over New York City without any clues about where she might be," I respond, determination in my voice. "I'm going to the office to see if I can find anything that might lead us to her."

"I can't say for sure," she continues, her tone

shifting, "but I think Tom has something to do with this."

"Tom?" I raise an eyebrow, confusion knitting my brow.

"Yes. Tom Hansen."

"Why would you say that?"

She rolls her eyes in annoyance, and the elevator doors slide open. I step out, her footsteps echoing behind me. Everything seems oddly normal, but as I glance toward Dani's desk, a wave of sadness washes over me at how empty it looks. Reality is settling in: Steven is hurt, Dani is missing, and all I can think about is our last conversation. I'm going to find her. I have to find her.

"Tom is a psychotic piece of shit," Isabella says, her voice rising with urgency. "You have no idea who he really is; he knows how to put on a charming façade. I kept pushing Dani to tell you, but she wouldn't. She was too damn worried about what that baggage would do to you and your relationship."

I try to keep up as she rambles, pacing back and forth on the floor. Her hands mirror her frantic words, and I finally reach out, touching her shoulder to bring her to a halt.

"What are you talking about, Izzy? What didn't Dani tell me?" I ask, desperation creeping into my voice, urging her to continue.

She turns to face me, and I catch a glimpse of moisture shimmering in her eyes. "Tom and Dani dated in high school."

"I know. Tom mentioned that."

"Well, did Tom tell you that on prom night, he

drugged her, took her to a hotel room, and raped her?" A wave of nausea rolls over me as I process her words.

"What?!" I exclaim, anger bubbling up within me as my fists clench at my sides.

"He raped her, Dean. Then he broke up with her and spread rumors around school, making her life a living hell. She never told anyone because she feared no one would believe her over him. And now he's been following her around here for months. Last week, he even came here when she was alone and kissed her. She told me he was upset when she pushed him away."

"You're saying that Tom Hansen raped Dani seven years ago and has come back to stalk her?"

"Yes," she replies firmly. "That's exactly what I'm saying. He's not looking out for you, Dean. He was trying to break you two apart out of jealousy, and you fell for it."

"But her mother... I saw the photographs," I retort, an edge of defensiveness creeping into my voice as I struggle to rationalize my choices.

"Exactly. You saw pictures that don't tell the whole story. Yes, her mother visited, and yes, she asked for money. But Dani refused and kicked her out. And here's the kicker: Tom was the one who convinced her mother to come and speak with her."

My mind races with this overwhelming new information. As I reflect on the night when Dani and I wandered through the art museum, vivid memories unfurl before me. I can still hear her voice as she recounted the story of the man who shattered her heart, the anguish that spiraled into a desperate attempt on her own life. My mind is finally beginning to connect the dots of this intricate puzzle. I realize now that I was merely a pawn in Tom's game, easily manipulated and used. I had unwittingly played into his hands, becoming no better than the man who had once broken her heart so many years ago.

Tom never seemed interested in being a client; he merely wanted a way to get close to Dani. Maybe he thought he could hit two birds with one stone. But the most painful realization is that I feel utterly foolish. The thought that Dani had to confront her rapist ignites a furious anger within me. I wish she had trusted me enough to share that burden. I could have helped her. I could have protected her. As much as I need time to process this deluge of information, I know I have to find her now.

"If you're right, and Tom did this... if he took her," I say, determination rising within me, "I think I may know where he went. Let's go."

We rush down the stairs, and the officers survey the scene—their backs turned to us. Seizing the opportunity, I slip outside without raising any questions. I quickly text Jay to inform him of my plan.

Isabella and I stand outside the shadowy shell of Tom's building, which looms ominously in front of us, still shrouded in the chaos of construction. To an unknowing passerby, it appears abandoned and foreboding, yet it serves as the perfect refuge for someone seeking to avoid interruption. My instincts scream for action; I want to charge in, guns blazing. But caution holds me back. We have no idea what Tom's intentions might be, whether he is armed, or what state of mind he occupies—and that uncertainty is chilling. Yet, the fire of my anger and the desperate need to reach her overshadow any fear I might have of the unknown.

"Do you think she's in there?" Izzy asks with concern, her voice breaking through my thoughts.

"There's only one way to find out," I reply, stepping closer to scrutinize the building's exterior.

"Should we call the police?" she asks, her anxiety evident as she glances back at me.

I turn to face her, the weight of the moment settling heavily between us. "She may not have that kind of time. You don't have to come in. You can stay right here."

Without hesitation, she shakes her head. "No. If my best friend is in there, then I'm going to help get her out."

I nod, meeting her determined gaze, realizing that her mind is set. There's no swaying her now.

I squint through the tinted glass of the large front windows, straining to catch a glimpse of what lies inside. The door, as expected, resists my efforts to open it, so I turn toward the alley beside the building, searching for an alternate entry. Frustration mounts as I find nothing but shadows and silence. At the back, however, a wooden door catches my eye. I try the handle, but it remains stubbornly locked.

"Move over," Izzy says, nudging me aside. She pulls a few hairpins from her messy bun, letting strands tumble free, and kneels by the door, deftly inserting the pins into the keyhole. A satisfying click echoes in the stillness, and she pushes the door open with a triumphant grin.

"Should I ask how you know how to do that so well?" I inquire, stepping around her to take the lead. She offers a smirk, but our playful banter is cut short as we step into the unknown. A sense of responsibility weighs on me; I must keep Isabella safe while we search for Dani. If anything were to happen to her best friend, my chances of winning Dani back would be obliterated, if it wasn't already.

The hallway is cloaked in darkness, and I press myself against the wall, peering into small rooms with ajar doors. I see nothing and hear only silence, but as we venture deeper, a sudden thud followed by a gasp sends adrenaline coursing through my veins. My heart races at the thought of that gasp belonging to Dani. Without hesitation, I move toward the sound, with Izzy right on my heels.

We enter a corridor that opens up ahead, revealing a large room bathed in natural light spilling through the expansive front windows. Each step forward heightens my resolve; we are closer to finding Dani, and I won't let anything stand in our way.

A sudden noise ahead jolts me to a halt. To my right, a closed door stands silently. I strain to listen, catching the sound of a thump. I turn to Isabella.

"I'm going in. Stay here."

Her expression shifts to concern. "You think she's in there?" she asks, her voice trembling.

"We've searched the building. He wouldn't keep her where anyone could see. We don't know what's happening inside, so I need you to listen, Isabella. Please, stay here."

She crosses her arms, muttering something about "bossy" and "masculinity," but ultimately stays put. I turn back, stealthily approaching the door, pressing my ear against it, desperate for any indication that we didn't just fuck everything up by breaking and entering.

"Wake the fuck up, bitch," a familiar male voice sneers. "First time, you weren't coherent. This time, I'm going to make sure you fucking remember it."

That was all I needed to hear. I step back and kick the door open, the sound of Isabella's gasp echoing behind me. The thought of him thinking he had any right to touch her ignited a fury within me that felt primal. The door crashes open, revealing what appears to be an office repurposed as a bedroom, but my focus quickly shifts to Dani, sprawled on the bed. She looks peaceful, yet the dark red stain in her hair betrays the truth—she'd been struck and was unconscious.

Tom kneels over her, his pants unbuttoned, her shirt hiked up. It takes only a handful of strides for me to reach him, my hands wrapping around his neck as I hurl him off her and onto the floor.

"Dean?" he stammers, surprise etched on his face. "It's not what you—"

I don't allow him to finish. My fist collides with his face, his eyes widening in panic.

"You don't understand," he pleads.

Once again, my fist connects, blood gushing from his nose. "You think hurting women makes you a man?" I sneer. "Try going against a real man to see what a pathetic little bitch you really are." I finish with a solid punch to his gut. He rolls over on the floor, the air knocked out of him.

Isabella rushes in, her hand clamps over her mouth, her eyes wide in shock as she takes in the scene. Spotting Dani, she dashes over, calling her name, desperate to wake her. Tom sees my distraction and seizes the moment, landing a punch that connects squarely with my jaw. He pulls his knees to his chest and kicks out, hitting me in the gut, and forcing me back against the wall.

He scrambles to his feet, grabbing the front of my shirt and yanking me down to the ground. With Tom on top, I can see the echoes of my words replaying in his mind, his eyes darkening with hatred and rage. He unleashes a flurry of punches; some I deflect, while others connect, but I barely feel the blows, likely due to the adrenaline surging through my veins.

People may see me in my tailored suits and doubt my fighting skills, but I trained with professional MMA fighters back in college, even stepping into the ring myself when the stresses of school and work became overwhelming. I know how to fight, and I know how to endure pain. Though I may not fight anymore, those lessons are etched in my memory.

With grit, I grasp the collar of his shirt and his waist, even as he continues to rain down punches. I lift my hips, pulling his upper body toward me with a firm grip, starting to rotate our bodies. Leaning my weight against him, I manage to flip Tom onto his back, reclaiming the top position. I seize his hair with both hands and slam his head into the ground, a loud thud reverberating through the air, momentarily stunning him. I pull back my arm and let my fist connect with his jaw, then strike his cheekbone, splitting the skin. My knuckles begin to bleed, but the pain is a distant whisper in my mind. I lift my arm again, ready to strike, when suddenly, someone holds me back.

I glance over my shoulder and see it's the officer I spoke to earlier. I didn't even notice anyone else enter the room.

"That's enough, son." His voice is firm. I'm breathing hard, my gaze locked onto the face of the man who hurt my girl. A primal urge to kill him surges within me. I could break free from Dixon's grip and finish this, but as I look around, I see paramedics attending to Dani. I realize it's not about what I want; I need to be there for her, and I can't do that from a jail cell. I nod, and he helps me to my feet.

"It's over," Dixon reassures me, gesturing to an officer who strides into the room, pulling Tom to his feet and snapping handcuffs onto his wrists. The officer begins to read Tom his rights as they escort him out.

"How did you know we were here?" I ask, but before Dixon can reply, Jay enters the room.

"You texted me your location. Plus, I can track your phone, remember? We checked the cameras, and they were off. We would have been in deep trouble if it weren't for that old-school camera we have hidden behind the front desk. It captured most of what went down. I was about to call you when I saw your text. So here we are," Jay explains.

Despite my urgency to discuss the next steps with Dixon, my gaze drifts back to Dani, now on a stretcher, still unconscious. I rush over and grasp her hand.

"How is she?" I ask, my heart pounding with desperation for good news.

"Her vitals are stable, but we need to get her to the hospital to evaluate that head wound," the paramedic replies as they push the stretcher past me. Isabella glances at me, reaching out to place her hand on my arm.

"I'm going with her. Meet us there. You should get checked out, too," she insists.

"I'm fine. I just need to know that she will be," I respond. She nods and hurries to catch up with the paramedics. Dixen turns to Jay and me.

"I'll drive you both to the hospital. We can talk on the way, but I'll need a formal statement from you sooner rather than later," Dixon says.

I nod, trailing behind them. My mind is fixated on reaching the hospital. I need to know she will survive this. She deserves to hear how I've messed up and how fucking sorry I am for doubting her, even if she never forgives me. Dani used to tease me about how money could fix everything, but if I lost her, no amount of money would erase the guilt and regret I would carry for the rest of my life.

****

I sit in the waiting room with Jay and Isabella, our hearts heavy as we await news from the doctors. I've already arranged for Dani to have a private room when they're ready to transfer her; she deserves a peaceful space to heal, away from the disruptions of a roommate.

Suddenly, Izzy stands, her movement catching my attention.

"Chad!" she calls, arms outstretched, ready to embrace him in a hug.

"How is she?" he asks, worry etched across his face.

"We don't know yet. She's being checked out now," Isabella replies, trying to reassure him.

Chad runs his fingers through his hair and lets out a long sigh as he settles down next to Izzy, finally noticing me sitting across from him. His expression hardens, jaw clenching, eyes narrowing as he locks onto me.

"You have a lot of balls being here," he snaps.

"Easy," Isabella interjects, placing her hand atop his. "He saved her, Chad."

"Just because you played hero and took a few punches doesn't mean any of us forgives you for what you did to her," he retorts, crossing his arms in a clear display of intimidation.

"Understood," I reply, keeping my voice steady.

"Why the hell are you here anyway?" he presses, irritation lacing his tone. Izzy rolls her eyes at his persistence, and I sigh, not wanting to engage in this right now. I glance at Jay, who seems amused by the unfolding drama. I turn back to Chad and decide to be straightforward.

"I fucked up. I know that. And I can list all the reasons why I'm here, but I'd like Dani to hear those reasons first."

Izzy's expression softens, understanding breaking

through her tough exterior. Beneath her fierce loyalty lies a sweetness that explains why she is Dani's best friend. Despite Chad's hostility, I can appreciate the fierce love her friends have for her.

"You look like shit," Chad adds bluntly. Jay bursts into laughter, causing the corners of Chad's mouth to twitch upwards ever so slightly. Izzy shakes her head but can't suppress a smile. I should be offended, but honestly, I probably do look like shit.

The doors swing open, and a doctor emerges, exchanging words with a nurse who gestures in our direction. He begins to approach, and we all stand, our hearts racing with anxiety to learn about her condition and an even greater urgency to see her.

"How is she?" Isabella asks, her voice trembling slightly.

The doctor takes a breath before responding. "She had a large laceration on the back of her head that we stitched up, along with several minor lacerations and contusions across her body. She did wake up, but she has a significant concussion, which accounts for her prolonged unconsciousness. We asked her a few questions; she recognized her identity, but the details of the attack were hazy, which is typical in such cases. We conducted imaging tests, and thankfully, everything came back to normal. We've given her a sedative to help her rest, and she's already settled in her room."

"When can we see her?" I ask, the desperation evident in my voice.

"Are you immediate family?" he inquires, scrutinizing each of us. My heart sinks at the thought that

I might not be allowed in.

"Yes, we are," Isabella asserts confidently, clasping both Chad's and my hands. Our eyes lock for a moment; I nod in silent gratitude, and she squeezes my hand in reassurance.

The doctor studies us, his skepticism lingering, but I can sense that he has more pressing matters to attend to. He explains where we can find her, cautioning us to refrain from disturbing her while she sleeps. Jay pats my back, informing me he would check in on Steven before heading out, and asking me to keep him posted on any changes.

We step into her room, forming a circle around her still figure. I have a torrent of words swirling in my mind, but I decide to hold them back until she is awake and we can have a moment alone. I offer to fetch coffee for her friends, who nod in gratitude—more for the prospect of privacy with their friend than for the caffeine itself. This small errand provides me with a much-needed moment to gather my thoughts.

Her face and arms are marred with bruises, stark reminders of the suffering Tom had inflicted upon her. Yet, I understand that the wounds run far deeper than the visible marks on her skin. The video footage, the chaotic scene, and our statements have all painted a grim picture. Dixon had reassured us that Tom would be facing significant consequences for his actions. He requested that I return to the station in a day or two to provide my official statement, promising to share whatever details he could about the case.

My jaw tightens, a wave of frustration surging

within me as I contemplate her lack of trust. The thought of her withholding the truth about her past and Tom's identity gnaws at me. Had I known the reality, I would never have accepted him as a client. Each interaction replays in my mind like a haunting melody, revealing the impossibility of discerning the darkness hidden beneath his polished exterior. He had an answer for every question, meticulously crafted to assure me of his intentions. I can't shake the feeling that his grandfather was merely a pawn, Tom orchestrating this elaborate charade, convincing him that his aspirations to expand in the city were genuine.

I pay for the coffee and wait for them to be ready. Now, her distaste for wealthy men made perfect sense. Tom should have faced the consequences of his actions long ago, but Dani, believing that the only way to escape the lowly and shameful expectations imposed by her mother was to graduate from this prestigious school, had not fought for herself. She thought that, as a girl with scant resources, she stood no chance against someone who seemingly had it all. Despite her silence, he had a way of making her feel weak and insignificant in front of the entire class. Even now, for months, he wielded his power over her, exploiting her vulnerability.

"Here you go, sir," the barista calls out, breaking my reverie. I take the coffee and make my way back to the room. I knew what kind of person Dani truly was. She would do anything for anyone, always putting others first. She had given leftovers to the homeless and paid it forward during her coffee runs—something I was aware of because she often used my credit card to do so. She charmed everyone she met, often unaware of the profound impact she had on those around her. The fact that I had allowed myself to believe she could orchestrate such a convoluted scheme simply to access my money was both laughable and humiliating.

Regret clings to me like ivy, its roots deep and unyielding. I would give up everything I owned to be with her, and I would dedicate every second of the rest of our lives to making amends for being one more man on a long list who hurt her.

39.

Dani

My eyelids feel heavy, resisting the urge to open. Everything from earlier today is a blur; I can't even be sure it's still the same day. As I glance around the dim room, I notice the curtains drawn back, revealing a world outside cloaked in darkness, illuminated only by the soft glow of the moonlight spilling into the space. My gaze lands on a large figure sprawled across the small couch, and I'm momentarily taken aback—surprised that he's here.

I try to piece together the fragments of my earlier memories: the doctors' soothing voices summarizing the extent of my injuries, their gentle questions that seemed to roll off my tongue effortlessly. They had asked simple things – my name, the date, and how I felt – but when it came to questions about how I ended up in this hospital bed, everything went fuzzy. The fear creeps in, causing a tightness in my chest when panic begins to claw at me. Tom's threats echo in the back of my mind. I can almost feel the burn of his touch, his hands like fire against my skin, branding me with every painful memory.

The sudden creak of the door jolts me from my thoughts, making my heart race.

"You're awake!" Izzy exclaims, rushing over to me.

She carefully sets her drink on the side table and wraps her arms around me in a gentle hug. "Sorry if I scared you. I need to let Chad know. He was here earlier, but he needs his beauty rest—you know how he is."

She settles into the chair next to my bed, popping the cap off her iced tea and taking a long sip before setting it down. Her eyes are on me, waiting.

"How are you feeling?" she asks – her tone quiet but filled with concern.

"Sore. But I guess I'm okay," I reply, trying to muster a smile.

"I'm sure you're sore. That's not what I was asking. How are you really?"

I lean my head back against the pillow and close my eyes, drawing in a deep breath and slowly letting it out. "I don't know. I feel confused – it's like I'm watching a movie that's skipping through all the important scenes, and I'm left with this strange sense of... detachment."

Izzy nods, her gaze softening. "Well, why don't you tell me what you remember? I'll fill in the blanks for you."

I take a moment to gather my thoughts. "I remember going into Stonebrook this morning and grabbing my things. Then I came downstairs and saw Steven on the ground. After that, everything gets hazy. I remember being tied to a chair, and then Tom came in. I think he was planning to kill me, Iz."

Her face hardens at the mention of his name, and she remains silent, her eyes never leaving mine, giving me the time to gather more of my fragmented memories.

"I remember being dragged to this room. I tried

to escape, but he caught me. I hit my head, and then everything went dark. The next thing I remember is waking up here in the hospital."

"I'm so sorry, Dani," she says, her voice filled with empathy. "I'm so sorry you had to go through that, but you're safe now. That piece of shit is going to prison. The police arrested him."

"How did they find me? How did they even know I was there?" I ask, trying to piece it all together.

"See that man sleeping on the couch?" She nods toward the man who has barely moved. I blink and nod back, still processing. "He came for you."

"I don't get it. He hates me. Why is he even here?"

"If I believed for even one second that he hated you, even a little bit, I would have kicked him out on his ass. But a man who hates someone, does not do what he did today," she said, folding her legs beneath her. "I called him this morning. I got your note, well after you had left. I was worried. I figured since it was his building, he could let me in and see what was going on. That's when we found Steven and your things sprawled on the floor. Dean called the cops. While Jay dealt with them, we went upstairs to see if you were up there." Izzy gazed at the wall, biting her lip.

"What's wrong?" I ask, sensing her hesitation. She turns her head back towards me, still chewing on her lip as if weighing whether to share. Raising my eyebrows, I silently urge her to continue.

"I'm sorry. I told him, Dani. I told him everything. I had a bad feeling about Tom's involvement. Dean needed to know everything."

I swallow hard, stealing another glance at him. He stirs for a moment, then falls still again. He knows. He knows everything and yet he remains here. I would have expected him to distance himself from me. By now, he must realize I'm not the gold digger he once thought I was, but I had hidden things from him—significant things. I may not have lied outright, but I hadn't been entirely honest either. That kind of baggage would send any man running, yet not him.

"I'm not angry, Izzy. You were right; I should have told him from the start."

"Well, anyway, so I told him. He remembered that Tom had a building in the city, so we went there, broke in, and found you."

"You broke into a building and just found me?"

"Well, Dean might have... well, he may have beat the shit out of Tom while I was trying to wake you up."

"He what?" I lean forward, my eyes wide with disbelief.

"Yeah," she laughs lightly. "It was a bit scary at the time, but honestly, it was kind of impressive. It looked like Dean knew exactly what he was doing. But he was worried about you. He's been here the whole time." She glances in his direction. "I know he did you dirty and that was really fucked up. But, Dani, that man loves you. I'd do anything for a guy to kick down a door with those big muscles and rescue me," she says, her voice dreamy.

"Okay, please don't start imagining steamy porn scenes in your head while sitting right next to me."

"You're such a buzzkill," she teases, sticking out her

tongue. "I'm really glad you're going to be okay. I mean it. You will be okay. I'm going to head home for a shower and some sleep. Call me if you need anything; otherwise, I'll be back here tomorrow morning. I'll bring you some real coffee."

"Thank you!"

As Izzy rises, a gentle rustle fills the air, drawing my attention to Dean, who is now sitting up, his hands running over his face in a daze. Our eyes meet, and a rush of breath catches in my throat. He's undeniably handsome, and despite the anger that should simmer between us, I realize how much I've missed him. His eyes widen in surprise as he registers that I'm awake.

"Alright," Izzy chirps cheerfully. "I'm heading out now." She leans down to envelop me in a warm hug, her voice a soft whisper, "You deserve to be happy." With a final wave to Dean, she makes her way to the door, leaving just the two of us in the tension-filled space.

"Dani," he begins, moving towards the chair that Izzy had just vacated. "Can I get you anything?" I shake my head in response. I study him, noticing the discoloration and swelling on parts of his face that I'm certain will bruise. "Listen, I know you probably don't want to see me right now, but I need to get this off my chest." His hand hovers over mine, an instinctive gesture, but he withdraws it, reconsidering. I notice the cuts that run along his knuckles, confirming Izzy's description of what happened. I nod, urging him to continue.

"I'm so sorry, baby. I'm sorry for everything. I believed his lies. I doubted you, thinking that you could ever do something like that. I regret the way I spoke to you, the way I pushed you out of my life, for not protecting you," he choked out, his voice thick with emotion.

"Dean," I start to say.

"I don't expect your forgiveness," he interrupts. "I don't expect you to take me back, but I couldn't let you go without apologizing. You needed to hear this."

"I heard you broke into a building, kicked down a door, and threw some punches for me." A slight smile appears on his lips, and he chuckles softly.

"Actually, Izzy was the one who picked the lock."

"Of course she did," I laugh, a moment of levity breaking through the tension.

"I would have killed him, Dani," he declares, raking his fingers through his disheveled hair. "In that moment, I would have done anything to save you. I'd do anything for you because I love you."

My breath hitches at his confession. He just said he loves me. Growing up ensnared in a web of lies and manipulation, I find myself battling a deep-seated wariness and distrust. Yet, Izzy's words echo in my mind: I deserve happiness.

I study the man before me, a figure of power and privilege, possessing everything money can buy—except love. Money cannot buy love. It cannot buy me.

He stands before me, looking utterly exhausted, both disheveled and defeated. In the battle of emotional baggage, I may have come out on top, but we are both bruised and shaped by the very people we once trusted. We've poured our hearts into others, only to be left empty and broken.

"I should let you rest," he murmurs, shifting to rise. I grasp his hand, halting him.

"I love you too."

A rare, genuine smile breaks across his face. It reaches his eyes.

"Yeah?" he asks, leaning toward me.

"Yeah," I reply, meeting his lips with mine, sealing our unspoken promises at that moment.

Despite the imperfections of my childhood, a spark for life always flickered within me, one I envisioned would grow into an unstoppable wildfire, spreading my talents across the world. However, one fateful night altered everything, extinguishing that spark like a flame snuffed out by the wind. Yet, the man sitting beside me breathed life back into my soul, saving me in ways I never thought possible. He rekindled the spark that had long lain dormant, and in this moment of clarity, feeling the warmth of his presence, I know I truly deserve happiness. Together, we can ignite a brilliance that lights up the darkest corners of our lives. The anticipation of this journey fills me with eagerness, and I can hardly wait to embark on it.

40.

Epilogue

Dean

(One Year Later)

"Where are we going?" Dani asks, her voice laced with suspicion.

"You really need to learn to relax and trust me," I reply with a teasing smirk curling on my lips.

"You really need to learn that I hate surprises," she shoots back, her brows furrowed in that adorable way she does when she's frustrated with me.

"This one will be worth it," I assure her, hoping to quell her apprehension. She is likely bewildered by my decision to drive us, as we typically rely on my chauffeur. However, viewing this as a brief escape for us, I deemed it important to grant my staff a well-deserved break as well.

She leans back and gazes out the window, her mind clearly racing as she tries to piece together the scenes flashing by. I can't help but admire her; the way her dress hugs her curves, the cascade of her brown curls spilling over her shoulders, framing her face. A light touch of makeup highlights her expressive eyes, making them sparkle with curiosity.

I never imagined I'd be sitting here with Dani, on the brink of one of the most significant nights of my life. She had no idea we were escaping the city for a few days—a well-deserved break after the tumultuous year she'd endured. My heart tightens at the thought of what could have been. Although she had physically recovered quickly, the emotional scars lingered, a testament to the challenges she faced.

That day could have ended in heartbreak. The mere idea of mourning her instead of celebrating her presence is a weight I carry. If Izzy hadn't reached out, if we hadn't raced to find her—those thoughts haunt me. It was all too easy to imagine a world where we were not here, together, on this journey.

After Dani's hospital stay, we chose to take things slowly. She expressed a desire to return as my assistant, and while I would have preferred she focus on her recovery, the idea of keeping a close watch on her brought me some comfort. We both agreed to avoid putting pressure on our relationship, more for her sake than mine. Hell, I would have married her that day. I had never anticipated that she would find it in her heart to forgive me. In the coming weeks, however, we had several conversations in between our makeup sessions. We discussed her regret over not being open with me sooner and my own regret for not trusting her. While we seemed to have forgiven each other, forgiving ourselves proved to be a far more complex journey.

With the demands of work and the ongoing trial, we had little time for ourselves, which is precisely why I had planned a special outing for just the two of us.

Tom was charged with first-degree kidnapping and

attempted murder. His lawyers attempted to negotiate a deal, but Dani was resolute in her decision to confront him and share her story. We took our chances in court. Although the trial dragged on for months, the outcome—Tom Hansen receiving a life sentence—made it all worthwhile. Dani showed incredible strength throughout this ordeal, and I couldn't have been prouder of her.

As we near our destination, a comfortable silence falls between us. I can feel her curiosity bubbling beneath the surface, but she knows better than to push me for answers. When I finally stop the car and get out, I circle around to open her door. Her eyes fall on the cabin in front of us, and for a moment, she's speechless. I can see the wonder in her gaze, the soft way she takes it all in.

"What is this?" she inquires, her eyes fixed on me as I pop the trunk and retrieve a large suitcase.

"Looks like a cabin," I reply, watching her expression narrow into a skeptical glare.

"No shit. I mean, what is all of this?" she gestures toward the suitcase and the quiet beauty of the surroundings.

"This," I say, wrapping my arms around her, "is for us. For you. A sanctuary of tranquility. A few days to unwind and rejuvenate." I release her from the embrace, take her hand, and lift the suitcase, leading her toward the cabin with a sense of anticipation.

When we step inside, she scans the expansive open space, her eyes wide with wonder. Before us stretches a generous living area, where several armchairs and a leather couch are arranged in a semi-circle around a television and a crackling fireplace. To the right, the dining and kitchen space gleams, outfitted with modern appliances.

"It's beautiful," she breathes out.

"You haven't even seen the whole place yet," I reply, watching as her gaze lands on the dining table, elegantly set for a romantic dinner for two. She turns to me, a spark of excitement in her eyes.

"You mean you really set all of this up for us? A romantic dinner?" She sounds almost incredulous, but the joy in her eyes is unmistakable.

"Of course," I reply, my tone light, though I feel a flicker of nervousness. "I can be romantic," I say as I wrap my arms around her.

"The most romantic you get is when you're deep inside me," she retorts with a playful smile.

A smile tugs at my lips, and I step toward her, pulling her close. "And you fucking love it when my dick is inside you," I whisper into her ear, kissing her neck, feeling her shiver with delight. "And my fingers." I trail kisses along her jaw. "And my tongue." Our lips meet in a passionate kiss, and I feel a rush of desire flood through me.

I feel the connection between us, the love that has only deepened since we began this journey together.

Later, in the privacy of the master bedroom, everything shifts. The world outside fades as we find ourselves again, not just in the physical sense but in the emotional one as well. As I lower myself to her, everything else disappears, and we are simply two people, in love, sharing something raw, beautiful, and deeply intimate. I gently lay her on the bed, the anticipation crackling in the air between us.

"I love you," I whisper against her skin, the words coming easier than they ever have before.

She smiles, her eyes softening with affection. "I love you, too."

I hold her close, the past year's struggles falling away, leaving only the promise of what's to come.

I bend down, my hands slipping around the back of her heels, sliding them off her. I kiss and nip at her feet, making my way up her calf. As I reach higher on her leg, I pull her dress up, following with my tongue and lips, teasing her as I bite softly on the soft inner flesh of her creamy thighs. I hear her breath become heavier with need.

"What do you need baby?"

"I need you to touch me, Dean. Please." I fucking love it when I have her begging for me. My cock is already straining against the confines of my pants, the fabric tugging uncomfortably. I lick the entire length of her slit, motivated by the moans it elicits. My fingers find her entrance and I start to pound into her as I lick and suck on her sweet spot. I can already tell she's close before she even says anything.

"Oh fuck, Dean. I'm going to come!" she yells. I gently bite her clit, sending her over the edge. I take my fingers out and hold them out by her mouth.

"Let me show you how sweet you taste." She maintains eye contact with me as she parts her lips, allowing me to slip my fingers in for her to suck on them, tasting herself. I nearly combust right fucking then. When she's done, I pull my fingers out and grab her dress, pulling it off her. I unhook her bra, tossing it to the side, teasing her tits with my mouth and hands. Her head leans back on the bed, eyes closed, moaning and grinding against me. I reach down to release the button on my pants and let them fall to the ground. I grab my dick with my hand and pump it a few times as I kick my pants completely off. I open her knees, pushing them to the side as I line up with her entrance and tease her.

"Please, Dean! Fuck. I need you inside of me."

"That's right, baby. Beg for this cock."

"Please. Please fuck me!" She gasps as I thrust hard inside of her. I lift her legs over my shoulders to hit her deeper. She feels so fucking good and I tell her so.

"God damn, babe. You feel so fucking good. I love it when your pussy squeezes my cock." Just as she's about to cum, I pull out, despite her disappointment. I push her higher onto the bed so I can get on top, pushing myself in again, both of our orgasms building. I push her knees toward her chest and fuck her harder. She grasps the nape of my neck, drawing me closer as our lips meet in a fervent kiss. In that fleeting moment, she reaches her climax – I follow behind her.

I rest my forehead against hers, both of us panting as we regain our breath. Her smile lights up her face, and in that moment, my previous plans dissipate. Patience has never been one of my virtues.

I pull back slightly, my heart pounding in my chest. "Marry me, Dani," I say, locking my gaze with her big brown eyes, now half-hooded from the passion we've just shared.

Her eyes widen with a mix of surprise and tenderness, and then she smiles – a smile that could light up the entire world.

"I told you, you're the most romantic when you're inside me," she replies, laughter bubbling up as she speaks. I let out a nervous chuckle with her.

"Is that a yes?" I laugh along with her, my chest swelling with hope.

"That's a yes," she whispers, leaning in to kiss me, her hips rising to roll me over. She sits up, and I feel her begin to grind against me, my cock ready for round two. My hands instinctively find her nipples, teasing them between my thumb and index finger.

She throws her head back, a soft moan escaping her lips as she continues to move. This is one of my favorite views—a sight that eclipses even the most breathtaking landscapes. The woman I love is coming apart for me. My present and my future. My wife-to-be.

In that moment, with her in my arms and the promise of forever in her eyes, I know one thing for sure: this is just the beginning.

41.

Epilogue

Dani

(Nine Months Later)

"I have a little something for you," I say, extending a wrapped box toward him. "What do you give a man who can afford anything that he wants?"

Dean unwraps the box with caution, lifting the lid to reveal its contents. "A snow globe?" he asks, curiosity etching his brow.

"A promise," I reply, my voice soft but steady. "No matter how fiercely life shakes us, we will weather the storm together. Chaos, no matter how overwhelming, will always give way to tranquility."

He smiles, a warmth spreading through the moment, and leans closer to kiss me softly. "Now, let's take a look at this," he says, pulling the globe from its box. He gives it a vigorous shake, and I watch intently as the snow begins to swirl within. I don't have to look at the globe to know when the snow settles because his eyes, filled with wonder, widen and begin to glisten as he takes in all the details.

He finally glances away from the snow globe, which contains a crib cradling a teddy bear, and asks,

"You're pregnant?" I had engraved the globe with the news of our baby's due date, a small token of the joy I hoped to share. I nod, my heart racing as I anticipate his reaction.

Setting the snow globe gently on the coffee table, he rises, running his hands through his hair, the weight of the news settling in.

A wave of nervousness washes over me, and doubt creeps in – a tight knot forms in my stomach, and I hesitate. "Dean?" I call out, standing to meet him. He halts, his pacing ceasing as he turns to face me, my voice trembling just a bit.

"We're having a baby?" The words come out low, almost disbelieving, but underneath is something softer – something hopeful.

"Yes," I whisper, my voice barely audible – it's all I can manage.

His face transforms in an instant, his radiant smile spreading like the sun breaking through clouds. Before I can blink, he lifts me off the ground and spins me around, laughter bubbling between us, our joy undeniable. It's a new beginning for us both.

"We're having a baby!" He bellows, his voice thick with happiness. He repeats the words, quieter now, as if savoring their taste. "We're having a baby..."

Tears well up in my eyes as I watch him kneel before me, his hands gently cradling my belly, his lips brushing the skin there with such tenderness it takes my breath away. This was the same man who, not long ago, had been impossible to understand – hard, cold, seemingly unbreakable. Yet somehow, through the chaos, he had become the one who healed me, who made me believe in love again, and in the future – my husband, the father of my child.

He had stolen my heart, mended my spirit, and reignited the flame that had been extinguished far too soon in my life.

"I love you, Dean," I whisper, feeling a rush of emotion swell within me.

He rises slowly, his hands cradling my face with such reverence, his thumb tracing my cheek.

"And I love you, baby," his voice full of sincerity. He pulls me close, and when our lips meet, the world feels like it stops – every spark of desire, every unspoken promise lighting up between us.

ACKNOWLEDGEMENT

Wow! I am thrilled to reflect on this extraordinary journey and deeply appreciate your decision to join me on this path. Writing this story has been a dream come true and I'm only getting started.

I extend my heartfelt gratitude to my husband, whose unwavering support has been my foundation since he learned I was writing a novel. Balancing the demands of raising three children with my passion for writing is no small feat, yet his enthusiasm has inspired me to pursue this dream of mine.

Thank you to everyone who played a role in preparing this book for publication. I am immensely grateful to collaborate with such talented individuals.

Lastly, I wish to express my sincerest appreciation to my readers. Your trust in me to guide you on this journey means the world. I cannot convey how much I value your willingness to take a chance on my work.

ABOUT THE AUTHOR

A.m. Roberts

About the Author A.M. Roberts lives in a small town in Pennsylvania. When she isn't writing, she enjoys spending time with her husband, three children, and her husky, Athena. She is a teacher by day, but at night, you can usually find her at a sports field, cheering on her children or playing a little softball herself. Two of her obsessions are iced coffee and true crime documentaries. Her ideal evening involves curling up with a good book, a warm blanket, and the flicker of candlelight nearby.